Santo Santo

A NOVEL BY
MICHAEL JOHNSON

ISBN: 978-1-961879-18-8 (sc)
978-1-961879-19-5 (e)

Publishing rev. date: 10/04/2023

Santo Santo

Santo Santo

"Well, we're finally on our way." The loudspeaker system of flight 418 of the *Compania Santense de Lineas Aereas* had just announced that they were in the air for a flight of ten hours between Los Angeles and San Santo, the capital of the high Andean country of El Santo.

"Where?" The Reverend Oliver Francis Wallby, former Vicar of the Episcopalian Church of Saint Henry the Eighth of Westwood, Los Angeles, lay slumped in his seat. He seemed, at least to his travelling companion, sort of caved-in.

"To El Santo, of course. That's where you wanted to go, isn't it?"

"Oh yes. Quite simply. It is the place where I …" Reverend Ollie dozed off before completing his sentence. It was understandable. He had been through an ordeal, and he wasn't that young either. In fact, he was old. It seemed to Elliot that his minister friend had never been young. At least since they had met, which was more than twenty years ago. But now he was unwell to boot. Once obese, chugging a forty pound surcharge that made comings and goings from Eighth's altar an ordeal for his unexercised lungs, he was now almost skinny. Trauma and age could do that.

"We're going to El Santo to begin our new life, remember? Besides, it would be quite unwise to remain stateside."

Wallby groaned. This too was understandable. If you had been sacked from one of the most prestigious Episcopal parishes in the colonies and forced into exile because of a charge, really unsubstantiated, but already tried in the press, of molesting, you would groan too.

"I mean," Elliot hastened to add, "because of the need to begin *The New Life*." It would be cruel to taunt the elderly clergyman when the press and commentators had already raked him over the coals, before drawing and quartering him. Enough was enough.

"In Sano." Wallby pronounced, stressing the second syllable.

"No. El Santo. We have to learn to pronounce it like the locals. We too will be speaking Spanish before long."

Wallby made no sound, but his lips moved. From the shapes formed by his upper and lower lips, wrinkled and shriveled though they were, Elliot guessed that he was reciting passages from the New Testament in Koine. He had been at it a lot lately. Now almost defrocked (it was unclear whether an Episcopal minister *could* be defrocked. You would have to invent at least a dozen new sins), he had left off his attraction to the Bhagavad Gita, to the Pali texts of Buddhism, to a dozen solar and chthonic sects of eschatological tendency to return to his seminary past. He had mastered the common Greek of the early centuries so well in those school years that he was able to suggest corrections to the reference dictionaries. His divinity thesis itself had argued that the New Testament was a fake.

Outside the porthole window dispersed clouds floated by. Elliot had the window seat, so that the Reverend could more easily gain the isle in case of an evacuant emergency. Elliot looked around the plane while the holy man snoozed. The passengers were mainly Santanos returning to the homeland for a brief visit before going back to their jobs and businesses in L.A., plus some tourists and a few odd travellers, like themselves. Most were still shifting about in their small seats, examining and then stowing away and then re-examining small bags and parcels. They kept an eye on the stewardesses (mainly male), probably wondering when the first meal would be served. Elliot was thinking how he might decently approach a steward-person with a request for a cocktail. Since no steward type who was not obviously busy and overworked came near, Elliot got up in the odd, perpendicular way required by seat and cabin space design, then inched past Ollie, being careful not to disturb his deep slumbers (his face was turning just a trifle purple around the nose. It could be the altitude). He went to the tourist section restroom.

Inside, Elliot took a piece of paper towel and carefully slid the lock. You could never be too vigilant against international germs. He looked at himself in the mirror. Elliot Spenseric, now. He was beginning a new phase of his life, but he was not particularly new. He shifted a lock of hair to hide his bald patch, at least from the front. Elliot Spenseric, formerly of Beverly Hills, where he had lived lengthy years of youth, stretching late into his thirties, in the house of his mother, poor deceased Maxine, and where he had first made the acquaintance of Rev. O. F. Wallby, Vicar of Westwood. The years had taken their toll on that once admired Elliot face, but it was far from bombed-out. Those sharp lines of jaw and cheek were still clear and the skin still taut. It had wrinkled a bit under the eyes and had discolored somewhat with sallow tones and dark spots, nothing that could not be cosmetically covered, to some extent. That was the surface. Underneath, there was the same question that the Reverend had asked him years ago. Where to? The earlier Elliot had had goals to furnish his life. Born to wealth, raised in luxury, he had also felt a desire to do things to help. He had a religious side, dating from his college years at Tarzana University, where his senior thesis had been "The Origins of Protestantism in the San Fernando Valley".

Now they were going toward a New Life, in El Santo. Reverend Ollie had furnished this interpretation. Ollie, who had traveled the world in search of ever newer spiritualities, but had come back to help Elliot in his hour of need. Another explanation was that, despite an early finding of no evidence, press and popular personalities were still pounding the drum against the Reverend for charges on that molestation incident. You could not be extradited from El Santo, except to Cuba.

Elliot regained his minuscule tourist section seat just in time to observe Ollie in conversation with a stewardess/steward.

"And of course we will want to explore the peaks of the Andes and the craters of available volcanoes. Otherwise, it is to learn the culture and the folkways of all the people and ..."

"You want the chicken or the beef for dinner?"

"Chicken." Of course Ollie chose chicken. It was much less violent than beef. "This is my traveling companion, Mster Spenseric." Ollie introduced him to the stewardess. The term "Mster" was the Reverend's own invention. It meant a male who might or might not be married. Elliot disliked it.

"Hello." The stewardess moved off. She was not impressed by either of them.

"Glad to see that you're awake. I was afraid you were coma-ing out on me again."

"No. I am much better now. We are high already, physically and spiritually. I feel moved so much, as if the Andes were already below us." He fell into a quick snooze.

Narcolepsy. The doctor had diagnosed it. It was rare for Ollie to be awake for as long as half an hour non-stop. He began to snore through mouth and nose. Due to the angle of the Reverend's head, Elliot could see two large nostrils clogged with bristles and transited by pressured flows of air exhaust.

I warned him, Elliot thought. I warned the old bastard. But he would go through with "the momentous spiritual innovation" that he called Naked Mass. The first and last celebration of this religious performance, inspired as it was by the nude hippie stage extravaganzas of the sixties, had been at St Henry's. Elliot had not attended. It turned out that among the thirty or so participants, New Age seekers and, no one doubted it, a few exhibitionist and/or voyeurist adults, was a seventeen year old. As part of the Naked Mass, Ollie had included a Stone Age fertility ritual actually practiced in New Guinea. The scandal press had described it as a "gang bang". The parents of the seventeen year old had pressed charges. Arrest was avoided when police records revealed that she had a long history of prostitution. But a scandal was born and would live forever. Faced with an avalanche of negative publicity, the Bishop had reacted, although privately he told Ollie that he didn't know what all the fuss was about. He suggested a lengthy leave of absence in missionary territory.

At the airport, before embarkation, they had been hounded by a dozen yapping vox populi from the tabloid press.

Elliot was at his porthole seat again, looking at the clouds. They were gaining altitude. The fasten seatbelt sign flickered on as the plane shook from the effects of turbulent pockets of air. He looked again at the large section of tourist class passengers. On the whole, they might have been the passengers of the average Los Angeles bus, only older and better dressed. The plane climbed and climbed. They seemed to be stuck at a forty-five degree angle relative to the surface.

Rev. Oliver flickered on. "I am reminded of my trip from New Delhi to the Himalayas. So high, so advanced in feeling and thought."

"You mean when you spent three weeks in a hotel in Kathmandu with diarrhea?"

"My experience was earthy as well as high."

"I got high myself a bit after your Nepal fling, remember. I joined the Brothers of Perpetual Sanctity and got taken for my last dime. Every cent that Maxine left me, and that was quite a bit, including the sale price of my childhood Beverly Hills home." A saddened Elliot nodded. "I'm still grateful that you came to rescue me when I fled the monastery in Mendocino. And you gave me bread and succor." This referred to the job at St. Hen's as personal assistant to the Vicar that Ollie had provided in order to keep his newly indigent friend afloat financially.

"Such is my vocation. I believe that it is the duty of all men to give each other succor." A steward-person passed in the isle. "Attractive fellow."

"You mean the short swarthy one with a low forehead and tiny ears?"

"He reminds me of an adorable little character in the old Tarzan films."

"Cheeta?"

"Boy."

The stewardess/stewards were starting to serve lunch. It was not chicken or beef, but apparently iguana/llama.

"In El Santo, iguana is often called chicken, that is, *pollo*." Ollie had read several guide books on El Santo, as well as a great deal of political literature.

"Delicious." Elliot made a face. "Nothing like grilled lizard for lunch."

"You are incurably provincial."

When the steward-person had pushed the heavy lunch cart to their row and asked the eternal in-flight question, Ollie opted for llama.

Revolting. Llamas were such attractive animals. Little supercilious snouts, so laughably cute.

"Can I have a ham sandwich?" Elliot at least tried.

"Sorry senor, it is forbidden. We have very many Moslem people for our flights today."

"Iguana, then. But please take the iguana part out and give it to the poor. I'll eat the fixings." Anyway, iguanas were not mammals, unlike the more evolved llamas, which must have feelings at least vaguely like those of humans.

Ollie ripped the aluminum cover from his hot lunch tray. He speared a piece of llama with his plastic fork. "In pre-Columbian times, llama meat was reserved to the Inca nobility. It was reputed to be an aphrodisiac."

Elliot looked at his elderly clerical friend. It was difficult to imagine him now under the effects of an aphrodisiac. He was shriveled, reduced, wrinkled, meatless—except for what came in through his mouth.

"Take it easy. You'll soon be at the steward persons."

Elliot's tray was served minus the pieces of cooked lizard tail. It was not bad. Rice, some vegetables, largely unrecognizable as to species, and two sections of flat bread. The flat bread might have been intended to placate the Middle Eastern passengers, thus making up for the threat of ham.

For a drink, Elliot chose one of the tiny bottles of pisco and a six-ounce bottle of Peruvian wine. Cabernet, the label said. Ollie had only the pisco. He drained his bottle quickly.

A very small sip of pisco from a plastic glass made Elliot gag. "Nasty." He looked at the Reverend for a reaction, but Ollie had narcolapsed again into dream time.

Clouds wafted across the window space. Clouds and more clouds. They were climbing and climbing.

After the trays had been collected---"little ears" had been delegated to this task and Elliot gave him a dirty look—Ollie turned back on.

The Rev grabbed the locket that hung from his neck and opened it. On opposite sides it bore matching cameo portraits. Jesus and Che Guevara. This was a principal reason for their trip to El Santo. Wallby began. "Since its inception, Christianity, brought by the Spaniards with fire and sword, has meant little except oppression and slavery to the Andean peoples. The Church took their lands, their labor and their souls. It gave them guilt and penance. In the later twentieth century, however, things began to change. Che brought the hope of a new future, where the people would work for the people and receive the fruits of their free labor." This was the new gospel, the doctrine of Che-su. Reverend Wallby had given the same sermon many times before. Elliot was not sure he believed in it. He was not sure what it meant. But he had come along with the Rev, out of gratitude, and because he had no alternative. The idea was that they would "take root" in the local society and make contact with the liberation movement. Once accepted by FARS (Frente Armado de la Revolucion Santense), they would begin to spread the idea of joint Jesus-Che spirituality. Ollie called it, rather blasphemously, Che-su. Of course, at their age, especially Ollie's, they could not be expected to shoulder arms and march through the jungle. They would operate at their own level, but in total solidarity with FARS and related freedom movements.

Rumors about FARS had been dismissed by Wallby as contra-revolutionary propaganda. Even if they did kidnap people and hold them for ransom and occasionally assassinated wealthy bourgeois and robbed banks and stores, it would only be for the good of the revolucion. To protect and preserve the people, providing food and medical care to those adorable little Andean babies, was the goal of FARS, along with seizing political power. Ol' had always—almost always—been right in the past, so why not this time? Elliot too had ploughed through an enormous amount of literature on the subject, mostly from university presses. They had given FARS high marks.

Night came on quickly. They were now in the tropical latitudes. The cabin windows were dark. Like most of the other window seat passengers, Elliot pulled down the plastic cover, shutting out dark and cold.

Elliot's mind went into dreamtime. He thought of his last years in Beverly Hills, living with his mother in the large house. His well furnished bedroom/study. The servants. Maxine was hitting the bottle pretty heavy at that time. She spent her days in the ground floor "den", a sort of parlor to the left of the entry, watching television—she adored daytime programming—and draining quarts of the hard stuff. Elliot had more harmless activities. In the daytime he would frequent coffee shops and explore used bookstores. He had a large, largely unread collection on medieval history. In the evenings he would cruise the boulevards in search of romance. Early one morning, in the second floor hallway of the mansion, Maxine had encountered a naked prostitute—male—invited home by Elliot. Elliot claimed he was doubtless a burglar. Thereafter she had referred to the incident as "Elliot's love burglar". But he had tired of his drone existence and asked for work. Not paid work. This was almost impossible to obtain, but volunteer work for the good. He had gone to work at the headquarters of a Pasadena organization that helped bring immigrants to the Southern California basin by freely giving such things as grants for airplane tickets and subsistence. It seemed an odd sort of charity. After all, millions made their way to L.A. unaided. Anyway, it was *helping*. But the helping did not last because of a personal dispute between the Director and Elliot in bed. How was Elliot to know that Mr. Director was entirely passive? The real tragedy came on soon. Maxine's cirrhosis reached crisis stage. The estate went into probate. Then a few years of comfortable wandering in northern cities like San Francisco before Elliot decided he had a vocation for the papal order of the Brothers of Perpetual Sanctity. He had donated his entire fortune to obtain a novitiate in the Mendocino monastery with its gothic architecture and luxurious furnishings.

Once again a misunderstanding involving the "chastity thing" forced Elliot to flee. Oliver found him on the road that led away from the monastery. Elliot was broke, abandoned, weeping by the wayside.

That was a few years before. Now events pushed toward a new future, new hopes aroused by the humanitarian Wallby, who foresaw a mission to convert the Indians and mestizos of the southern continent to the religion of Che-su (Che and Jesus). It was more than a little dubious from Elliot's viewpoint, but you had to hope, didn't you?

Turbulance. The bell sounded, the fasten seatbelt sign lighted up, the plane bobbed up and down heavily. Elliot clutched the armrests of his seat. Ollie snoozed oblivious. It was a mercy that he was developing a capacity to sleep deeply at almost any moment and often for long periods. This reduced his psychological and physical suffering caused by "the events".

They had been in the air for at least five hours when Wallby opened his eyes suddenly. "Then we have already landed. Tell the taxi driver that we wish to go the Hotel de Carlos."

"No, Ol'. We're still in the bright blue. We won't be there for two or three hours."

"Oh. The countryside looks so much like what I expected from the brochures and guide books."

"The window cover is down."

Wallby looked more closely. "So it is. Difficult to tell at a distance." He was wandering. Elliot recognized this fact and made his calculations. He would have to watch his clerical friend closely, to try to prevent him from straying into danger, e.g. stepping in front of a bus or similar object.

"We're staying at the Hotel de Carlos?" Elliot enquired, partly to change the subject. Ollie had talked about this hotel before. He had found the name in the Hollywood Tourist Guide for El Santo. According to the guide book, the hotel was "hot and secret".

"Yes. I have made reservations. Or, rather, reservations are not really necessary, because they are seldom full. Except during theatre season."

Ollie had explained about "theatre season", too. San Santo, the capital of the country of El Santo, had one of the most highly developed transvestite theaters in South America, in fact, in the entire planet. Classical pieces such as "La Paca" and "Un Jueves de Todos los Jueves" were regularly performed. Theatre season was generally from December to March, the hot season.

"We will have a two room suite, including bath and W.C. As well as the use of the common areas, such as the massage room and sundeck."

Elliot thought of his "common area" experiences in Hollywood. They had not been entirely pleasant. You never knew when you might pick up a loser.

"Tomorrow we will begin. We will live for others and with others. Now I understand that my last years at Westwood were dominated by self-involvement. It is the people who must be our center." This was Che-su doctrine, although it was far from original.

"To live with the poor, for the poor, by the poor …" Then Wallby was out again. His head lolled backward, allowing his nostrils to fill from pure vertical air. A relief for both of them. It seemed the Rev had been on the verge of reciting the Gettysburg Address.

An hour later the loudspeaker announced the beginning of the descent to the San Santo airport. Elliot nudged the ancient theologian. "We're going to be landing before long. Make sure your seatbelt's connected."

"The hotel? Give my name at the desk. They will understand. I sent a letter three weeks ago. Reservations were confirmed."

"No. It's only the airport. We'll be landing in about forty minutes."

The touchdown was difficult. The plane bounced three times on the tarmack. At last, when they were firmly on terra firma, the passengers broke into applause. Several prayed and crossed themselves. Many wept. Lineas Aereas pilots were not highly reputed for their tactical skill.

The passenger group was waved through immigration and customs. No one tried to sneak *into* El Santo. As for contraband, the country was an open highway for drugs and arms via Andes and Amazon. When they were in the open zone of the airport, Reverend Wallby stopped. He stood watching.

"Our new country, Elliot, our new people. Let us begin to love them now. Can you?"

"I think I can, although we don't know much about the place yet."

"It will be a land of miracles."

Crowds waited just outside the barrier. Many wore derby hats. These were the women. They held little signs in front of their abdomens. *Guia Touristica. Productos Locales.* Bags of goods for sale lay at their feet. Probably filled with peanuts or mangos or children's clothes. Hopefully washed. Ollie was emotionally concerned by the general appearance of poverty. Elliot winced at the looks of misery and misfortune on their faces. Later he would learn that these were "lo ricos", the lucky ones.

"We have come with hope. We will share whatever they must suffer."

"I can't eat too many peanuts. They give me gas."

"A small sacrifice, my dear. Some gave all. All can at least give some."

"Okay."

They located a cab outside the International Terminal. The driver spoke some English. He wore a hat that was not a derby and not a llama wool toque. It was something original and in four colors. At first the driver tried to bargain for cigarettes, eight, or at least six cigarettes for the trip to San Santo, the city. When he learned that Wallby was prepared to pay dollars in cash, he fell to his knees, he wept. He took out his rosary and began to pray. Ollie hinted that they did not have a great deal of time. Ten Hail Marys, a single decade, okay, but no more. Ollie retained an anti-Catholic prejudice from his seminary days. Then they were on the road. Elliot was agreeably surprised to find that it was paved. Potholes there were, but not too bad, except one that almost wrenched the left front wheel off and knocked Wallby's head on the car ceiling. Large crowds moved along the opposite roadside toward the airport: men, women, llamas, children, monkeys, dogs, a total menagerie, but not happy, all clad in drab, worn skirts, baggy pants, and loose but once colorful blouses, only a few quaint hats. Some carried banners with the images of saints.

Ollie took it in. Just what he had hoped. The revolution had broken out already! They would be receptive to Che-su. *"Viva la Revolucion!,"* Ollie shouted.

"No, sir. It is not revolution. It is transportation," The cab driver explained.

Most of the foot travelers did not have two mangoes or half a cup of rice to pay the bus driver, so they walked to the airport. It was one of few places where you could hope to wrangle some coins in actual money.

Wallby nodded. He remembered reading an article in an economics quarterly that argued that El Santo was not doing as badly as generally thought. According to the IMF, the per capita gross national product declined by only fifty-three percent last year, the most favorable result since the Alliance had taken control five years ago, and despite the new Constitution, which outlawed private money. Anyway, trade was now largely by barter. Maize for sweet potatoes, sex for drugs.

They were getting nearer to the capital, that was clear. Each time the cab stopped a horde of beggars, window washers, trinket hawkers and prostitutes surrounded the car, tried to open the doors (the driver had carefully locked all four before starting), screamed for custom and sale, showed their festering wounds and pressed their faces horribly against the window glass.

"Do not be afraid, senor. They only want food. It is like everywhere."

The cab started again, tearing away from the faces. Mustache and beard hair stuck to the windows. They had been women, mainly.

Then they were in San Santo, the capital, the center of political, cultural and economic life. The mainly low, two story buildings probably dated from the mid-nineteenth century. The same crowds covered every street corner, overwhelmed every major intersection of avenidas. Then they were in the Centro Historico, the Old Town.

"Soon we are at the Hotel de Carlos," the cab driver said. He looked at them through the rear view mirror and grinned. Naughty naughty.

They were pushing in heavy traffic through a large square, the Plaza de la Revolucion. The guide books said that this was in many ways the heart of the city, even of the country. Historic buildings covered each side of the square. Churches, palaces, colonial era buildings. In the center was a large equestrian statue mounted on a twenty-foot base. Astride the horse was a military figure in ornate costume, sword raised. Ollie and Elliot gaped at its grandeur.

"Si." The cab driver grinned. "This is the statue of the General. He bring to us independence, freedom, joy, prosperity two hundred years ago. All Santanos love him like the father."

Ollie nodded in sage agreement. Elliot was too discreet to say what he thought. Joy, prosperity two hundred years ago? What the *hell* had happened since?

Past the square, they turned down a side street. They pulled to the curb in front of the Hotel. Ollie grandly took a five-dollar bill out of his wallet and handed it to driver. The driver stared at it with incredulity. He looked as if he might faint. With such an amount one could buy an estate in the countryside, one could retire for life!

Half a dozen bellhops ran toward the car. In seconds they had Wallby's and Elliot's luggage out of the trunk and were assisting the two toward the hotel entrance. They had time only to glance at the façade. It was nicely decorated with multicolor banners and little statues of cupids and nymphs and naked athletes. Hotel de Carlos. Bienvenu Wellkommen Welcome Bienvenido to the world famous inn. Two sturdy doormen in chartreuse uniforms were there to guard against unwelcome visitors. Wallby and Elliot were already inside when a mob of sidewalk people rushed the cab, being tipped off by eagle-eye vision to the five-dollar bill, and began to rock it from side to side. *Limosna! Limosna!*

The lobby of the Hotel de Carlos was impressive. Colonial style dark wood furniture occupied attractive niches. Tapestries hung from the walls. An ornate, gurgling fountain adorned the center. A few odd individuals, standing or seated, turned curious glances to the newcomers.

To the desk. "Welcome, Padre." Reception smiled, bowed. He was a thin brunette man in his late forties with a wispy moustache and sparse hair damped to his scalp and parted in the middle. Wallby's letter of reservation must have tipped him to the old boy's clerical status. Although the truth was that Ollie wasn't really a "Padre". Episcopals were not canonically ordained and were certainly not celibate. They did not accept historic church doctrine.

"We feel blessed to be here in this very high country." San Santo was at nine thousand feet above sea level.

"We are so please to have receive you."

The formalities over, the 6 bellhops bore the travelers and their luggage to *piso tres*, the third floor. The head hop unlocked with his passkey, grandly pushed the door open and revealed a large, elegantly furnished room. Ah. It was almost like home, Elliot thought.

"Las maletas en el dormitorio," Ollie ordered. The hops rushed into the bedroom with the bags. There were two huge beds. Three of the bellhops immediately began to disrobe.

"Gracias, no. Demasiado fatigados." No thanks, they were too tired, Elliot explained politely.

With a very good tip in hand they retired smiling, bowing, sweeping the traces of their common shoes from the room.

In fact, they *were* tired. Elliot's legs felt heavy, as if invaded by lead. His arms were weak and difficult to raise. His head drooped. It was the altitude. The guidebooks had warned about it. Those unused to extreme altitudes would need a few days to become acclimatized to the rare atmosphere. The excitement of arrival had masked it. Ollie was already stretched out on one of the beds. In fact, he seemed to be breathing with difficulty.

"You okay, Ol'?"

"In this height of … gasp, snort … we shall surely reach … gasp … closer to heaven." He was delirious.

Elliot grabbed the bedside telephone. Reception picked up.

"Hello, yes." They usually answered in English, the first or second language of most of the guests.

"It is my friend. He's not well. I think you should call an ambulance."

"Ah. This is altitude sickness, senor. I will send the doctor at once."

Five minutes later there was a precipitate rapping at the door. Elliot opened. A short man wearing a dark suit rushed into the room. A stethoscope hung from his neck.

"Bring me please to the seek man."

Elliot pointed to the bedroom.

"Ah."

The doctor loosened Wallby's shirt and applied the stethoscope. He shifted the cup to various positions on the Rev's chest. "You will please to bring a glass of water for your friend."

Elliot dashed for the bathroom. He looked for a glass. There were towels, soap, but no glasses. He rushed to the main room, tore open a suitcase and retrieved a little souvenir cup they had bought at the airport. It was in the shape of a llama and would hold three or four ounces. In the bathroom he turned the faucet, then noticed a sign. "Agua no potable". You couldn't drink the water. There were plastic bottles of distilled water on a shelf above the sink. He grabbed one and headed back to the bedroom, arriving just in time to see the doctor easing a few twenty dollar bills out of Ollie's wallet.

"What are you doing?"

"I must look the passport for identification."

"Well you won't find it in there."

It was no surprise to find the medico pilfering, and almost excusable. Even before the currency reform, doctors in El Santo earned barely a thousand dollars a month. Policewomen-men five hundred. Peons and workers 60 (partly paid in kind). Now payment was usually in "social scrip" in return for work or the delivery of goods to the state. Real money was reserved to high government officials. The doctor dropped Ol's wallet, coughed, stood up.

"It is the altitude seekness that have you fren. Most time it not too bad, but he old and not too good. Lung congest. Maybe diabetes. He get better in a few days. He not really in coma."

Elliot was relieved. He was happy not to be alone in this strange land. He smiled.

"You tell them give him the soup. Just put the head up so he no swallow to pulmones."

With two additional dollars from Wallby's wallet in hand the doctor left smiling. "I come tomorrow. You telephone if he go bad."

When the doctor closed the door, Elliot looked at his ailing friend. Elliot was almost smiling even after a frightening emergency. "Not really in a coma." He sat down on the bed beside Ollie, who was breathing noisily, but breathing.

The doctor had described Reverend Wallby as "old". In fact, he looked old, but then he had always looked old, since he and Elliot had met twenty years ago. Ollie was indeed seventy, maybe past eighty (he never divulged his actual year count. "Spirit is our age", or something like that, was his motto). When they met Ollie had already been the Vicar of Westwood for many years. He was enthusiastic about new forms of spirituality, because "all spirit is one". Now the prophet of Che-su, he had brought Elliot to a "high land" where they would learn and teach a new life, with the yapping dogs of scandal far behind. Elliot looked at the prophet. Appearances were deceptive, but his general looks inspired little confidence in his prophetic ability. Eyes shut, his mouth was open to suck in more of the thin atmosphere of El Santo. The skin of his face, thin and blemished with scattered moles and small warts, was loosely drawn over large facial bones. His nose had lengthened with the years, increasing the crook of his hawk-like beak. The mouth was large with fleshy lips. The dark rings under his eyes gave an almost raccoon appearance, his most endearing feature. The tissues of his neck spread out in wrinkled formlessness. His large chest sprouted abundant white hairs, visible through the half-open shirt.

For a moment Elliot dozed. The nine thousand feet were affecting him as well. His eyes opened abruptly. He was there, sitting on a hotel room bed beside a not really comatose Wallby. Suddenly he had a thought. What Wallby reminded him of was … Maxine in her last years. Maxine, Elliot's mother. For years they had lived and fought together in their Beverly Hills home, bought with the millions provided by Elliot's prematurely deceased father. Her perpetual sarcasm. His constant violations of "propriety". He had cried when cirrhosis finally claimed her after ages of a diluvian intake.

His life had not been all partying. Elliot's interest in the religious, in the charitable, had sprouted early. The impulse to help the helpless was there, but it always seemed to go wrong. The "helpless" were appealing only in one sense. And his groping for spirituality always seemed to end in the discovery of corruption or bland mediocrity. Still, he followed a shepherd whom he had never completely trusted.

Wallby rolled a bit on the bed. "Call taxi after touchdown." His eyes opened.

"Rest, Ollie. That's what you need now. You have altitude sickness. We're already there."

"Oh. It is a wonderful land." Eyes shut again. Loud snoring, like the wind blasting through Andean canyons, trumpeted forth.

Outside, as glimpsed through the bedroom window, night was falling. It fell quickly. This was a tropical latitude, even if it was at nine thousand feet. He had to care for Ollie.

"Hello desk? Would you please send up a bowl of soup for my friend? He is too unwell to go down to the dining room."

"Of course, senor. It will be send immediately."

"And someone to feed it to him." Elliot was no nurse.

Half an hour later there was a knock at the door. A middle-aged woman dressed in a colorful Indian skirt, manta, bead necklace, psychedelic head cover, was standing in the doorway. She carried a tray with a bowl on it.

"Donde esta el enfermo?"

Elliot pointed to the bedroom. Pointing was the easiest way of communicating here.

She bustled into the bedroom. "Ah. Bueno. El pobrecito. Tan pobre viejecito. Necesita comida." She nodded as she pronounced the last word. Comida. He needed food.

"But you must raise his head, the doctor, el medico, said so, so he doesn't choke."

She looked confused. "Choque?" Probably she had flunked English.

"Cabeza arriba."

She raised her head.

"No. Su cabeza de el. Para que pueda tragar correctamente la sopa."

"Ah. Si. Comprendo. Usted tan buen amigo del viejo. Y el tan enfermo en la cama y no puede moverse ni hablar ni nada ni mirar la television siquiera."

She would soup him up. There was no reason Elliot shouldn't go down to the dining room now. According to the guidebooks, the Hotel de Carlos had one of the best restaurants in San Santo.

"Me back soon." He started for the door. After a few steps he stopped, returned to the bed and grabbed Ollie's wallet. She seemed such a nice, sweet, charitable old thing. But you could never be sure.

In the elevator framed photographs showed scenes of performances in the adjoining nightclub. Nearly naked muscular males danced or wrestled on stage while an audience of largely man/woman couples looked on smiling. "The mens enyoy see atletas in dance artistic." This was the caption under the photo.

The Hotel restaurant was known on six continents for its unconventional entertainment and clientele. The elevator dropped to lobby level and the door opened. The restaurant was just to the left.

The dining room was furnished in Spanish colonial style. In fact, with its heavy furniture and the dark woodwork skirting the walls, the antique tapestries and baroque portraits of seventeenth century viceroys and bishops and saints, the room might have been unchanged since colonial times. Not so the waiters. Dressed in red jackets and tan trousers they scudded across the room in large numbers. Elliot was shown to a table.

He considered the menu. He was determined to avoid iguana and llama. There were beef dishes. Carne de res. This too was disagreeable. Wallby had convinced him that animals must be loved, not eaten, although the Reverend did not always follow his dictum literally. Pollo was the best bet. High quality protein. And the poor chickens were not mammals and probably would not have grieving relatives.

To start, Elliot ordered a glass of pisco. Adopting local customs was important. "And I'll try the pollo."

"Si, senor." The redcoated waiter winked at him. "And will you require companion?"

"Companion? No. My companion is in our room on the third floor. He is indisposed."

"Ho ho. No, I mean food to eat with pollo."

"Oh. I understand. I suppose a beer and a bottle of wine."

"Excellent, senor."

Within minutes he was served with a small glass of pisco, as well as a bottle of beer. He tilted a drop of the pisco onto his tongue. Ugh! Aagh! It tasted like something fermented from mummies. And probably was. Nearby Peru was famous for its mummified corpses of the Inca period. The drink was very strong, almost unpalatable to the neophyte. A swallow of beer helped to cleanse the palate.

He looked around the room, checking out his fellow diners. Most were men dining alone or by twos. He recognized a few odd birds who had been in the lobby when he and Wallby made their entrance. A tall man with whitish blond hair returned his gaze and nodded. Elliot looked away. You had to be careful. They were not in Beverly Hills anymore.

The first dish served was a sort of soup or potpourri with beans and vegetables and corn meal. Elliot took a small spoonful, then washed it down with a swallow of beer and a sip of pisco. Odd flavors from everywhere. But not entirely disagreeable. There was a plate of flat bread on the table and he bit the corner of a triangular piece. It was rather tasteless, but filling. Probably this was what Santanos lived on, when they could. Other diners seemed to be revelling in huge plates of iguana flesh covered with red vegetables. One group was hacking away at a whole side of llama.

The local beer was good. It helped wash away the taste of the pisco.

The waiter brought Elliot's dinner, accompanied by another glass of pisco (later Elliot learned that pisco was often called "wine"). Exotic gourds were among the vegetables. The guidebooks had explained that each province of El Santo had its own varieties of squash and gourds, although most tasted alike, being equally bland, which is a worldwide characteristic of squash. The pollo was nicely glazed with a red sauce and spices. Elliot tore a small forkful from the carcass. It tasted … not bad, but it wasn't chicken. He washed it down with pisco. Oddly, this improved the flavor of both the pisco and the pollo. He scraped another piece of the red-tinged animal muscle away from the mass. Another sip of pisco. He was getting nutrition.

The waiter placed a small carafe in front of him. Pisco. "It is from the gentleman." He indicated the whitish haired man who nodded again in his direction. This time Elliot nodded in return. Politeness required.

Elliot was chewing through his fifth piece of animal tissue when the tall man presented himself at Elliot's table.

"Jonathan Winthrop Belcher." He put out a long blond hand.

"I'm Elliot Spenseric. Of …" he started to stammer in confusion, Belcher was so impressive, " … Beverly Hills." He swallowed more pisco. It brought confidence along with its largely nasty taste.

Jonathan eased into a seat at the table. He refilled Elliot's pisco glass. "I'm glad to see that you are taking advantage of the local products. They are excellent. I'm here with People's Watch."

Elliot looked at the timepiece on his wrist. He did not need a new one.

"We're observing the local rights situation."

"Oh." Jonathan's long face, with its straight and protuberant nose above a wide flat mouth, was not handsome. But it made an effect. He was self-confident and aristocratic, but he also had that "common touch". He looked like someone who should be working for the United Nations, negotiating the end of mutual bombings for the thirty-seventh time. "I am here as a tourist." Elliot lied. It was the safest thing. El Santo was not Beverly Hills.

"You are traveling alone?"

"No. My friend, the Reverend Oliver Francis Wallby, is here with me."

"The floppy looking fellow you came in with?"

"You saw him? We arrived on a flight from L.A. this morning. Ollie has not adapted to the altitude yet. He's resting in our room." Floppy described old Ol' pretty well.

Jonathan rubbed his long chin, where a few whitish hairs had escaped the shaver. "Wallby? Isn't he the gent who was in all the newspapers?"

Elliot grabbed his glass of pisco and swallowed half an ounce of nasty. "Sort of. You see, most of what the newspapers wrote was highly exaggerated and not too accurate. Ollie never touched anyone under the age of forty." For Ollie, a forty year old was infantile. "His bishop had to protect the appearance of propriety, so he fired Ollie. So much donation money comes from people who never lived the Cultural Revolution."

"Is that what it was? The press was full of all kinds of graphic descriptions. There was no bondage or whippings? Transvestite frolics?"

"The last part maybe a little. No whippings, though. Ollie is absolutely against whippings of any kind."

"Oh." Jonathan was surprised, disappointed.

"You see, he grew up in a different age. His mother used to whip him when he was a lad. It influenced his personality drastically, that's why he turned to religion. Although, from what he has told me, I think those naked whippings by his mother were justified."

Jonathan drank pisco from the glass he had brought from his table. He swallowed it as if it were water rather than a vicious, highly alcoholic syrupy dregs. "'Violence is never justified'. I see you're enjoying a portion of forest pig. It's a popular dish here."

"No, this is chicken. Pollo."

Jonathan laughed. "Pollo is the word used here for forest pig. It's actually a type of porcupine, but much bigger."

Elliot gagged. He tried to reach into his throat with a finger to retrieve the pollo and almost vomited. He felt sick. Pisco helped him over the nausea. "I'd never have … aagh aagh argh … eaten it if I'd known. I'm a vegetarian."

"I admire your sentiments. 'Eat peace, save the planet'. Is your Reverend here as a missionary? The press said something about a 'nude Mass' in Los Angeles. Has he gone over to Rome?"

"No. You can rest assured. It was not a Catholic ritual, only an ancient fertility rite. They do it in New Guinea."

"They do it here," Jonathan quipped, smiling.

Elliot speared a large piece of provincial squash with his colonial fork. He bit another edge of flatbread. "You say you're here to watch rights? Ollie gave me a rundown on the situation. He's read all the books. I know they need it."

"But not exactly in the way many people think." Jonathan kept giving him a look that was flattering as well as disturbing. "You see, since the Correo brothers took over here, foreign powers, especially El Norte, have tried to prevent reforms. The Correos have given everything to the people, so naturally the former possessed classes and their foreign allies resent them and wish to sabotage their efforts to provide basic essentials to the masses. We're keeping a watch on that."

The Correo brothers, Stalin and Lenin. Wallby had given him a summary version of them. The Alliance, their party, was now the sole political organization. Almost everything had been nationalized, sometimes more than once. Money was outlawed. Social values were foremost. Among the two Correos, Stalin was the nicer one. Lenin was said to have an orgasm when he witnessed the execution of contra-revolutionaries. Elliot was savvy enough not to let on that he and Wallby had come to help FARS. FARS and The Alliance were ideologically identical, but they were deadly enemies. FARS wanted to overthrow The Alliance and establish a *real* people's dictatorship.

"People's Watch is here to make sure that the imperialist powers do not grab the people's right to run the country their own way."

"I see." Elliot drank a swallow of Peruvian wine of a different sort. It wasn't bad. At least not after the pisco. "Ollie and I have come to see this country and its people. Ollie is excited about the volcanoes. Such enormous holes. He thought he could see them from the airplane."

"The Times said he was arrested. He isn't on the lam, is he?"

Elliot tried to laugh. "Oh no. Not at all. Charges were dropped, at least in L.A. County. He did get a letter from the Federals, though. All very vague stuff."

"Why don't you come up to my room after your meal. I'll give you some literature that explains what PWO is and why we're here. You and Wally might want to help us. We need all the extra eyes we can get."

"It's Wallby. Reverend Oliver Wallby. In the days before Naked Mass he used to do the sermons and things at Saint Henry's Church in Westwood."

"Never been there. I'm not a great one for religion. Come up to my suite and I will offer you a glass of aged pisco. Most of the stuff they serve here at Carlos' hotel is straight off the llama train. Manolito is out for the night. That's my young Santano companion from the local Watch group. We share a hotel suite."

That look. What did he have in mind? "I have to look in on Wally. I mean Ollie. A health worker was feeding him soup when I came down to the dining room. She seemed a nice woman, dressed in some sort of provincial or cultural outfit."

"Ah. Yes. Probably you met Influenzia. She often has to change Manolito. Sometimes, when he uses the white powder for more than two or three days running, he drops into a state of exhaustion. Diarrhea attacks can occur. I'm trying to get him to give up the habit, but ..." Jonathan shrugged.

"That's not Ollie's problem." Elliot was emphatic. "It's just the altitude. He's a little bombed out. He should recover in a day or two, everyone says so."

"How old is the floppy guy?"

Elliot thought for several minutes. In fact, he wasn't sure. Ollie was sensitive on the subject of his age. Probably seventy or eighty, at least. "He's not exactly a spring chicken, or pollo. I think he said about seventy-five." A nice compromise. "He's spry for his age, though, whatever it is."

"I only ask because I know that elderly people have a hard time adjusting to the altitude here in El Santo. Sometimes they never do."

"I think Ollie will. He once lived in the Himalayas for several months."

"Come to my room. I can show you a number of interesting handicrafts made locally in San Santo province and in Amazonas. That's the Amazon. Autochthonous erotic traditions are amazing, far in advance of the Naked Mass."

Elliot was wary. He did not want to decline, since Jonathan's contacts might be useful for promoting Che-su, but he suspected an ulterior motive. "I must look in on Wally first. I may be able to introduce you."

"By all means. But have the dessert, after you finish your forest pig. It's a local specialty."

"Not made from iguana?" Elliot was suspicious.

"Oh no." Jonathan laughed a broad free laugh. "It's a sort of custard made from squash and sweetened with honey. They add forest spices. It tastes like nothing on this planet."

Great. Martian food. Just what he needed. "Sure. What have I got to lose?" He used a finger to clear the remains of the pollo from his pharynx.

In fact, the custard was not bad at all. It was a bit too spicy and had small, black pieces of fruit or something—they couldn't be raisins, not at this altitude. It complimented the forest pig and pisco in a strange but effective way. "Umm. It's tangy. I guess they eat a lot of it here."

"When they can. Because of the stratagems of the major capitalist powers, natillas are rare today on the average Santano table. Although, strictly speaking, they don't eat at tables."

Elliot drained his pisco glass. It wasn't really too nasty, when you got used to it. They walked to the elevator.

Jonathan faced the framed picture of the wrestler/dancers. "Have you seen the show yet? It's incredible. Bring your friend to the nightclub when he feels better. If that doesn't start him up again, nothing will. Monolito auditioned for a part, but he is, well, too thin for big time."

At floor three Elliot led the way to the shared room. "I think this is it." He put his key in the lock. It refused to budge. "No, wrong door." He moved down the hallway. "Ah! This is it." He opened the way into the luxury suite, then tiptoed to the bedroom. At a gesture, Jonathan followed. Reverend Wallby was still sleeping. A healthy snore came from his open mouth. He was still wearing his dentures.

"Ollie looks fine." He pushed the inert figure with a hand. "Ol', I want you to meet someone. He's involved in rights and liberation. This is Jonathan."

"Charmed," Jonathan said in the direction of the open mouth.

"He's usually more alert. He must still be very tired. He's not really in a coma."

"No doubt. Well, come along to my place now and I'll give you a show."

"I'll be back, Ollie." Loud snorts came from the hair-filled nose passages.

The elevator moved up slowly to floor four. "Here we are." Jonathan stepped spryly out into the corridor. "It's a shame Monolito is out. He is really a talented dancer, especially folkloric and pre-Columbian. Something like in the nightclub, but not nearly so hefty. His mother taught him. He resembles her in many ways."

The entryway to Jonathan's hotel room was graced by a large framed print of Mahatma Gandhi. "I decorated the rooms myself. People's Watch Organization has a long lease on the place." Beneath the Mahatma were smaller photos of the Correo brothers, Stalin and Lenin. They were autographed. "Stalin's the nicer one," Jonathan explained. "Although Lenin is probably the more passionate. I've met both of them twice."

Elliot peered closely at the photo of Lenin Correo. There was something fervent and twinkling about the eyes. The nose was grimmer. While they were examining the pictures they became aware of a heavy breathing sound coming from the bedroom.

Jonathan picked up on it immediately. He was not happy. He walked quickly toward the bedroom door, which was half open. Elliot followed. From the doorway they could see two naked male figures, both prone on the bed, one on top of the other. They emitted groans in tandem to a rhythmic movement about their waists.

"Manolito!" Jonathan called. He was ignored by the naked figures

"Which one is Manolito?"

"The one on the bottom."

"With the thick neck and small ears?"

"Exactly. I distinctly told him not to bring his friends up here, paying or not! He'll hear about this when he's 'finished'." Jonathan closed the bedroom door. "Watching his antics is even more disagreeable than participating." He spoke as if from experience. "Let's go to the salon."

The larger room was decorated with local curios and works of art. The furniture was hard and modern. On the floor in front of the sofa was a leopard skin. "This is from Africa, from my previous mission. Please sit." Jonathan went to a large cabinet and came back with two glasses filled with a dark liquid. "Pisco, almost one hundred years old." He handed a glass to Elliot.

With all due caution, Elliot tried a sip. Suddenly he spat the liquor out and began coughing from deep in his throat. It was like fire, and there were small pieces of a hard substance, possibly charcoal, that he spat repeatedly for several minutes.

Jonathan tried to slap him on the back, but Elliot warded off the helpful blows. "You must have swallowed the wrong way."

"Aagh. Aagh. Urgh. Urf. Maybe I aagh urgh did."

"I'm dreadfully sorry. Try holding your nose as you drink."

Suddenly Manolito emerged from the bedroom dressed only in a pair of shorts. Later Elliot would learn that he had probably been attracted by the smell of pisco. He was a long-term aficionado.

"Here is my wanton little champion." Jonathan playfully grabbed the younger man at the back of the neck and tried to bend him from the waist, but without success. "Naughty naughty."

Manolito looked shorter standing. His torso was disproportionately long for his small legs. An especially thick neck and a small head did not improve his appearance. "I do wark today."

"Tonight," Jonathan corrected. "His English is coming along, but he still needs lessons. Verdad, campanero?"

"I do wark. For the peece."

"Of course. Such an adorable little internationalist. Mano', would it inconvenience you to put some clothes on over your jockey shorts? We do have company."

"Ya ya. Yes. I do the dress. You me excuse." Manolito skipped out of the room.

"He's really quite intelligent, even if he doesn't learn the first time. But I promised to show you some artifacts of anthropological interest. Besides Manolito." Jonathan laughed at his own joke. He rummaged in a large chest, pulled out several objects and brought them to the sofa where Elliot was sitting.

"These are Guajirano, mostly, as well as from several related ethnic groups." Jonathan held up an oblong wooden object with crisscross carvings and pieces of feather stuck at various spots. "This is a totem ritual object." He handed it to Elliot, who held it with his fingertips. It was disagreeably sticky.

"In fact, it is used for fertility rites intended to insure reproduction."

Elliot handed the ritual object back to Jonathan, who held it in a vertical position, the better to explain its use. "During the rituals the totem priest will grasp it firmly at one end, then …" Manolito suddenly reappeared. At first he was smiling. For some reason he was wearing a blue dress. When he saw the totem object he screamed.

"Aiee! Aiee! No no no senor. Nunca mas. Por favorrr!" He ran from the room, somewhat ackwardly because the skirts were too long for his diminutive legs.

When his little companion had tripped out of the room, Jonathan explained. "He became frightened because of ingrained conditioning, you see. His people have been detribalized for barely more than a generation. He has an innate fear of the taboo, of ju-ju, of witchcraft connected with the totem object. I am attempting to wean him from these irrational beliefs, but it is a slow process. At the same time, I am trying to give him a positive image of his people's culture, which is really very marvelous in certain aspects."

Elliot could see Manolito's head peeking around the doorway. He was still too frightened to come into the main room.

"For instance, transvestitism. It is an essential part of Guajirano culture. Not effeminate, of course. Many of their greatest warriors and hunters have been transvestites. The Guajirano believe that some males are inhabited by the Kwi-Kwi spirit, which allows them to mediate feminine powers into the masculine world of hunting and combat."

"So Manolito may be inhabited by this qui-qui thing?"

"Possibly. At least he thinks so. In fact, I discovered Mano at El San Basas, where we have an agency. It was during the garbage emergency."

Elliot looked disturbed and confused.

"You were not here at the time of the emergency and it was not reported in the international press, so naturally you are unfamiliar with it. The garbage emergency occurred just after the Alliance, the Correos' party, initiated the currency reform. The unsophisticated Guajirano were stampeded into the belief that because money was now outlawed, their needs would not be provided for. They rushed to seize the mission trash containers because metal, plastic and glass objects that are thrown away can be redeemed for cash. The crowds at our El San Basas station became unmanageable, as well as creating an epidemiological nightmare. We called in a local army detachment. They fired in the air, but that only made the scavengers more frantic. We were forced to abandon the mission. I rescued Manolito, who had become stuck under the steel fence that protected the garbage area. He has been with me in San Santo for eight years now."

Elliot sorted this information for possible use in Wallby's Che-su campaign. It wasn't going to be easy. "Then, is Manolito now working for the People's Watch Organization?"

Jonathan sneered. Mano, still in his blue dress, was standing in the doorway, keeping out of reach. "Hardly. He still has not grasped what our organization is about. He works on his own in the streets of San Santo, sometimes in ways that I disapprove. But his antics are really a survival tactic, a recrudescence of the conditions of the *ancien regime* of the former ruling classes. It will take some time to get the people on their feet. Or, in this case, at least off their bellies." He laughed and glanced disagreeably at the blue dress.

"We are naturally dependent on the Alliance government's help in carrying out our mission. At this moment one major problem is an imperialist backed terrorist organization called FARS. They proclaim revolutionary goals but in fact are tools of the external reactionary powers."

Elliot was glad that he hadn't let slip that he and Wallby were there to work with FARS. They might have been facing a firing squad.

"More pisco?"

"No, thank you. Uargh!" Elliot spat out one final charcoal pip.

"Mano," Jonathan called to the evanescent blue dress. "Quieres pisco?"

The blue fabric rushed forward. Mano grabbed the pisco flask and drained it at a gulp. It might have been water and he a Sahara camel. He smiled, burped just slightly.

"Mano grew up with the traditional liqueur, so he is highly accustomed to it."

"Mu' b'en."

"In fact, his father and uncles and cousins were involved in the commercial production of pisco. On a small scale, of course, before the reforms. Now all work is for the people."

"Make much pis'o."

"That's right, Mano. He really is learning English fast. Quite brilliant, despite a lack of formal education. Verdad, amiguito?" He grabbed Mano's skirts and pulled him closer. Mano was apprehensive. "Now, what I would propose is that Mano and I reenact the ancient Guajirano fertility rite. You could participate, Elliot. It is an unbelievably intense experience, spiritual and sensual. With profound sexual-religious overtones."

"I must check in on Ollie. And I'm feeling the altitude a bit myself."

"It would take only fifteen minutes, half an hour at most." Mano made a rush toward the door, but was stopped by Jonathan's firm hold on his skirts. Mano slipped. He lay on the floor looking up at Jonathan with an expression of terror.

"Aiee aiee!"

"Really, I must be going."

"He is only enacting the role of one possessed by the Kwi-Kwi spirit. Pure theatricality."

"The Reverend Wallby is under my care. I must leave."

"If you have any interest in anthropology and in folkways, you will stay. Despite his apparent clumsiness, Manolito is a very nubile actor or actress. He has known the ancient tribal rites since early youth. I think his chronological age is twenty-three. The native peoples usually have sparse facial hair."

Elliot looked at Manolito as he lay sprawled in the folds of the blue dress. He might be twenty-three. Emotionally, subtract twenty. "I must check on Ollie. Some other time."

Jonathan sighed. "You really don't know what you're missing. But I will not insist since you clearly are not in the mood. Take some pamphlets with you. You and the old gent may want to help with our mission." He went to a cupboard and came back with a dozen booklets. He handed them to Elliot.

"The Struggle against Imperialist Exploitation", "El Santo Its Own", "How the Alliance Broke the Chains of Class Rule", "Sexual Liberation in National Liberation: the Santano Example".

"Thank you. I'll certainly study these." He opened one and skimmed a page. "I'm sure we can—might—help."

"We'll be in contact. I hope your friend feels better. By the way, don't let Dr. Zapatero out of your sight. He's a bit of a kleptomaniac."

In the bedroom of the third floor hotel suite, Wallby had opened his eyes. He was still snoring. He was not really in a coma.

"Ol'? How do you feel? Still a bit under the altitude?"

"Arrange meetings with the leaders. We must begin. Begin. High, dreadly high …"

"Of course, but rest for now. I don't think you're well yet."

"I will preach on the peaks, before the multitude, for Che-su."

"Of course, Ollie. Just as soon as you are well."

Oliver dropped into unconsciousness. His eyes even closed.

Elliot took Wallby's wallet out of his pants pocket and counted the cash. Five hundred and eighty- five dollars. From what he had seen, you could buy half the country for that. He lay down on the other bed and was soon unconscious.

The next morning, Influenzia brought the breakfast tray. There was soup for Ollie and a piece of bread and some coffee for Elliot. "You fren look much de better. Like he well soon."

"Yes, he does look improved." Elliot spoke from under the covers. "His left eye is partially open." Ollie was still making a lot of noise when breathing. He was using the sparse local oxygen at a prodigious rate.

"He get the altitude. That why he sleep like de gringo touristas. He pretty old, though, maybe fifty, sixty. He not young like you." She gave Elliot a strange look. She might have been signalling that he could make some money.

"He is well preserved for his years." Reverend Wallby was into his seventies. "Possibly because of his religiousness. Es pastor. Tiene iglesia en Los Angeles."

N.B.: "Pastor" means a Protestant minister.

"Ah. Que bueno. He ver' goo' man. Make pray to de God. Mi seester work in Los Angeles, bu' not in de church." She giggled.

"He does indeed 'make pray to de God'. Although he can't always decide which god he is praying to."

Influenzia did not understand. She began to ladle spoon loads of soup into Wallby. "Dese make he feel bien. Tiene legumbres y verdes." She loaded in as much as he could swallow. "Wha he need is de coca. Tha' make no feel de high mountain. I have the coca me." She opened her mouth to show that she was indeed chewing coca leaf.

Elliot looked away. He had lost his appetite. "Yes. Possibly. He will have to regain full consciousness first, in order to chew properly"

"Yah. He get the chew quick."

"He's not really in a coma, you know."

"Como?"

"Coma. He's not really in one. Not now."

"Ah. Comprendo." She did not understand.

"El medico, el Doctor Zapatero, says that he's almost conscious now."

At the mention of Zapatero, Influenzia drew back, spilling soup on Wallby's chest. "I go now before Zapatero come. He see me he do the beat." She looked around the room, possibly trying to locate personal objects that had not yet been purloined.

Since Wallby had already been stuffed with as much soup as he could absorb at the moment—you could tell because he was drooling—Elliot did not insist that she stay to feed the Reverend further. Her fears of Zapatero were of course irrational, but natives were like that. You couldn't force them to accept reason, it was a matter of observation and slow learning for them.

"Thank you. Muchas gracias." He gave her a one-dollar bill. Influenzia looked at the banknote in disbelief. She started to whimper in gratitude. The Santano people were well known for their almost universal sense of gratitude.

"Oh gracias, senor. Usted es mi padre y el padre de toda mi familia, de todo mi pueblo."

"No need to exaggerate. You'll be back this evening, for more soup?"

She nodded, bowed her way to the door.

The locals were an obliging bunch. You couldn't accuse them of a lack of politeness. He took another close look at Wallby. Ollie was still sleeping, but he really did look better. Color was sprouting on his cheeks. It was probably the effect of Influenzia's soup, a very nutritious concoction no doubt.

"Ollie?" He shook the elderly divine's shoulder. "Ollie! Wake up!"

Oliver Wallby sprang to life. "Yes. Yes, my boy. You are absolved of all sin. *Ego te absolvo.* Let us bring the flocks to Che-su, *per secula saeculorum.*" He was still raving, but at least he was conscious.

"How are you, Ol'? You've been asleep for a long time."

"I ... yes ... have felt ..." He dropped back into snooze land.

Although still suffering from the altitude, Wallby was clearly coming around. Since there was no need to watch by the bedside, Elliot decided to take a look at San Santo. It would be their home for an indefinite period of time.

It would be unwise to dazzle the locals with a display of wealth. Elliot dressed casually and modestly. A pair of slacks, not new, a sweater, a jacket. He stuffed all of the cash and most of the valuables into his pockets. No need to expose Zapatero to the *near occasion of sin.*

Just before exiting the hotel lobby, Elliot took a long look at himself in the large mirror that hung on the wall just above a vase stuffed with local flowers. More than dapper, almost youngish was his self-evaluation. His clothes stylish but not garish. Not for anything in the world would he wear the costume jewelry hawked on the sidewalks in Hollywood.

There was a crowd outside the hotel. Maybe there had been an accident and these were gawkers. But many of them held little signs. "Guide Touristas" "Guia Speak English" "See Wanders of San Santo" "Naughty Nights". They were offering their services. The women wore the customary derby, the colorful manta. Some offered curios. Imitation shrunken heads. Plaster busts of Columbus. Photos of undressed women/men. At the sight of a foreigner, a cry was raised. "Aqui aqui. Senor, see ladies. Watch the naked dance. See palacio, catedral, monasterio."

Elliot snaked his way through the crowd, hitting at intrusive hands, guarding his valuables. Then he was free in the street, followed by only five or six die-hards. "Desnudas, completamente, baratas, todas horas." He left them behind, like a horse running ahead of a swarm of flies. He tore down a side street, ducked behind a pillar of a colonial style building. While recovering his breath, Elliot caught sight of a familiar figure. It was Manolito. He was in his blue dress, quite becoming. He was leaning against a wall, taking a break from his work. He smoked a cigarette. A little mustache was visible on his upper lip. It was not unbecoming either. Then Manolito noticed him. At first Mano' drew back, but then, probably twigging to the fact that Jonathan, whom he had seen several times in the company of Elliot, was somewhere else, he relaxed, signaled Elliot to approach. Elliot showed his wristwatch and pointed at the dial with fingers of his other hand. He didn't have time, not right now. Maybe later. Mas tarde, quizas. He moved away. Manolito followed anyway.

A few yards away, Elliot ducked into a church. Mano wouldn't dare follow him into a church to press his services. Not in that dress—it was cut excessively low and used padding to enhance breast development. Inside the church it was dark, except for the light from a few votive candles placed in side altars before holy statues and pictures. A few bundled figures prayed on their knees. The hum of rosary recitation wafted on the air. This was very interesting. It was Culture. No naked dancers, no pisco, no fertility rites, just good, plain, historically endorsed Culture. Elliot lit a candle to Santa … he hasn't sure which Santa it was, but she was impressive. The earnestness of suffering, the plain marks of devotion, of abnegation. He lit the candle for Wallby. May he recover from his illness. As far as Che-su, Elliot offered no particular request. It was a formula that he would have had difficulty putting into words.

Elliot left by a different door. Outside, he blinked in the sunlight, then wandered into a café. It was only minutes since he had left the Hotel de Carlos, but already he felt a need for rest, for refreshment.

The Altitude. He sat down at a small round table, not particularly clean. After a thirty-minute wait during which Elliot observed the bottles on display behind the bar—there were six of them—and the lack of other patrons, and the wall decorations (bullfight posters from the fifties or seventies), a waiter approached. From appearances it seemed that he had not changed his uniform since long before the end of the oligarchic class rule society.

"Senor." His fatigued tone seemed to indicate that he was disillusioned by foreign tourists and their so often belied tipping potential.

"Pisco. Grande. Vaso limpio." Clean glass. That was important.

Ten minutes later Elliot was served with a large glass of dark liquid. He took a sip. It tasted better than Jonathan's pisco and better than the pisco served in the dining room of the Hotel de Carlos. Maybe it had been diluted with Coca-Cola. Just possibly he was getting used to the taste. He gazed at the posters, the bottles, contemplating. It was a strange land, this place where they were to begin their New Life. But stranger things had happened. In a few months or years they might be swallowing pisco like Coca-Cola. While this meditation was going on, a little figure rushed into the bar. The bartender noticed first. He charged at the little blue figure, a dirty, wet bar towel swinging in the air.

"Vaya, puta, hijo de madre de puta! Vaya! No vuelvas nunca o te mato!"

"Manolito! Whatever are you up to now?"

Twigging to the fact that his only customer was an acquaintance (customer?) of the little blue one, the bartender let his towel fall to a flaccid state. He moved back to the rear bar area, grumbling as he went. Elliot could make out only one word, expressive as it was. "Mierda!"

Manolito came quickly to Elliot's table. He understood that the foreigner's influence gave him protection.

"Buenos, senor. Hello you, sir."

"Jonathan would be upset if he knew what you were up to. But in any case, I have to say that blue suits you better than red."

"Gracias, senor. Jo'nan sabe I here. He know all for it. Bu' me no like him. Dese man he with the Alianza. An' he make me do dese work wi' de guy for him."

Elliot twigged that Mano had something to say. He would have invited him to sit down, but there was only one chair in the café and he was occupying it. In any case, Manolito was so short that, standing close to the table, he looked like he was sitting. Elliot was upset by the information about Jonathan. "You mean he is a chulo?" Chulo: pimp.

Manolito laughed. "Of course he chulo. Here ever'one chulo or puta. But that nothing. I do wark for him, cuz me, I got wife an' fife hijos. I gi' dem de food."

He was married and had five children at the age of twenty-three, or possibly thirteen. Elliot was not surprised. Wallby had read the books on sociology and anthropology and had mentioned the custom of "premature nuptiality". "I understand. You are only doing a job. I admire your courage and initiative as well as your sense of parental responsibility."

"Than you. Wad I hate is de Jo'nan with de Alianza. He make me do de thing for de Correos, de Stalin, de Lenin." Mano spat on the ground. "He take de mitad for pay de impuestos." [mitad: half. Impuestos: taxes] The bartender shot him a rapid, angry look, then smiled as at an enfant's prank when he saw that Elliot was watching. "Me, I do wit' de FARS, for make de big hard for de country. De crazy Jon'an make me do thing for the Alianza, but I do all time for FARS."

Elliot was gratified to find a FARS sympathizer. He was not sure that it would be wise to uncover himself and Wallby as friends of FARS so soon. This was dangerous ground. "So you want to help erect your country. That is wonderful. You are a true patriot."

"Si! si! 'Rec' de country! When we ged are leader on de top, den we have revolucion. All the people have free. Food, car, womens, mens."

Manolito's notions of the political aims of the Frente Armado de la Revolucion Santana were caricatural and distorted. His idealism was beyond doubt.

"Me, I no like dese wark I do wi' mens, bud no hay otro trabajo. Dey no pay you in money for work for Alianza. Dey gi' you de scrip. It not word nuding. No vale nada. Dey wipe de butt wid it."

"Social scrip. Yes, Jonathan informed me. It replaces money."

"It replace de shit."

Alert to possible betrayal, Elliot looked rapidly around the room. The bartender was polishing glasses, his head bent over his work. There was no one else in the room. "You must be more discrete, Mano'. These are dangerous times for all of us."

"De street? Yeh, I bedder go back to de street. I gotta make de money for mi familia. Dey gotta eat too." Mano had received the equivalent of a B- in his *primaria* school English classes.

The blue dress swished toward the bar door. Mano' was in fact so short that, attired in the admittedly becoming blue dress, he appeared hardly to have any legs at all. This was the result of childhood malnutrition, which was endemic in El Santo. All of the books mentioned it. Without sufficient protein in the diet, growth during childhood was stunted. You couldn't live on pisco alone.

He would meet Mano' later, no doubt. Today Elliot's goal was to explore the city, the terrain where they would begin the struggle to teach Che-su to the masses. He paid for his drink and left a tip. Five cents plus five puntas of social scrip. He had a large wad of scrip in his pocket.

After he was out the door the bartender picked up a cell phone. He punched a number. "Diga! Servicios policiales!"

San Santo was a city that Elliot could love. Its buildings, old and old looking, contrasted with his native Beverly Hills. The luxury and other excesses of B.H. were ultimately tiring. Although Elliot was a pragmatist and understood that poverty could also be a drag. The people in the streets, whether in native costume or in modern attire, were so endearing. The People, with their age-old, customary, domestic, conjugal habits. So dear. Families always had numerous children. Usually the father was absent. Probably at work looking for work. Handicraft and lottery vendors were legion on every street corner. Food vendors were also numerous, although Doctor Zapatero had warned against street food. It was dysentery bait. Although not, of course, for the locals, who were immune by long use. Roast corn hawkers traded their wares with those selling bits of cooked pollo. It was quite a little picnic. Coca-Cola signs were everywhere, a vestige of the old regime of "class domination". In any case, a bottle of Coca would cost a month's wages for the New Santano.

In San Santo, the capital city, there were many palaces, cathedrals, historic buildings, convents and monasteries from the colonial period. They were beautiful. Elliot wished that he had brought his camera, but Wallby told him that it would only lead to trouble with the authorities—rightfully vigilant against imperialist snooping. He bought a postcard featuring a photograph of the main cathedral. He paid the itinerant postcard vendor with scrip. The vendor in his colorful manta and llama wool cap looked at the scrip— ten puntas—blew his nose on it and tossed it away. The people with their age-old customs were so dear. Elliot bought a small ceramic burro.

It was high time to check on Ollie. Elliot hurried back to the hotel. He walked quickly and as unobtrusively as possible through the lobby of the Hotel de Carlos. The desk clerk noted his entry. Jonathan, standing in a corner with a newspaper around his nose, lowered the news sheets and nodded in recognition.

Piso tres. Elliot exited the elevator. After having been away for the afternoon, he was anxious about Wallby's condition. He might not be as well as the doctor claimed. He entered the bedroom. It was a happy surprise to find Ollie sitting up and talking.

"God is manifested in the Person of Jesus but He has seen fit to give us a reminder in the appearance of Che. All shall not be Caesar's. It shall be given to the poor, who are with us always."

"You're well again, Ollie, what a relief!"

Wallby impatiently waved his hand. Elliot understood. This was practice for the Sermon on the Andes. It must not be interrupted. "And so, my humble ones, make the sign of the closed fist to signify that you are one in this, your first free revolucion." Suddenly Ollie's head lolled back onto the pillow. He started to snore.

The Reverend was coming around, but what was probably his first lengthy essay back into consciousness had been too much. He required more convalescence. Elliot was so glad to see that Ollie was on his way back to the living. You could hardly have a revolution without him.

As Wallby slept, Elliot looked around the room. There was a folded piece of paper on the table beside the minister. A note from the doctor: "Hello Senor. You frend do much the better. He well soon, but he need lot more the care. I come again ever day. My small fee is add to hotel factura."

Wallby snored on. His mouth was full open. The inside of his mouth had taken on a curious white color. Possibly a result of the altitude. Elliot noticed that the older man's wristwatch was missing. He hardly blamed Zapatero. Being a doctor in El Santo wasn't easy.

Since Wallby was resting peaceably, Elliot decided to use some of the time before dinner to take a bath. San Santo (the city) probably was much cleaner than it looked, but you still got an urge to wash from looking at the garbage in the streets and the puddles that reeked of something worse than excrement. The water from the bathtub tap itself was not clear. It wasn't brown, but it had a greenish tinge. The altitude, once again, most likely. He was scrubbing every surface and angle of his body with white soap—jabon blanco—provided by the hotel establishment, Producto de El Santo, as the paper wrapper proudly declared, when he heard sounds coming from the bedroom. It seemed that Influenzia had returned to soup Ollie up again. He regretted that he hadn't closed the bathroom door, but he was already soaking in the tub.

"Una vez mas, hijo, sorbe, sorbe, si si, la sopa deliciosa!"

Gargling noises.

"Bebe, hijo mio, bebe. Te ira mu ben."

Coughing, hawking, gurgling.

Maybe she was forcing the soup too much. Elliot thought that he ought to supervise the fluid application, least Wallby swallow too much the wrong way, which, at high altitudes, could be harmful. He raised himself from the bath water. Only partly covered with clinging bubbles, he rushed toward the clothes rack on the bathroom wall. Before he was halfway there Influenzia appeared in the bathroom doorway.

"Ah senor. Que guapito eres. Todo desnudo como estas. Mi amor." She rushed toward him.

Elliot backed toward the water. "I only wanted to make sure Ollie did not take the soup the wrong way. He sounded like he wasn't swallowing right."

"He not swallow. Me swallow." Influenzia tried to embrace him.

"Mrs. … Influence. At least let me get dressed first!"

"You no de dress. I de dress."

Elliot ducked her large encompassing arms. He grabbed a towel and quickly fixed it about his waist. "I have to check on Ollie." He rushed out of the bathroom.

Influenzia followed. "My love is not cost mucho, amorcito!"

He stopped at Ollie's protective side. Ollie's open mouth and his nostrils emitted strange noises, like the last water draining from a bathtub. "This doesn't look good. I'll have to call Doctor Zapatero."

This threat had the desired effect on Influenzia. "I come later for de bowl. I do no more goo here now." She fled.

Elliot went to retrieve his clothes. He glanced at himself in the bathroom mirror. No, he was not guapito. A little guapo, maybe, around the waist.

Decent at last, he went to look at Wallby. Ollie was snoring now without aqueous sound effects. He must be all right. In her over-excitement, Influenzia probably pumped the broth too fast.

"Ol'! Ol'! Please wake up. I need spiritual advice. I just almost sinned!"

The dining room was almost deserted. An American couple were offering toasts with the local wine while a huge plate of smoking meat simmered on their table. Jonathan sat quietly in the company of a Santano, a small man, very aquiline in features. Probably a pharmacist or a lawyer, maybe a teacher, definitely not a doctor. No Santano doctor could afford a meal at the Hotel de Carlos. Elliot scanned the menu. It hadn't changed since last night. He was determined not to order pollo of any kind. Unfortunately, there seemed to be nothing else on the menu. When the waiter arrived, he requested a carafe of pizco, and some legumbres, vegetables. Plus bread. No one could make any sort of bread out of "pollo".

There were pamphlets on each table. "See the famous Inca ruins of San Santo". "See the famous naked men/women wrestlers". "Free El Santo: the Challenge of Imperialist Intervention". This one was from People's Watch. The organization's logo, two mild and concerned older persons holding binoculars, was on its cover. Elliot read a few pages. It was familiar stuff. Wallby had clued him in the weeks before they left L. A. The basic idea was that the gringos were an imperialist power. Their history involved the destruction and exploitation of native peoples on a grand scale for the benefit of a class of narrow-minded imbeciles. The gringo empire was now making eyes at El Santo, hoping to add it to their necklace of shrunken heads/nations. The difference between the pamphlet and the version preached by Wallby was that the Reverend proclaimed FARS (Frente Armado de la Revolucion Santana) as the hoped for resistance to the greedy and bloated Northerners while Jonathan's pamphlet identified FARS as a Trojan horse for "Junky Sam". Jonathan was naturally unaware of the promise of the Che-su movement.

The waiter, all smiles as usual, brought the pizco, a plate of bread and what must be vegetables. When the server had bowed out, Elliot drank directly from the carafe. Pisco tasted better all the time. You only had to get used to it and to the altitude. The bread was basically bread-like, but it was flat and had little bits of something green and red mixed into the dough. The vegetables resembled a baked rutabaga or similar root crop swimming in a thin tomato sauce.

Suddenly, as before, Jonathan let himself down into a chair he had brought with him. Elliot looked up. The pharmacist had vanished. Brother Jonathan was smiling and offering his hand.

"I'm glad to see you have survived your first day in San Santo. But you haven't seen the wrestlers yet. The manager told me."

"No. I … had to care for Ollie."

"Of course. I admire your selflessness and sense of friendship. Not many would do the same."

"He's not really in a coma. He's just convalescing from the altitude."

"Zapatero told me. And you went to a church and then to a café where you drank pisco."

"How did you know?" Elliot was confused and apprehensive. Jonathan knew everything.

"Ha ha ha. Manolito told me. He happened to see you in the street. Naturally he followed you. He has a family to support, you know."

"Yes. Five darling little innocents."

"They will follow in the footsteps of their father."

Elliot tried to look at the floor.

"I see you have ordered the local pollo bread. It is excellent. It actually contains pieces of forest pig. Fully cooked of course."

Elliot dropped the piece he had been nibbling. "And the rutabaga?"

"Fried in forest pig fat."

Elliot took a large swig of pisco. It was the only consumable item available.

Jonathan laughed. "You still have the food prejudices of an American. Before long, you will become acclimatized. Actually, I was just talking to my friend Jaroy. He is a druggist and sometimes sees tourists with complaints about the local food. Although fewer and fewer these days, as a matter of fact. Most tourists have shied away since the Revolucion. Apparently they have been scared by what they have heard about the Correo government. Imperialist propaganda. In fact, both Stalin and Lenin are moderates interested only in improving the lives of their people. Stalin is the nicer one."

Elliot nodded. He really wasn't very interested in local politics. Beyond a commitment to helping Wallby spread the Che-su idea.

"Have you visited the cathedral yet? And the palace? The convents and monasteries?"

"Just from the outside. I didn't have enough time to go in."

Jonathan laughed. "Typical turista. I simply must take you in hand and make you into a genuine connoisseur of San Santo. Even though we are in the midst of a cultural revolution that is remaking the social, political and economic climate, much of old San Santo remains to savor."

Elliot savored from the carafe of pisco.

"Bravo! You are starting to do like we natives do."

"It tastes better now. Kind of like Coca-cola."

"Ha ha ha. Droll. But you're not eating anything. At least take a little of the rutabaga. A little forest pig grease never hurt anyone."

Elliot tried a small forkful of Santense rutabaga. It wasn't too bad. Something like yam, but stringier and spicier.

"Excellent. Take care of yourself or you'll be consulting Jaroy before long. Codeine helps a great deal with moderate cases of dysentery."

As a precaution against worse disease, Elliot swallowed more pisco.

"Mmm. You're learning. What I have come to say is that you and the clergyman—Wally?---could be of great help to our humanitarian movement, People's Watch. If you are going back to the states in the near future, for example, you could help us by carrying a small package to our people there. We have to sidestep the Yankee embargo."

"It's Wallby. Reverend Oliver Francis Wallby. We plan to stay indefinitely. We hope to spread the word of ..." He was about to mention Che-su, but stopped himself in time. You couldn't be too careful in these days of social upheaval.

Jonathan was disappointed. "In any case, we will keep in touch." He was off.

Elliot took a few nibbles of rutabaga and even a bite of pollo bread. He drained the pisco, then headed for the elevator. The framed pictures reminded him. He must see the famed men/women nude wrestlers. It was a cultural duty.

He unlocked the door to their third floor suite, then quickly relocked it from the inside. On the floor was a piece of paper with writing on it.

"Hello Senor. Done believe the lies of this guy Jonathan. This guy cheat me. He give you big trouble. Monolito."

Elliot sighed. The poor little tyke had even misspelled his own name. It wasn't surprising. During the period of rule by the class dominated parties, education had been reserved for the children of the wealthy, or at least the middle classes. Mano's origins were somewhere between the lower classes and the lower lower classes.

Elliot could hear the reassuring sounds of Wallby's heavy breathing as he lay in bed. Elliot decided to be an exemplary tourist. He would show respect for the cultural achievements of the Santano people and their past. After all, he and Ollie had come to guide the people to the paradise of Che-su and FARS. After visiting the cathedral, etcetera, he would look at the local markets. There were still goods for sale in the streets and squares. Local handicrafts as well as the heirlooms of the formerly wealthy classes. They didn't accept scrip. Cash or barter only.

Elliot swallowed a piece of forest pig bread in lieu of breakfast. Beyond any doubt Wallby was better. Last night he had turned over onto his side on his own power. Now he was not awake, but he was not snoring loudly. Instead, his breathing had taken on a chug-chug rhythm, like the Andean trains described in the brochures. Elliot wondered if he should remove the clergyman's dentures. They contained bits of gold that might tempt the staff. He decided to leave them. Zapatero and Influenzia would certainly have too much decency to stoop to denture robbery.

A rain-like mist was falling in the streets. The beggars, hawkers, guides and propositioners outside the hotel huddled looking damp and even more discouraged than before. Elliot was able to head toward the cathedral with little difficulty. He deposited a penny into the lap of an elderly beggar woman sitting on a paving stone with her shriveled hands formed into a bowl. She swooned from surprise. Probably she hadn't received a real coin since VP Nixon's visit in nineteen fifty-eight.

The cathedral was one of the national treasures. All the books said so. The Correos had declared the site to be under the special protection of the regime. A large sign on the church steps informed visitors of this. Inside, the altar was a baroque glory with multi-layered images of saints and viceroys and angels. Small portraits of Stalin and Lenin Correo had been added at ground level, probably to be nearer to the people they were leading. A dozen side altars lined each side of the nave. Candles provided a reverential glow. Many small hunched figures knelt in prayer. A sign attached to the altar rail announced that the next Mass would be celebrated at eight-thirty in the morning two months from now. This was not surprising. Real clergy were in short supply. Too many had to be executed during the takeover. Briefly, Elliot had the notion of contacting the cathedral authorities and offering Wallby's services, but he quickly realized that this was impractical. Even if Wallby recovered sufficiently to perform religious services within a week or two, Zapatero and Influenzia would probably have to hold him up. Besides, traditional rites, based on ancient Catholic practice, had nothing at all in common with the Naked Mass or any other Episcopal invention.

Elliot lit a candle, prayed briefly on his knees in front of a shrine, crossed himself—he was imitating the natives—and left. To the market! Piety and respect for local religious practices were well and good, but there was a sensual side to life as well.

Petty markets were in fact everywhere. Street vendors hawked everything from used plumbing fixtures to young relatives. Partly smoked cigarettes were prized highly. Whole crowds of petty entrepreneurs scrounged them at the airport or outside major hotels. Pollo in every shape, form and color was on sale. Handicrafts made of colored thread and little sticks had a wide following of vendors who pandered to the tourist predilection for infantile curios. For the local "consumers", however, these petty objects were of limited interest. What, after all, was the attraction of bric-a-brac in a society just barely above subsistence level? One advantage was that handicraft curio vendors would accept scrip for at least part of the purchase price. Elliot chose two "thread sticks" to bring back to Ollie.

One thing that Elliot had already learned about San Santo was that you could buy cups of pisco from outdoor bars that sold doses of the stuff for a few pennies. They were a welcome source of refreshment during a street trudge. As for non-liquid sustenance, baked sweet potatoes were a cheap, nutritious and just barely palatable supply. When he had loaded enough trinkets for Wallby and taken on a few odd ones for himself, Elliot hurried back to the Carlos. It was time to check up on the holy man.

Elliot was crossing the lobby, receiving the usual nod from newspaper draped Jonathan, when he was hailed by the check-in clerk.

"Oh Mister Spen, please could you have talk now?"

He went to the reception desk. "A detail, senor, please, but it is policy to pay each three days of resident."

"Oh." Elliot had assumed that the bill would be settled when he and the Reverend Wallby checked out. "Of course." He had the contents of Ollie's wallet in his pocket. "What is the amount due?"

The clerk produced a handwritten tab. "Merely seventy-two dollars and forty-six cents. Three nights of residence, four meals, and the women/men wrestlers."

"I have not yet had the pleasure of viewing the club act."

The clerk checked the tab again. "Excuse this error, senor. Sixty-nine dollars and forty-three cents."

Elliot peeled a few bills from the wad in his pocket and received the change. To the stupefaction of the clerk, Elliot left five cents on the desk counter.

On floor three, Wallby was still recuperating in dreamland. There were a few new soup stains on his shirt front. Another folded note was in evidence.

"Dear senor. I am have to take the superior dentures from the friend mouth. He must not be in danger of the eating of them." Dr. Zapatero.

Wide snoring showed that Wallby's upper teeth were missing. The advantage was that a clearer corridor for air was now opened in the reverential mouth.

"Ollie?" He shook the sleeper from the shoulder. "Ollie, wake-up, I've brought you some really nifty stuff from the street market! Besides, it's high time we got on with our mission. You know, for the New Life."

Ollie snorted in a way that seemed to indicate that he understood the message. He did not answer. His eyes were still closed.

"Ollie! I know we are at nine thousand feet and you have to get used to the altitude, but it's been three days now since we got here. You haven't even seen the women/men naked wrestlers."

The response was a new sort of rapid nose exhalation. Then the audio kicked in. "Ah ah ah I I shall speak to the ma ..."

"Yes, of course, Ollie, go on. You will speak to the masses, yes, it's what we came for."

"To the ma ... ma ... martians." The Reverend gentlemen returned to a deep snore.

This would not do. There was definitely something wrong with Ollie beyond the usual altitude sickness, even if he was more than seventy, even if he did have a bit of diabetes. It was very disturbing. Elliot would call Zapatero immediately. Ollie ought to be in a hospital, maybe even a clinic or sanatorium. He picked up the telephone.

"Recepcionista? This is three oh six. I must talk to Doctor Zapatero right away. My friend is still not well. He's not getting any better."

"Si senor. I hell im too soon. He not very slow to crumb."

The doctor would soon be on his way, if Elliot understood correctly.

"Oliver? Try to wake up, my dear friend. You ought to see these trinkets I bought in the market. They are wonderful examples of the people's handicraft art. If you saw them you would be inspired."

"Aargh. Ahng. Urghag."

There was a knock at the door and Zapatero rushed in.

"I am received you call, Mr. Spence. I understand your urgency." The doctor connected the stethoscope to his ears and applied the receptor to Wallby's chest. "Um. Um. Ya." He grabbed the minister's wrist and felt for a pulse. He measured it with his wristwatch. What was now *his* wristwatch.

"You fren is maybe too fast. His pulso. What I think is maybe he got a little infection in the pulmones. When they get the high up and they so old, then maybe they get infection in the lunges. I see theese lotta time."

"You think he has pneumonia? Once when he was in Nepal he had a massive case of dysentery, but nothing like this."

"Si. Pulmonia. I give him a medicine. He feel better the soon. Antibiotico. He are not allergic to penicillin?"

"No. Well, I mean, they didn't have any in Nepal."

"This make him feel so the better. I think it only he age and high up, but now maybe he got infection." Dr. Zapatero took a glass syringe out of his black bag. He wiped the syringe with a handerchief from his jacket pocket.

"I feel we ought to transport Reverend Wallby to a hospital, where he could receive the best possible care." Elliot.

Zapatero considered this. He wasn't happy. "No, you doan wanna go to hospital. All de doctor on de strike. They no wanna work for no money. Anyway, de hospital got all the disease from the sick people. De Pastor no much good in hospital. They make wait three day before see the doctor."

This was doubtless true. Lines in front of the San Santo Hospital emergency ward stretched for blocks. Elliot decided not to push the subject for now. "Couldn't we at least have an I-V bottle to make sure Ollie is receiving adequate fluids?"

"Ha ha. We got no ivy on the bottle, senor. We not that backward." Zapatero nodded and left the room. He had enough decency not to wait for the customary tip.

What now? Elliot had come with the Reverend Oliver Wallby to this high land to start the New Life—he didn't fully understand what it was—and now his shepherd was unconscious, except for brief moments of nonsense. Fortunately he had bought a small bottle of pisco in the market. He drained it at a gulp. He had to think. What could he do? Hospital was a bad idea. Zapatero must know what he was talking about. If Wallby continued semi-comatose, then the mission was aborted. But they could not go back to L.A. Even before take-off the press had been talking about law suits filed by the "victims", that is, those who had chosen to participate in the Naked Mass, especially the Young Innocent, as she was called in the Times. Criminel charges were still quite possible. So they had to stay in El Santo. But what could they do? He looked at Ollie, looked down those hirsute air holes in his nose.

"Ollie, please. Try to wake up. This is El Santo, capital San Santo. Remember? It's the place to go."

Rumblings from the air passages of the reverend gentleman indicated that at least unconsciously he was processing data. His mouth moved. He was trying to talk. He was about to talk.

"Yes. Yes. What is it? Say it."

"Hossblank. Snublich. Ingreditch forg."

In dispair Elliot slumped onto the bed. No good. No bueno. Ollie was in dreamtime. Hospital was out. L.A. was out. Zapatero was doing his best, which wasn't much, a little penicillin. The last best hope came into Elliot's mind. Influenzia. Yes. She had tried to crank him, Elliot, up, why couldn't she do the same for Wallby? He grabbed the room phone.

"Reception? Yes. Hello. Thank you. My friend in three oh six is still not well. Could you contact the Senora Influenzia? She has given him a lot of soup, but now he needs much more."

"She help udder clientes. Maybe I find her. You wait some minutes?"

"Oh yes. I'll wait. Tell her it's an emergency. Tell her Wally needs her."

In the mean time Elliot curled up on the bed. The pisco bottle was dry. He grabbed a book that Ollie had brought from the states. "Obras Coleccionadas de Carlos Marx". No, no good. They had had all that in college. It was practically all their English teacher talked about.

There was a knock on the door. La Influenzia!

"Ah, Senor. They tell me you got so many much bad the poor Pastor. Que lastima! Hombre tan bueno, tan santo, tan guapo."

"I'm so glad you came—that is, arrived—quickly." Wallby "guapo"? This Elliot found hard to understand. Maybe she liked father figures.

Influenzia looked intensely at Wallby. "Ya. I see he no very much good. Ya he make noise in de nose like no respira bien. That not goo. I try give im de massage. Make loose so he res an get bedder." Influenzia began to rub and stretch the tissues of Wallby's abdomen and chest.

"Ay, si, todo va bien bien. Todo ira mejor. You make relax. Ya ya." Influenzia was pushing and twisting Wallby's muscles every possible way. She was panting with the exertion. It might have been partly the altitude, even though she was a long time resident. "Senor, maybe you leaf de room, so I not distract from de work him up."

"Yes. Certainly. I think the treatment is already starting to have an effect." Wallby's toes had started to twitch. He was groaning in a regular, rhythmic manner.

Elliot went into the main room. He sat on the cream color sofa and took up a brochure from the coffee table. "San Santo Visitors Guide." The headlined article recounted Stalin and Lenin's highly successful campaign to replace banned imperialist exploiter tourists with fraternal guests from socially progressive neighboring states. But Elliot could not concentrate on the text of the article. Strange moaning and cooing noises came from the bedroom. Influenzia was working her magic. Elliot caught snatches of words like guapo and grande and fuerte. There were sounds almost like a bellows being worked. It was possible things were going too far. Elliot rushed back to the bedroom, but the door was locked.

"Guapissimo senor ay ay ..." This came from behind the bedroom door.

He pounded on the door. "Mrs. Influenzia, please don't overdo it. The Reverend is still in a very fragile state. He is an ordained minister, even if he almost got defrocked!"

"Pillo. Haces groserias!" She could only mean Wallby.

More pounding. "Influenzia! You are going too far! Remember his age and condition. What if the Times found out?"

"Ay que pillito!"

The moaning reached a crescendo, then subsided quickly and stopped. Elliot listened with his ear to the door.

"Tu eres como joven. Todavia lo tienes todo."

Wallby said something, but it was muffled. Suddenly the door opened. Influenzia bustled out.

"Now you fren much de better. He got much stren."

Elliot peered into the bedroom. Wallby was sitting up and breathing quietly. He looked happy.

Obviously Influenzia had done good work. Elliot reached into his pocket and pulled out a dollar. He handed it to the care worker.

"Ah gracias senor. You so generoso. He git good now. I come again." She grasped his hand, winked, left.

There was something gooey on her hand. Elliot's fingers were sticky from the touch. He raised his hand to his nose. It smelled like fish. In the bedroom, Wallby still was lying raised against the pillows with a contented look on his face.

"I see Miss Influenzia has helped you quite a bit."

"I ... I am grateful for the intervention. Immeasurably sympathetic. The people are so ..." Wallby dropped off.

"We must begin to think about preaching to the poor dear people, Ollie. That's why we came. Remember the Che-su idea?"

Wallby was snoring. But he was certainly feeling better. Elliot smoothed the blankets around the reverend gentleman's waist. There was something sticky, smelly ... He forced himself not to think about it. It was dinner hour down in the restaurant and he wanted to arrive early, before the other guests snatched up the best pieces of pollo. He went to the bathroom to wash his hands.

His reflection in the bathroom mirror was reassuring. He wasn't exactly guapito, but he certainly had Wallby beat.

In the elevator Elliot noticed a detail in the nightclub advertising photo that he hadn't seen before. The male men/women wrestlers wore a sort of covering at waist level but the female men/women wrestlers were entirely unclad. Doubtless, this was a cultural expression.

Half a dozen tables were already occupied in the dining room, mostly tourists and the inevitable Jonathan. Elliot tried not to look at the tall New Englander. Jonathan's ancestors, from Ohio or Ontario or somewhere, had once purchased thousands of acres of what were then trees for a few bottles of adulterated fire water, or so he claimed.

He didn't need to look at the menu. It would never change. He ordered bread, sopa sin pollo and a large—mu mu grande—carafe of pisco.

"Gracias, senor." The waiter sped off. He too was tearfully grateful for the tips Elliot had left. At least five cents each evening, once a dime and a handful of scrip. The latter, as Elliot had had the opportunity to observe, were usually transferred to the bathroom stalls.

Elliot was studying a brochure about the local Inca ruins when Jonathan dropped into the vacant chair. "Dear friend. You have my greatest sympathy."

Jonathan signaled to the waiter. "Pisco doble, rapido." He reached out and grasped Elliot's hand. "It is a terrible thing to lose a friend, a great friend, one well known in the world of philanthropy and charity. He was a philosopher and a theologian as well. We will all miss him and his influence."

The pisco came. Jonathan swallowed his glass at a gulp. "There are practical things, too. You will no doubt be sending the body stateside for a decent burial. It just happens that People's Watch needs a method of communication with our adherents in the U.S. that cannot be censured and monitored by North American government agencies. If we could insert a small package into the box that will carry your dear friend's remains, we would even be willing to compensate you for the extra expense and trouble. This would in no way be disrespectful to his earthly remains."

"Whose?"

"Your friend, the Reverend Wally, of course."

"Reverend Wallby is not dead. He's not even in a coma. Ollie showed intense signs of life earlier this evening."

"Mm." Jonathan was disappointed. "My apology. Truly sorry. That miserable Zapatero has given me inaccurate information once again!"

The waiter brought Elliot's soup. He smiled, bowed, smiled, bowed. "Gracias. Que tenga buen apetito."

"You have my sympathy about Zapatero," Elliot told his guest. He took up his spoon. The soup was crawling with large bits of pollo. They seemed to be moving under their own power. He dropped the spoon, grabbed a piece of bread and tore it with his teeth. "Good bread they make here. Except it's almost like Wonder Bread in consistency."

"Same company. Wonder set up an El Santo affiliate years ago. Thank you for your expressed feelings about the local products, Elliot. And I hope your Reverend Olby recovers quickly. Just a tip: don't rely on Zapatero. Get Influenzia to help with her native methods." He was gone. Elliot saw his back in the exit doorway.

Small packages in coffins, what was Jonathan up to? People's Watch was trying to help in the struggle against Imperialism, but it seemed they might have other chestnuts in the fire as well. Elliot took a large swallow of pisco. He was beginning to love the stuff almost as much as the natives. He was starting to acclimatize. When his legs kicked involuntarily from the effect of "pis", as expatriates called it, he became aware of an object under the table. It was softer than wood, harder than a human body. Suddenly a head emerged from under the tablecloth. Manolito. He must have done the Australian crawl from the doorway in order to reach Elliot's table unobserved. Now he was crouching under the table. Although, due to his short stature, he might almost have been standing.

"Psst! Psst! Senor! I gonna tell you someteen queeck. You gotta lissen. Dese Jonathan, he play you no good. He sen droga wi' you dead fren. Psst! He know this guy who know a lady who know somebody who know Correos. So de policia don make no trouble wid im. He cheat me mucho. Don let im sheet you. I with the FARS, make de big revolucion terminar all dese crazy guy."

Elliot was about to repeat that Ollie was not really dead, when Mano made a break for the dining room door. He clearly did not want to encounter Jonathan. Elliot watched him scuddle away. He might very well have been standing under the table.

Since the pollo was definitely unappetizing, Elliot made a meal with half a plate of bread, some vegetables that looked like fried gourds and a great deal of pisco. Then he decided to retire early. It had been a fatiguing day. If only he could get to his room without anyone else popping up or dropping in.

The elevator rose slowly, noisily. Taking the outside stairs would have been faster, but much more exposed. According to Jonathan, prostitutes plied their trade near the fire exits, as did coca retailers and other petty capitalists. Elliot got off on the third floor and was nearly home when a familiar figure jumped into view. Zapatero.

"Ah, senor. I jus take look at you fren. He maybe some better. I jus wan let you know that maybe you make a little much money when you sen im home. Put a little paquete in de box wid im. De People Watch sen de paquete to you country so de CIA no watch im."

"Box?"

"Ya. De coffrin."

"Reverend Wallby is not dead. You just said he was better."

"Ya, he maybe some better but he not too well. It don matter. He go in coffrin in de plane even life, it much cheaper and you got more espacio. Stret de leg."

Elliot handed the doctor a dollar bill. Zapatero smiled, bowed, walked away backwards. Elliot unlocked the door and went into the hotel room. He knew he had had too much pisco. There was no reason to give the doctor money for suggesting such an outrageous thing. Live patients transported in coffins with packages doubtless containing illegal powder.

"Ollie? Ollie? How are you, dear old friend?"

Ollie was sleeping, but his eyes were still open. At least one of them was. He made a mental note to have the Reverend examined by an oculist when possible. The snoring sounded deeper and fuller, without that chest rasp that had been so worrisome earlier. Maybe he really was better. Zapatero was a petty crook and a scoundrel, but he knew something about medicine.

Elliot lay down on his own bed, close to the one where Ollie lay semi-unconscious. He had to admit that the room was well furnished with its heavy, dark, Spanish colonial furniture, its framed paintings (the one of a cart pulled by oxen was particularly enchanting) and photographs (San Santo from the air. The Correos in battle fatigue uniform). If you half-closed your eyes, you might almost be back in Beverly Hills. But life in Beverly was very different. There, you drove your car along the boulevards, speeding from one stoplight to the next. You went to cafes and bars. Here, you manoeuvred on foot along narrow streets full of ambulant vendors and beggars to get to ancient churches. In Beverly your job was to enjoy yourself. Here you were closely pressed by the bleeding sores of poverty. With his head on the pillow, Elliot stared at the picture of the ox-cart. Much of life was certainly a drag. But it was our duty, wasn't it, to help others? Wallby had often preached on the subject from his pulpit at Saint Henry's. The objects of our concern did not necessarily have to be naked. As he turned the bedroom light off, Elliot heard a quick, incisive snort from the direction of Ollie. The Reverend was very likely in agreement.

Mornings at the Hotel de Carlos were pretty much like mornings everywhere at tourist enclaves in poverty ravaged zones. The maids came to clean the room and to make the beds. If you were still in bed they forced an entry with their passkeys. They wanted to get over with the dreary, obnoxious and ill paid work of hotel room cleaning as quickly as possible. They had other things to do: go home to the hovel to care for the ninos (on average 6.4 children per woman according to the published statistics); go to second jobs (prostitution was popular as well as ambulant vending, maybe even agriculture on the outskirts of the city), or simply to beg, the easiest and the most widespread occupation after prostitution. Elliot showered quickly and dressed, only briefly glancing at himself in the bathroom mirror. No, he was still not really guapito.

The maids knew how to work around Wallby. Three of them lifted him from the bed while two more changed the sheets. They knew he was in a state of lethargy and almost constant sleep.

"Este duerme mucho. Tiene algun enfermedad."

"Es que toma mucha droga la noche."

Elliot sped to the elevator. It was already eleven-thirty and he had to get to the restaurant before they shifted to lunch service. He had learned to make a meal with the local bread and a few vegetables. For breakfast he would add a large glass of orange juice generously laced with pisco, a drink that gave you energy against the altitude and cultural problems.

"Senor Spense! Senor Spense!" The desk clerk was calling. "Please you would pay bill now for de tree days?"

Elliot went to the reception desk. The clerk itemized the bill. Three nights of a double room, six meals (breakfast and dinner), the services of Doctor Zapatero and of Influenzia. Influenzia's service was described as "massage treatment", "tratamiento masaje". The total: one hundred and sixty-eight dollars. Elliot paid.

Wallby's cash was running low. Not much more than two hundred dollars remained. Elliot was not worried. He knew Wallby had a large amount on deposit with North American Express that could be accessed through the local office. He had put twenty-five thousand into an international account before they left L. A.

The dining room was almost deserted. Even Jonathan wasn't there. The waiter arrived quickly.

"Jugo de naranja con pisco, pan y verdes." He did not specify omission of the pollo. He knew that this would in any case be ignored. Instead he had brought the wastebasket from their hotel room. He showed it to the waiter. "Para el pollo." He set it on the ground.

The waiter nodded. He understood. He was not happy. Everybody ate pollo. It was a costumbre.

After the waiter left Elliot looked under the table to check for Manolito. He was always sneaking around—easy enough when you were well under five feet. For once, Mano' was away attending to his legitimate, that is, illegitimate, business. But there was something under the table. Elliot bent down, reached with the stretched end of his arm and pulled it up.

It was a pamphlet. "Santanos y Peruanos Juntos con el FARS". Elliot skimmed the text. His comprehension of written Spanish was not too bad. It was very nice that FARS had invited the Peruvians, traditional enemies of the Santanos. The main point, apparently, was for everyone to get together to topple the Correos. Then everyone would be happy forever, at least on the El Santo side of the border. Doubtless the pamphlet had been left by Manolito as proselytization.

He had hardly returned to sitting position when a large orange drink was lightly deposited on the table in front of him. A plate of pan followed and another plate containing sizzling vegetables and something else, probably a new type of pollo. Predictably, the waiter had ignored his orders. Everyone must eat pollo. Elliot speared the pollo with his fork and tried to ferry it to the wastebasket. It struggled on the fork, turned and twisted and finally managed to sink small sharp teeth into Elliot's finger. He dropped the fork. The pollo ran across the floor, headed for liberty. The waiter had observed this struggle.

"Ay, senor, que lastima por el dedo. Voy a informar al Doctor Zapatero."

"No. No Zapatero. Gracias, no. Estoy bien."

The waiter bowed, left. The gringos were inscrutable.

In fact, Elliot had no desire to be treated by the El Santo specialist. Why pay to be poked with needles, injected with unknown solutions, massaged brutally and left to be shipped home in a "coffrin"? He drank his naranja/pisco mix at a gulp, stuck the bread in his pocket and left. At a second thought, he came back, took the plate of sautéed vegetables and dumped them under the table. Mano might find them on his next visit. They could be washed, warmed and served with a sauce *a l'orange*. Even better after the second cooking. Elliot looked at his aching finger. It was oozing plasma from two rodentine punctures.

By no amazing coincidence, only half a block from from the Carlos Hotel, Elliot caught sight of none other than Manolito himself. Mano was manoevring between curio and lottery vendors. It looked almost like dancing. He was smiling to passersby, obviously part of his trade. Even from yards away it was unfortunately quite evident that Mano's lovely blue dress was torn in back, exposing a large extent of muscular torso. Scraps of the dress fabric flapped with his every movement. When he caught sight of Elliot, Mano ran forward to enfold him in a brotherly embrace.

Manolito's arms just encircled his waist. Mano's face reached the level of Elliot's navel. "Migo! Que bueno verte. I lee sonthin for ju unner de table. You fine im?"

"The pamphlet. Yes, I found it. Very interesting."

"Ya, it tell we all go get again dese crazy guy."

Mano was obsessed with the idea of revolution. That is, *his* revolution, the revolution of FARS against the revolution of the Alliance and Jonathan. The ideological distinction was obscure, but Mano must be humored. And anyway, hadn't they come to help FARS? Moreover, Elliot admired Mano for his diligent although not wholesome efforts to support his large family. For some unfathomable reason, though, Mano had consistently refused to inform his "migo" of the whereabouts of FARS. Probably he still wasn't convinced that he and Wallby were not spies for the Alianza or the CIA.

"Thank you very much, Mano." Elliot rubbed lipstick stains from his shirt. Chartreuse would have been a better match to Mano's dress and general appearance than cherry red.

"Bu now I gotta tell you one ting. De guy you meet dat gonna help you mos' fine de revolucion, I tell you. Okay? Mama."

Now things were really getting confused. Was Manolito insisting that he, Elliot, was Mano's mother? Even with five children to support, there had to be limits to his efforts to obtain subsistence. "I don't think I quite understand you."

"Na. Ella se llama la Mama. She call de mother. She de mama for all de FARS in El Santo."

"Oh. But I'm not really in need of a mother or substitute mother at the present."

"Lissen. See, she gotta stay in leetle calle, in a leetle place dey fix de broke up car. Mecanico."

"Broken car?"

"Dat jus to keep de Alianza not know de hole ting."

"A cover."

"Ya ya ya." Mano was getting excited. "De Mama is lider of movimiento. I tell you how you gonna get there." Elaborate instructions followed, with many names of streets honoring generals and revolutionary anniversaries and writers who admired revolutions and generals. Elliot could hardly make out a tenth of it, but he nodded with a smile.

"So you godda get dere, you meet wit' de Mama. She already know about you."

"She already knows about us? Could you provide me with a letter of introduction?"

"No, no. No de riting. Wi' de riting de policia git de guy an' maybe shoot im." Mano pretended to hold a rifle in his hands. "Bam bam. He he." Manolito skipped away. A group of tourists was approaching, pale young men, probably Americans. Mano would give them his best shot.

The existence of a shadowy revolutionary figure with the enigmatic name of "La Mama" was intriguing. He and Wallby must surely make contact with La Mama. She was the lider of the armed revolutionary group, the FARS. For the first time since their arrival, Elliot felt optimistic. They might succeed after all. The possibility of a New Life could be opening. From San Santo airport on, Elliot had had a sinking feeling about Wallby's plan. The ghastly poverty and sleazy attractions of El Santo had combined to rob him of his—or rather Ollie's—idealism. Now there was hope. He was eager to tell the Reverend the good news. Within minutes he was back at the Carlos, taking the elevator to the third floor.

Influenzia was just leaving the hotel room. "Ay, you fren de much of better. I give im de missage."

"Very good, Influence. I'm sure we're on the right path now." Elliot fished in his pocket and pulled out a dollar.

"Ah senor. Que bueno es. Now mi dotter she go to de Universidad!"

"I thought you said she was helping the foreign tourists."

"Ya. Dat before. Maybe now she study de book."

Influenzia tripped happily to the stairs—staff were forbidden to use the elevators. The bedroom had that telltale fish odor. Wallby was again sitting up in bed with a smile on his face.

"Hi Ollie. You are finally getting used to the altitude, aren't you?"

"High. Yes. I have reached the climax of our climb. It is ..."

"Don't flop off now, Ollie, please. I have something very important to tell you."

"I receive your words."

"Well, I just met Manolito on the street. You don't know Manolito yet, he's sort of a young scamp who 'works' with tourists. A bit naughty, but he must do it for his family. Anyway, he is connected with FARS."

Reverend Wallby sat to attention. The word had resonance with him.

"He has given me information about a revolutionary leader, the head of FARS. Her name is the Mama."

Wallby was in ecstacy. His eyes had that cool, blank expression that showed he was reaching the higher levels of consciousness. Perhaps he had been like this in Kathmandu. Then he began to snore.

Elliot was disappointed, but he now knew that Wally was still in touch, even if his narcolepsy had been exasperated by the climate.

While Wallby slept, Elliot continued his explanation, talking to himself as much as to the Reverend's unconscious. "From what I understand, Mama stays far from the eyes of the police. She lives in a little side street from where she helps direct FARS activities in El Santo. Mano gave me directions. If we can make contact with La Mama, I think we'll be well on our way to building the New Life here in El Santo for the people."

He listened to Wallby's breathing, trying to discover the expression of an opinion. There was nothing obvious. A few loud snorts, but there were always those, two or three rather forced exhalations, and a word, incomprehensible, spoken in sleep. It sounded like "garnog", but Elliot couldn't be sure. It might have been "nargog".

It was still early afternoon, far from the time to think about struggling with pollo in the hotel restaurant. Elliot decided that he ought to go out to visit a church, or at least a café or bar. Getting in touch with the local life was the necessary beginning to everything.

Elliot managed to avoid the crowd of beggars and would-be guides in front of the hotel by putting a coat over his head, as if he were a white collar criminal being taken to a waiting police car. Apparently the crowd was used to this sort of thing, at least for hotel guests. For locals the police used more expeditious methods.

St. Jose's was the destination. The guidebooks and tourist brochures were ecstatic about it. A little seventeenth century baroque masterpiece. The ornate façade was beautifully crafted, the square bell tower was an extraordinary attraction. Elliot was beginning to pick his way through the squatting and standing beggars to reach the entry when the general attention was wrenched by a loud ruckus just inside the church. Two men dressed in black, one obviously a priest and the other perhaps a sacristan or usher, were manhandling an individual as they forced him toward the exit.

"Puta, hijo de puta, vaya!" A push sent the manhandled individual tumbling down the church steps. Elliot recognized the blue dress. Manolito. The poor little tyke had patched the back of his dress with a large piece of blue plastic. Elliot sped down the street. He sympathized with Manolito, but it was always unwise to become involved negatively with local customs. He would see St. Jose's some other day.

A glance back at St. Jose's showed that the altercation was continuing in front of the church. Police or some sort of militia had arrived. Several figures were gesticulating wildly and shouting. A blue dress was attempting to slink away. Elliot ducked into a bar. He sat at a table, after bending down to check underneath. Mano might very well have scattered ahead through some hidden by-way. But no, no Mano, only a few cigarette ends, possibly dead insects.

The waiter appeared. This might be his only cash customer for the day. "Senor?"

"Pisco."

"Pis'," the waiter repeated, dropping the final syllable of the word as in current demotic usage, or perhaps out of contempt. Maybe he had expected Elliot to order a whole roast pollo? Waiters got an automatic fifteen percent of the tab as a tip. The waiter lounged away, taking a desultory shot at a few flies with a wet towel.

Elliot was thinking that he ought to have ordered at least two glasses of pisco when he noticed a too familiar figure. Jonathan Winthrop Belcher. Jonathan was waving at him. Elliot waved back, then hoped that this would be enough to satisfy politeness.

Two minutes later the familiar figure brought a chair over to join Elliot. San Santo establishments of a lower social level rarely had more than one chair, if that. This was because café managements sold the chairs first, in case of financial need. If there weren't enough customers, why would they need so many chairs?

"I see you have discovered La Flor del Santo. Usually newcomers take some time to find this place. It's not in the guidebooks, but it is one of the gems of the local nightlife."

Elliot looked around the place. It was largely undecorated. The plaster of the walls was cracked and becoming unpainted. Behind the bar a few large bottles of pisco could be seen, and some dirty and broken glasses. There were a dozen other tables, empty except for the newspaper Jonathan had left on one of them.

"But there is something I must tell you." Jonathan bent toward his listener and lowered his voice. "Manolito has gone off the handle. I suspect he is using drugs. I advise you not to have anything to do with him until he straightens out. The police have him under surveillance and they might mistake you for a dealer or a buyer."

"I will certainly be cautious. I would never have suspected it of the poor little fellow."

"Yes, he seems a model citizen and paterfamilias. I suspect he has been depraved and led astray by imperialist agents. There is a group called FARS that is financed and controlled by the CIA. I know that he has been in contact with members of that group."

"Ung." Elliot made a clicking sound with his tongue to express commiseration. He knew, of course, about Mano and FARS. "They git rid o dese crazy guy," Mano had said.

"I understand that your friend Oldy is much better now. I'm happy to hear it."

"Wallby. Reverend Oliver Francis Wallby. He is a bit better, thank you. I wanted to have him taken to a local hospital, but Zapatero talked me out of it. He said they were not high quality institutions."

Jonathan laughed. "That's the least you can say. Even when the doctors and nurses are not on strike— although I don't blame them. Their rate of pay is truly sickly—the line of patients seeking hospital care extends for several blocks. If your friend made it into the waiting room, he would have to pay rent before he got to see one of the overworked doctors."

"I really think he is better now. He even talked to me today. Influenzia is giving him native treatments and they seem to be effective."

Jonathan laughed. "She's quite popular in that line with the more elderly guests."

"Very good pisco they serve here." Elliot took a large, embarrassed sip.

"Yes. It's the real stuff, Colombian, not one of those cheap Peruvian knock-offs. Unfortunately, the last pisco distillery in El Santo closed during the general strike, La Huelga. It was located in the part of the city that suffered more severe burning."

There was a grumbling noise at the entrance to the cafe. "Que puta, putazo. Sin verguenza!" A tall man in a black clerical robe came in. His long, serious, buff colored face spat expressions of indignation and disgust. This, Elliot would learn, was Monsenor Juan Antonio de las Vargas Vargas, parroco of St. Jose's. He was forty years old, although he looked more like fifty. Originally a franquista, he had made the transition to the Alianza without passing through the intermediate stage of social democracy. He was served at the bar with his own glass, a huge tumbler that was brimmed with pisco.

"Ah, migo!" He caught sight of Jonathan. "Que bueno verte. Como estas?" He came to join them. He had provided his own chair from the rectory furniture, carried on the back of a peon. The cloth seat was embellished with a representation of Saint Pordiosero, El Santo's patron.

"Padre. You are looking very well indeed."

"I am look well? Jona, what you are been smoking?" He raised his glass and swallowed a good mouthful. "I just have have a battle in the church to thrust this wretched one who does sacrilege almost inside our holy walls."

Jonathan was intrigued. He liked to hear a good scandal, even if there was no material advantage to be had from the information. "Do tell. But first, let me introduce you to a countryman. This is Elliot Spenseric. He and his friend, the *Pastor* Olliby, have come to El Santo for a long stay."

"Buenos," Juan Antonio scowled at Elliot. He was not particularly fond of *Pastores*, Protestant ministers. The market was too small even without competition. "But what I'm tellin' to you is that I haf now a big struggle to throw this sinful one who is polluting our Church of San Jose with the lustful sin of sex as prostituta."

Jonathan was shocked. Although thoroughly secular and even a bit anti-clerical, he respected the religious practices of allies of the Alianza. That a low prostitute should presume to ply her trade in a place of worship made him nauseous.

"There is worst. Thees prostituta is de *travesti*. She is really a mens."

At once, it clicked. Jonathan knew what had happened. Again, that naughty little Manolito at work!

"Wan Padre Alfredo harv seed this one near the altar of Santa Teresa, he is call me and we make fast him to door, but he kick and he grab on de columna, den he fight with his hand again my face." Padre Vargas had been hit in the eye. It was already swollen and discolored, although the discoloration was less noticeable due to his deep brown complexion.

"Shocking indeed!" This time Manolito had taken it too far.

"We are of summons the milicia and they are remoffaled of this unspeakable criminal of sacrilege."

"Quite right. I understand your indignation. Social progress has a great deal of work to do, although the Correos are certainly leading in the right direction." Jonathan.

"Camarada Stalin is mors simpatico. He is fren to the everybody."

"Yes, he is the nicest."

While Elliot was listening to this description of the events that he had partly witnessed, he felt a tug at his trouser leg. He shook it off, thinking it might be the establishment dog or maybe a very large fly. At the second tug, he glanced under the table. A hand reached up. It held a pamphlet. "La Alianza, Aliado del Imperialismo y del Capitalismo". There was a handwritten note scratched on the cover with a rock or stick. "Senor do you please give me one dollar for help the eat." Elliot looked down again and saw the smiling face of Manolito, still smiling although somewhat bruised and swollen on the left side. This explained the request for money. He could not ply his trade with the marks of a violent struggle on his face. That would attract only the lowest and most dangerous customers. Worse, a shoulder strap of his once beautifull dress was torn, letting the front fall away from a muscular and obviously masculine chest. Elliot fished a dollar bill out of his pocket. The poor fellow had to eat, after all, and his family too. A dollar would buy enough rutabaga meal to feed an entire village for a year. Mano put the banknote in his mouth. The pathetic state of his gown prevented the usual in-bosom storage. Ballroom dresses do not have pockets.

"De are de wicked time we live, senor. El diablo are lead dees personas to fight of with the imperialistas agen the holy people an de church. I pray of the hope to the peoples." The Padre took a large swallow from Elliot's pisco glass. He looked at the glass. "Colombiano? Muy bien."

Jonathan sucked up a bit from his own much smaller glass. "It's very good, yes. Tasty. Only the Colombians have the secret. But, to return to the scandal at your church, we at People's Watch are not affiliated with any religion, but we respect the right to worship." It was part of the program of the Alianza, to allow freedom to worship ... the Correos.

"Yaaah!" Suddenly Padre Juan Antonio jumped up and began hopping around the floor on one leg. At first, Jonathan thought he was doing a revolutionary dance to show his solidarity with the Alianza and the Correos and he began to clap his hands as at a flamenco performance. Then a small figure shot out from under the table and rushed toward the exit. The small figure was gone before anyone could make a positive i.d., but Jonathan and Elliot were in no doubt.

The Padre pulled up the skirts of his cassock and his pants leg. "He bite me in de leg!" He showed rather deep puncture marks with incipient bleeding. "He bite me like dog! Que puta de perro! Is worst than the worst puta of all the San Santo." Juan Antonio sat down. He poured a bit of pisco on the wound, probably to disinfect, then sucked it, so as not to waste.

"I be damn if he have de rabies."

"I don't think so," Jonathan declared. "I was able to get a look at his face. Although I could not identify the individual, I saw that there was no sign of froth or bubbling at the mouth, such as is usual in full blown rabies."

"Ah? Then I am not worry so. I see de vestido azul. Dees de same guy we tro from de church." Padre Vargas was thinking that if the police or militia caught the fellow, the dress could be confiscated and awarded to the Padre as partial damages. He could easily have it repaired and altered to serve as a gift to his girl friend, Paca. She too was short, but much larger around the waist.

He poured more pisco on the wound, then sucked it up again. "It not hurt too much bad. Later I go to comisaria to make complane. Voy a quejarme de esta puta!"

"I'm very sorry," Jonathan added. Elliot nodded in agreement.

Juan stood up. He began to limp away. "I go now. To the comisaria. Anyway, I thin I know dis guy madre." She could very well be one of his former girl friends.

When Padre Vargas was gone, Jonathan turned to Elliot. "Manolito is clearly out of control. If he continues in this path he will surely end up in a Reeducation Center. In fact, I myself will denounce him to the comisaria for summary trial. It would really be a kindness. At the R.C. he would be taught a trade and removed from the influence of organizations like FARS." Although Mano' formally supported the Alianza, he was in fact a promoter of the goals of FARS, at least when it was financially advantageous.

Elliot nodded. "Yes. I have seen him working in the local barrio, but I never imagined he would resort to actual biting." He signaled the waiter for another pis'. Ecstatic, the waiter brought another bottle. Today he would earn enough to pay a month of pollo. "The biting incident, obviously an act of oral aggression, could indicate hostility toward his mother. Perhaps he was weaned too early."

"Ha!" Jonathan commented. "If he stopped sucking too soon, he has more than made up for it late. I've tried to be a father to the lad. I have even let him use my hotel room for his business affairs. I had to stop because his 'guests' left my bedsheets in such a state that even the tintoreria—the dry cleaner—refused to touch them. The hotel management finally sent them to Disease Control."

"Ugh." Elliot had not thought of this aspect.

"For a while, he used the fire exit of the hotel for his customers, like many. But just imagine. If there were a fire, you'd have to choose between being burned to death or a dozen std's."

Saddened, Elliot nodded in apparent agreement. "He seemed such a bright, active young man." He reserved revealing the fact that Manolito had given him very useful information and that he was secretly a member of FARS, the outlawed organization that he and Wallby had come to join.

"Enough of Manolito. In fact, the sooner he is sent to *some* center, the better." Jonathan was now thinking of the "Freedom through Slavery" camps that the Correos had established deep in the Santano Amazon. "Your poor friend, Mr. Oddby, though, may be better. I hope so. Influenzia told me she thinks he is almost cured, although her idea of 'cured' is rather like what they do to make a ham. The best thing beyond any doubt would be to send this Oddy back to the states for treatment."

"He does not want to go. We just got here." They had a mission.

"Santano medicine is highly advanced and free for all, but in the current situation, with the trade deficit and the embargo blocking medical imports from the imperialist powers, he will not be able to receive adequate treatment in case of a turn for the worse. Now what I want to propose is that People's Watch will pay his airfare to Tucson, provided we are able to use his medicine containers for communication of a confidential material to our people back home."

"I'll talk it over with Ol' again. Perhaps he will agree. He's getting better, only very slowly." Elliot knew that Wallby would not even fathom the question.

"Do try. It's the best way. If your friend were to tank out here we'd all be immensely sorry."

Elliot hurried back to the hotel. The sky was almost dark. On the equator days are of nearly uniform length the whole year and sunsets are short. He was crossing the lobby on his way to the elevator when the desk clerk courteously attracted his attention.

"Yes, senor. We have the three day factura for you." He presented the paper to Elliot.

One hundred and ninety-six dollars for three nights in a double room, six meals and the services of Influenzia and Zapatero. Elliot took the wad of U.S banknotes out of his pocket and peeled off the correct amount. He was surprised to find that only about sixty dollars remained of Wallby's cash. The clerk took the bills, counted them and put them in a drawer. He greedily pocketed the twenty-five cent tip.

As the elevator ascended, Elliot tried to figure out their exact financial situation. Wallby had brought about five hundred dollars in cash to supply their needs during the first days in El Santo. Naturally, due to the revered gentleman's indisposition, Elliot had had to take charge of the accounting. The five hundred had gone much more quickly than expected. Perhaps tipping had been excessive, not to mention tippling. In any case, Wallby had also placed twenty-five thousand dollars on deposit with North American Express. It could be drawn on from their San Santo office. This would be enough to keep the whole country in pollo and pisco for a decade. Beyond the twenty-five grand, Wallby's brokerage account amounted to six figures. The brokerage firm had a branch office in nearby Peru.

Wallby was sleeping. This was no surprise. No new personal objects had been purloined from the hotel room, doubtless because Elliot now carried their remaining valuables with him at all times. The odd thing was that the pictures were missing from the bedroom wall. The blanket and top sheet were missing from Wallby's bed along with one of the pillows. He recalled the notice inside the closet door stating that guests would be held liable for the value of any missing hotel property. Were Influenzia and Zapatero mining the last resources?

He tried to shake Wallby into consciousness. There were serious things to discuss. He was rewarded by a barrage of snorts and puffs. Then a shock: under the blanket, Wallby was naked. His expensive pajamas had left with the bed furnishings.

Elliot sat on the edge of his friend's bed. The trip was not developing as expected. In fact, it had started to turn into a minor disaster after only ten days in the high country. He decided to cast up the balance of their advantages and disadvantages in his mind. In high school he had learned that this is what Benjamin Franklin would have done: on the one hand, they had come to lead the New Life according to Che-su philosophy and to lead the masses of impoverished and oppressed peasants to freedom under the leadership of FARS, the Frente Armado de la Revolucion Santana. Now Reverend Wallby, who alone understood the full intricacies of Che-su thought, lay morassed under the effect of a mysterious illness. It was not simply altitude sickness, that was now clear. Perhaps Zapatero's latest diagnosis was correct. Ollie was suffering from the combined effects of altitude, age, possibly diabetes and a respiratory complaint. Their cash money was running out. The local kleptocracy was making off with their portable possessions a few at a time. On the positive side, Elliot could affirm that he had met a number of unusual characters since his arrival in the picturesque capital, San Santo, that he had actually started to like the taste of the local drink, pisco, and that he had certainly begun to understand how the other half lived. They were far from the Hills of Beverly and his former lifestyle. Then the sum: What must be done? Simply to turn tail and run back to the states was as much a problem as a solution. Wallby faced legal difficulties at home. Abandoning the country of El Santo would mean the end of Wallby's vision of Southern Hemisphere salvation. If the Reverend woke up back in the U.S., he would probably be incensed and indignant as hell. He would accuse Elliot of disloyalty to Che-su and FARS. Wallby had explained it many times: the mission of Che-su was the spiritual zenith of our era. It was worth the sacrifices that would be required. They would receive their reward in the next society, after the old corrupt one had been laid to ruins. For now, Elliot had to draw money from the North American Express account and trust in Che-su.

Elliot stretched out on his bed. He wasn't hungry enough to go down to the restaurant. Besides, they didn't have anything to eat except pollo. He curled up on the mattress without taking off his jacket. Since the blanket and sheet had disappeared, sleeping fully dressed was necessary anyway. That's the way the people of the streets did it here.

The desk clerk in the lobby of the Hotel de Carlos gave Elliot the address of the local North American Express office. The clerk knew it well. Half of their guests were always running off to the NAMEX office to draw more funds. Even though El Santo was a country where the dollar was gold, it seemed always to go like water. Yes, the clerk could tell him where to go. Go down the street in front of the hotel until you get to the large Avenida, then follow the Avenida to the Plaza. In one corner of the plaza was the office of NAMEX. The sword of the equestrian statue of the General pointed directly at it.

Inside the NAMEX office, half a dozen clerks sat behind thick glass windows. A few customers stood waiting while banknotes were counted in front of them. The walls were decorated with travel posters of San Santo. The Catedral, the Palacio, the Museo. Elliot waited his turn with the clerks. He was getting nervous. What if the authorities had given the order to watch for FARS supporters? Perhaps the Klepto Liberation Army had made off with Ollie's funds? Finally a seated employee beckoned him to a place in front of the plate glass. He rushed up and started to explain.

"Yes. Well, you see, I came to make a small withdrawal for my friend, the highly respectable Reverend Francis Oliver Wallby of Beverly Hills. We need a short advance from our cash account because ..."

"Nombre?"

"Francis O. Wallby."

The clerk, a youngish man with a dark mustache and short dark hair, clicked on a computer keyboard. He clicked for several minutes, then looked up at Elliot with an expression of respect almost resembling love.

"Wallby account verified."

"Yes, then I would like to withdraw four hundred dollars in cash. No, make that six hundred. I wouldn't want to bother you every other day."

"I will need the identity papers of personal."

Elliot pushed his passport through the slot.

The clerk studied the passport and the computer screen, turning from one to the other several times. "Dese are not of the same names."

Elliot emitted a nervous laugh. "No, because, you see, I'm not Oliver. I mean, personally. He's sleeping at our hotel, so he can't withdraw money himself. It's the altitude. That is, the high level above the sea."

"We are not able to release funds without the identified individual in present."

Of course. Elliot laughed. He should have thought of it. Naturally only Wallby could get cash at the NAMEX office, because the account was in his name. "I will bring Reverend Wallby here. I mean, personally. I mean by himself, in person. Thank you. Muchas."

On the way out, Elliot noticed security personnel conferring and observing. He fled.

He had to go somewhere to think, somewhere safe from paranoid security and identity demands. He checked into a café bar on a side street. It was empty except for a slow moving waiter.

After twenty minutes of waiting at a table, which for some strange reason had *two* chairs, the waiter brought a glass of pisco. Elliot smiled and nodded. Clever fellow! He hadn't even had to order. They were really on top of things here. He took a sip, then another. He felt happy. Then the thought came that of course the waiter brought pis'. There was nothing else on the menu. It was what everyone drank. The problem, though, he remembered, had to do with Wallby. How could he manage to bring Wall to the NAMEX office when he could rarely even wake the holy gentleman up? Taxicab was an obvious answer, but there were problems. They were expensive and only about fifty-five dollars in cash were left. And a taxi could not help transport Wall down from the third floor of the Carlos to a car or out of a car into the NAMEX office. Then he found the answer. Mano had told him that sometimes when "peoples drink too many much many, dey get dere home in the carretilla." In the wheelbarrow. The temporarily incapacitated were brought home from bars in wheelbarrows. He had seen them on the streets. They were cheap and efficient. The carretilla driver could load Wallby directly on the third floor, then bring him right up to the NAMEX clerk's window. The problem was solved. That is, if Wallby could be brought to consciousness long enough to say his name.

Elliot was contemplating the various aspects of the problem when two customers walked into the café. This was a rare event and caused the bartender/waiter and the sole customer previously on hand to stare agape. They looked like a couple of retired schoolteachers, a gray haired man and woman, probably American tourists from Massachusetts or Michigan, one of those places. Elliot had only a vague notion of U.S. geography. Until a few years before he had believed that Missouri and Mississippi were the same state. Even now he suspected that they were in collusion.

"Why, this seems to be a nice restaurant," the lady schoolteacher said to her companion. "Ought we to just sit down?"

"I dunno, hon."

"Maybe I'll ask that nice looking gentleman over there." Mrs. Schoolmarm approached Elliot.

"Senoor? Ablaz inkless?"

"Hablo el espanol. Nada mas!" Elliot got up and stomped toward the exit. He muttered over his shoulder in a voice as loud as he dared, "puta de gringa!" These hated imperialist foreigners had to be shown their place.

Outside the café, when he was sure that there was no angry pursuit, Elliot regretted what he had done. His glass of pisco had been left with a quarter inch of the stuff still at the bottom.

On the way back to the hotel, Elliot sang to himself the words of the old song "I Love San Santo in the Springtime". In fact, San Santo had very little that could be called a change of seasons. No matter. San Santo would always be San Santo.

The streets were crowded. Ah! Elliot remembered he had been told that today Stalin Correo, the Executive Leader (Lenin Correo was the Legislative Leader), was to give a speech from the Presidential Palace balcony. The people were massing for the benefit of his words. Beggars and street vendors covered every sidewalk, blocked the intersections and made the streets unsafe for autos and buses. He put his hand in his pocket and tightly grasped the small remaining roll of bills. Pickpockets would be especially active.

In a small open area a newspaper vendor offered copies of La Verdad, the official journal. It was now the only newspaper. All the others had been closed for lying. Just to start a conversation with the young vendor (he was hardly older than forty), Elliot bought a copy. He paid for it with a dozen pieces of scrip. The vendor took the pieces of scrip, crumpled them into a ball and tossed them into the gutter. Merely out of politeness, Elliot looked at the cover page of La Verdad. It showed a huge photo of Executive Leader Stalin Correo. The shock headline: Estamos Construyendo la Nueva Sociedad!

Elliot asked the newspaper vendor, "Sabe donde puedo conseguir una carretilla con conductor?" Do you know where I can get a wheelbarrow with driver? Elliot demonstrated in pantomime what he wanted.

The paper vendor, who had no idea that Elliot had been speaking Spanish, shrugged his shoulders, then pointed toward the next cross street. It seemed a good way to get rid of the foreign pest. On the far side of the cross street, in a large hole in the paving that was partly filled with water from the last downpour, there was a wheelbarrow. The driver waited, resting in the barrow. She was dressed in regulation derby and poncho.

"Muchas." Elliot thanked the vendor and offered more scrip. The vendor, in a splendid display of skill, spat in such a way as to hit only the pieces of scrip that Elliot held in his open hand. Elliot dropped them into the gutter. He noticed that a trail of ants quickly changed course to avoid them.

When he was close enough to observe, Elliot saw that the barrow driver was not young. In fact, she had to be at least seventy, with white hair covering her head and a dark mustache on her wrinkled upper lip. From appearances, though, she seemed quite strong with well-formed limbs outlined beneath poncho and black skirt.

"Senorita? Hello, senorita."

"Si?" She had probably been chewing beetle nut. You could tell from her teeth, which were a uniform black in color.

"Would you be able to take on a small job? It would involve very little work and you would be helping two people who are in great need."

"Cuanto?" She made a gesture with her fingers like counting money.

"I can give you a dollar and all of my gratitude."

She jumped out of the wheelbarrow in a single bound. She really was athletic. "Vamos!"

Behind the handles of the wheelbarrow, she started off practically at a trot, even though she could not yet know where she was going. She turned her head back toward Elliot. "Venga, venga."

Elliot ran behind her, panting in an effort to keep up. "I'm not …used … to all this …altitude."

The barrow driver plowed ahead at a shocking pace amidst the scattering crowd. Several jumped aside just in time. Many shouted curses. At least one launched a large portrait poster of Stalin Correo at her head. Elliot followed at a distance now of twenty feet.

"Senorita! Por favor! I'm not used to the exercise! Where are we going?" Elliot was shouting and puffing.

The wheelbarrow did not slow. It did not vary in direction. The driver knew exactly where she was going. After ten minutes Elliot did too. She was headed to the Hotel de Carlos.

When Elliot, completely out of breath and nearly fainting, caught up with the senorita driver, she was resting outside the hotel, leaning comfortably against the upturned barrow handles. She was smoking a pitillo.

"How ow ow ow did you ou ou know … this was the the the place?" Elliot was still out of breath.

"I see how you look, then I know you are Hotel de Carlos. I have bring many dese mens here."

This was hardly flattering. However, to business. "Let's go into the lobby, sometimes the elevator is working. We have to go up to the third floor. That's where our room is. My sick friend Oliver is there. Then we have to take him in the wheelbarrow to the North American Express office in the plaza."

The senorita shook her head. "Ah, no. De peoples in de hotel no not let me come with carretilla. De hotel so fine so rico, dese men no wan so pobre mujer an' de leedle barrow. De alfombra so fine, rica."

"Then how did you manage with the other mens? I mean men."

"I got de way." She picked up her wheelbarrow as if it where a light backpack and slung it over her shoulder. "I go de fire stair. Wha room you live?"

"Three oh six." Elliot stared as she trotted off with the heavy vehicle on her shoulders. He was amazed and impressed. With such strength, speed and agility, she could have packed him as well on her shoulders up to the third floor with no difficulty. This method of travel, however, would not have been dignified for a gringo tourista like Elliot, although it was certainly economical. He rushed, as fast as he was able, to the elevator. He did not want to arrive at the third floor too much later than the senorita.

When Elliot got to the third floor hotel room, the wheelbarrow driver was squatting in front of the door, taking a siesta.

"Senorita? Hello. Senorita."

She opened her eyes. "Where you go? I tink you no wan now. Maybe you stop in café for pis'."

Elliot ignored this. Athletic, she was. Discreet, no. "I had to talk to the clerk in the lobby," he lied. He used his key to open the door. "Reverend Wallby is resting in the bedroom. Walk this way."

The senorita watched him cross the room. "I no walk dat way. It make me de hip duele mucho."

"Would you please just come in here? Do you want the dollar or not?"

The senorita followed. She looked around the suite of two rooms. "Muy rico."

"Not so rico as it looks. By the way, could you tell me your name? It would facilitate communication."

"Mi apellido es San Fermin." San Fermin was her last name. Naturally she did not want to tell her first name, in case the police became involved at some point. There were thousands of *San Fermines* in San Santo. Most were related.

"How do you do? My name is Elliot. I'm here to help the people."

San Fermin grimaced. She did not understand. Or maybe she understood too well.

Elliot led the way to the bedroom. Wallby, as expected, was deep in sleep. His snoring resounded in such a harsh, craggy way that Elliot thought of adenoid problems. He must ask Doctor Zapatero about it. "Ollie? Ollie? Try to wake up, dear. You must come with me to the North American Express office. Otherwise we will soon literally be joining the people in the streets." He shook the theological gentleman. After a long, hard session of shaking, Ollie's head wobbled on his shoulders but his eyes remained shut. "Let's get him into the barrow. Maybe the air outside will rouse him."

Fermin grabbed Wallby's legs and began to pull him off the bed.

"Not that way! He's not a sack of rutabagas. Gently. We are dealing with an ordained man of the cloth."

"Eh?" She seized Oliver's arm and tried to wrench it out of its socket.

Elliot slapped her hands. "Where did you work before? In a morgue? No. Let's take his shoulders and ease him into the barrow. Wait. Let me put a blanket in first. Ollie is very sensitive to jolts." Elliot dragged a blanket off the bed and folded it to fit into the hollow of the wheelbarrow. Then he used both of his arms to embrace Wallby's shoulder. He was heavier than imagined. "Get the other shoulder!" They worked him into the barrow. His head rested against the high end near the handles. Only his feet stuck out in front. "I think this will do very well. We can take the elevator to the lobby."

"Dat no good. No bueno. No marcha."

"Why not?"

"Dey no let pobre vieja mujercita poosh carretilla in de hotel. Is too many bad for rug and see the pobre in hotel de ricos, dey no like. I de say before. You no lissen."

"Then what would you suggest?"

"We go down de fire. We tie de padre to carretilla an' I brin een. Lo llevo de espaldas."

She was proposing to rope Wallby into the barrow and to carry him and the vehicle down the fire exit stairs on her back like some sort of gargantuan infant. "He's not really a padre. He's an Episcopal minister, as I have explained, anglicano, so he's not really ordained and knows nothing about the rites of the historic church. Your idea may work, though. Are you sure he's not too heavy. No es demasiado pesado?"

Fermin looked the padre up and down with one squinting eye. "Yah. He muy pesado, lotta heavy, but I brin dese guy all de time. No hay problema."

"Very good, then. We will meet outside the hotel." Elliot had considered going with them on the outside fire stairs, but was afraid of being seen by the staff. They would naturally think he was trying to sneak out without paying the bill. Then there was the danger of the prostitutes on the landings mentioned by Jonathan and all their std's.

They managed to secure Wallby in the barrow by using several of his shirts as improvised ropes. "There. We'll meet outside the hotel, since I have to go the normal way, then we will go to the North American Express office in the plaza. You will have well earned your dollar and a propina." A tip, too.

"He kina little heavy, eat too much, but no too much bad. One time I got dis one guy, yah, he hunner kilo, maybe maybe hunner fifty. He wan I take im to Peru. The policia look de train an de plane an all de carros for dis guy, so he gotta go wi de carretilla. Bu we ge maybe twunny kilometros an he die."

"He died? How did that happen?"

"He git de hard attack. I dunno."

This was not encouraging. "In any case, we are not going as far as Peru." Not yet.

With a quick lift and shift, Wallby and the wheelbarrow were on the senorita's back. She walked rapidly toward the fire escape. When carrying very heavy objects, it is important to keep moving in order to maintain balance. Her wiry frame of taut muscles seemed quite adequate to the task.

Elliot headed to the elevator. He had taken the precaution of pocketing their last valuable possessions, a clean change of underwear and a ceramic mug commemorating the Los Angeles Olympics. On the way down to the lobby he looked at the photo advertisements again and decided that it might be fun to see the "Mens-Womens wrestlers".

Outside the hotel, Fermin and the barrow were nowhere to be seen. Once again, the senorita had doubtless rushed ahead to save time, and money. When this job was finished, she would be available for another. Probably she was pulling down four or five dollars per day, not bad money even in L.A. for a lot of people.

He followed the streets to the North American Express office as fast as he could. Naturally, he could not keep pace with the senorita, even strapped with a hundred kilo papoose. When he finally arrived, exhausted and out of breath after a twenty-five minute walk, Fermin was again relaxing against the upturned wheelbarrow. She was smoking a little cigarette, doubtless handrolled. It did not smell like tobacco. Wallby's eyes were open, but he was snoring and, oddly, making hand gestures like a preacher in a pulpit.

"Whew! You really are a sprinter," he told San Fermin.

"Yah. Now I godda liddle time smoke pito. It make you forgit la fatiga, sabes?"

"Oh yes. I quite understand. You must recuperate from your burden. Now, if you will just help me push the Reverend into this office, it will be payoff time."

"Yah. No hay problema." This was a phrase often used in El Santo, although it seemed to be contradicted by the general state of the country. Fermin lowered the carretilla to the horizontal position and easily moved it through the glass front doors of the North American Express office. The clerks and a few customers looked up in surprise, shock, and fear. The eruption of a peasant woman with leather complexion pushing a wheelbarrow was an unusual event in tourist offices, even in San Santo.

"Let's maneuver Ollie to the clerk's window. He'll have to sign some papers."

Fermin gave the carretilla a final shove. "Okay. Now he here."

"Thank you, dearest. You have been irreplaceable." Elliot fished in his pocket and came up with a dollar bill and a quarter coin. "This is for you."

Fermin stuck a hand in her own pocket, perhaps to find change for an overpayment.

"No, no. It is all yours. You deserve it."

"I look for udder paper to see if is same." She suspected that a counterfeit note had been passed from Elliot.

After several minutes of squinting and comparing at different angles, she accepted the payment. "Yah. Look okay. What you do wit de guy later?"

She was hinting at employment for a return trip. In fact, there would be no need for return wheelbarrow transport. With a bit of Wallby's cash, they could rent a limousine.

"Very thoughtful of you, but it will not be necessary. Thank you infinitely." He looked toward the door with a chin gesture that Fermin, a very smart lady, picked up immediately.

"Okay. Bud you need this guy move one time more, you come to de plaza. I gi' you de discount."

Elliot turned to the teller without giving an answer to the senorita's pitch. "Buenos dias. You see, I was here before, but I was told that since the account in reference was in the name of my friend here, that only he could sign for a withdrawal."

"Numero de cuenta?"

A slip of paper passed under the glass window. The clerk tapped on a keyboard for at least three minutes, then he announced in a neutral tone, "Oliver Francis Wallby."

"Yes! That is my dear friend." Elliot indicated the Reverend, now sitting propped against a chair. "Here is his passport."

The clerk studied the document for a full five minutes. "His is not so good as before. Is same guy?"

"Oh yes, he is certainly the same guy. He has been unwell, mainly due to the altitude."

"Why he is not on de leg?"

"Oh, you mean standing, *de pie*? That is because he is not yet entirely well. He is still a little weak, un poco debil." The clerk had doubts.

"But he gotta sign so he git of de money."

"That is exactly why we are here. We will need only about 5000.00 dollars for our first withdrawal. Small bills will be preferable." Elliot noticed that the clerk was a rather handsome man, khaki in complexion. He was not as tall as he had seemed at first. In fact, he was standing at the clerk's window, not sitting.

The North American Express employee pushed a form under the window slot. "Que ponga su firma." The Reverend had to sign.

"Ollie, dearest. It is now time to do our duty for the people. You must write your name in this place." Elliot pointed to the signature line. Oliver stared into space, still snoring. Elliot shook his friend by the shoulder, gently but firmly. The whole Che-su movement was at stake. He shook again, then a third time. A grunt was emitted. Progress.

"I'll help you hold the pen, since you are still quite convalescent." Elliot put the pen between the ecclesiastical gentleman's fingers and helped the hand to move. Squiggles were produced. They might have to do. He returned the form to the clerk.

"No. I don tink so. Deese no look like he firma in de passpor."

"Of course it isn't exactly like in the passport. Mr. Wallby is not well. But you saw his hand write the signature, didn't you?"

"I gotta check wi de boss." The clerk moved off to the back office.

"This is critical, Ollie. Please try to pay attention. If we cannot make this withdrawal, we are going to be joining the people in the streets in an overly literal way."

Twenty minutes later the clerk returned. "Lo siento. I really sorry, bud de firma no look like de book. Mi jefe say it not de correspond."

"Give me another form." Elliot placed the form on a table in front of his friend. "Ollie, dear, let's try again. Since you are having difficulty coordinating your fingers, you could hold the pen in your mouth." Elliot had seen quadriplegics do this on television years ago. He put the pen in Wallby's mouth and guided it toward the signature line. "Try to move the pen so that the result resembles your ordinary signature."

Wallby's head, with pen in mouth, dropped precipitately, piercing the paper without marking it at all. Then a sharp contraction of the preacher's jaw shattered the writing device into many pieces.

Elliot sank to the office floor in dispair. It wouldn't work. They were stuck in Santo with hardly more than fifty dollars in the world. He patted Wallby's knee. "That's okay old pal. I know it isn't really your fault. It's just bad luck. Bad luck." Elliot started to whimper.

The clerk was moved by this pathetic scene. It was something like the gritos of the gitanos in Holy Week. "Senor. I see de Pastor no feel too much good. So you gid im have de terapia for de hands from de medico, den maybe he rite good. Okay?"

"Thank you. That is a very helpful suggestion." Elliot filed the suggestion in his mind for future consideration, then turned back to Wallby. "We shall suffer hunger and thirst, cold and heat, with the masses." Genuine tears washed San Santo inversion soot in runnels beneath his eyes. "But then, we did come here to share the miserable lot of the people. Although I, at least, did not expect it so soon." He whimpered loudly. The No Am Ex employee looked fearfully at the handful of other foreign customers. The company was getting bad publicity.

"We shall soon be reduced to begging. We may even be forced to the moral horror of prostitution!" He gave Wallby an appraisal of honest realism. "At least I may." He leaned against the Reverend's ample shoulder, he cried, whimpered, shook in anguish. He was dozing off when the clerk's voice broke into his consciousness.

"Mr. Wallopy? I ver' sorry, bu' you cannot esleep here. De Compania got de reglamento."

"We have nowhere to go-oo!" Elliot went back to his dreamy anguish. "The wheelbarrow lady left and we could hardly afford her services now anyway. My friend cannot walk. And I am Mr. Spencer, not Wallopy."

"Senor. I gotta ting to give you." The clerk unlocked the door to the cashier's room, a process that required fifteen minutes and at least six keys. At last he emerged in full stature before Elliot and Wallby. "Dese we gi you to de free." He shook out a blanket. It was imprinted with the slogan "El Santo Campeones del Mundo". This was an allusion to a soccer victory in the grand quarter finals thirty years ago. "You go get de guys in de strees. Dey git im in de blanket. Much more cheap dan de carretilla."

"Oh. Yes. I see what you mean." Elliot understood that the clerk was suggesting blanket carriage as a means of moving Wallby from the No Am Ex office. Any hands in search of a few coins could pack someone in a blanket, you didn't need a wheelbarrow. It was a locally recognized means of transportation, economical and convenient. A U.N. study had praised it as an environmentally friendly and employment producing method of moving heavy substances. Elliot calculated that he might be able to hire four blanket porters at a nickel each, but to what destination? They couldn't go back to the Hotel de Carlos. One more night at the Carlos would finish their meager cash supply. But the clerk was right. They couldn't sleep in the North American Express office. Even a millionaire would be booted out at closing time. Elliot had half an idea. Until he could figure out his plan, they might as well go to an inexpensive café. A drop of pisco would soothe his nerves and stimulate his thinking. Also, it was one medicine that they had not yet adequately tried on Wallby.

"I'll be back. May I park Mr. Wallby with you for a few minutes?"

"Si senor. We giv de half hour free park to all clientes."

Outside, Elliot scanned the calle for available blanket porters. There were several dozen who looked like they could use a few cents and about half of those might be able to support the load. He approached a group of four who were lounging near the sidewalk curb.

"Um. Ah. Senores? Quiero contratar a cuatro hombres para llevar a un hombre santo en una manta." He wanted four men to carry a saint in a blanket.

The smallest of the group, apparently the leader, looked up slowly from a long contemplation of the sidewalk surface. "Senor, wad language you are speak? We no talk de gringo lengua too much good." It was true that Elliot's Spanish was very imperfect.

"Lo siento. I mean, I—that is I and a sick friend—need four men to carry him in a blanket. He is really not very heavy anymore."

"Okay. Mu' ben. Where you gonna goin'?"

"I'm not sure. Just to a café perhaps, a un café poco caro."

"Ah. Senor. I am of unnerstan. We are you service. Where dis udder guy?"

"Oh. Yes. Well he's very close by. He's in the North American Express office just over there." Elliot pointed in the direction.

The leader shook his head. "Dis not go be easy, mi jefe. In No Am Ex, dey no like de riff-raft."

Elliot laughed. What a charming sense of self-deprecating humor! "They have already been informed of the problem. In fact, the No Am Ex jefe himself suggested I hire carriers."

"Lees go." The four got up. Their clothes were somewhat unpresentable. Rather filthy in fact.

"Make sure to carry him to a café where they serve good pisco."

"Yah. You gid goo pis'."

Elliot followed the band to the door of the No Am Ex office. Inside, the carriers understood their task at once.

"Ay! Dis one kinna big. We strong, senor, bu' we no supermens."

"Ridiculous. He's as light as a feather." Elliot demonstrated by giving the Reverend a good shove. "See? You can move him about as easily as a barn door. Use this blanket." He handed over the Campeones del Mundo blanket. They were impressed by the slogan and logo.

"Ah! Futbol!" They started to hop and to give phantom soccer kicks as if they were training for the World Cup.

"Dis senor, he doan watch de futbol in de television?" The little leader pointed suspiciously with a shoulder toward Wallby.

"Oh yes. He's absolutely a fanatic. He used to watch the partidos night and day. That is, before his unfortunate accident."

"Oh. I see. It is too much the sorrow. He wed bedder soon. Geev im wid de curandero."

The curandero, the native healer. It was a good idea. First, though, they had to get Wallby to a café. "We have to leave this office. They close rather early, so we must depart. Can you and your friends manage the pastor for a dime each?" Elliot felt that a nickel would have been rejected out of hand by the aspiring workforce.

"Dime? Yah, dat not too bad. You wait when I tell em de organize." The U.S. dollar was recognized as official currency in El Santo. This was necessary because the E.S. peso was in fact worth less than an equivalent amount of *papel higienico*. The leader started to bellow in very fast and guttural Spanish. "Hay que trabajarlo!" The others began to arrange themselves around Wallby. Further shouted orders led to a series of quick and deft movements in which the minister was tipped into the center of the blanket, with a carrier holding each corner.

"Now we go. *Siganos*."

Elliot followed. It was like being on a safari. He walked behind the carriers with their blanketed burden. They might have been the porters who carried Richard Burton back from his ill-fated expedition to find the source of the Nile. There was no chant from the carriers, however, no monotonous, age-old wail of misery and privation. Though it would certainly have been appropriate.

For several blocks Elliot trailed the blanket men on the sidewalks and half-paved streets of San Santo. He was near exhaustion when they entered a café. It was so informal, actually run down, that at first he thought it was a sort of warehouse. The bearers deposited Wallby on top of a table that had probably once served as a giant spool for thick cables. Typically, there were no chairs in the establishment. Elliot rested himself on top of a sturdy crate.

"Thank you, men." He looked around for a waiter. By experience he knew that it could be quite a long process to have the waiter come, take an order for pisco, then have the waiter find glasses, then a bottle, then the pouring, and the serving. A small glass of the "stuff" often could be had only after half an hour, sometimes half a day. But this was not a bar as such. In a corner of the warehouse, or bar of sorts, was a small collection of bottles. The waiters might be off working somewhere else between customers or begging on the street while waiting for drinkers. A large poster of the Correo brothers was patriotically plastered to the wall. It had received several dart punctures.

"Thank you, sir." The leader put out his hand. "The men mus go to feed hir familias dat are starving from no have de dollares."

"I sympathize terribly. Forty cents." He searched his pockets. He found a quarter, a dime and three pennies. He poured these into the cupped hand of the leader.

"No, senor. Dis Mr. Santo he is so heavy, pesisimo, dad he gi my men de backache. They no can work more for de week. An de familias have no eat now for a month."

Elliot was skeptical. "What exactly are you suggesting?"

"You gi' fifteen sense eech wun. Quince cada hombre."

Elliot was about to explode. This was robbery. They had come to El Santo to save the people, then because of circumstances they had been left with a bare fifty dollars, and now they were being overcharged by five cents per carrier! But there was really no choice. It was four against two. Besides, the spirit of Che-su must prevail. They had to love the people as well as to help them.

"Okay." Elliot excavated another dime. That made twelve and a half cents for each carrier. "It's all I have left in this world, except my poor sick friend." He tearfully indicated Wallby—Wallopy—with a jerk of his shoulder. "And you can keep the blanket. La manta es la suya," he told the three subordinate carriers. They seized it immediately, then triumphantly exited, waving the bandera to the chant of "cam-pe-on-es de el mun-do, cam-pe-on-es de el mun-do!" Elliot was astonished by how short and dark they looked in recessional. Except for the very small ruling class, former and actual, the Santanos were generally low statured and suntaned in complexion. They were all the more lovable.

The leader knew he had been had. "Very smart, senor." But he accepted with resignation. Perhaps he had been touched in his heart by the spirit of Che-su. "Here you get you own drink, bebida, in the corner, el rincon." He pointed to the far end of the warehouse where a few bottles rested on the floor.

"Thank you."

When the leader had followed the banner-waving group, Elliot went to investigate the liquid supply. "Stay here, Ollie. Just shout if anyone comes back."

The warehouse or café (it might have been a café of a sort), was empty of employees and customers. The only very mild light came from the filthy windows fore and aft of the room where large pieces of cloth partly blocked the daylight. A dozen "tables" lay scattered in a disorder of empty bottles, pieces of lumber and abandoned rags and paper. In the far corner, as predicted, were bottles. At least one was almost entirely full of pisco. A little handwritten sign had been placed beside the glasses. The English message was obviously intended for tourists. "2 cent for one glass. Or 550,000,000 scrip." Ha ha! Despite the enormity of their socio-economic problems, the Santanos really managed to keep their sense of humor! Elliot put a nickel in the little box and poured out two large glasses of good old pis'.

On the way back to the table where Wallby was resting, Elliot sampled the liquor. "Very good!" He savored a larger sip, then drank a full swallow. This was from an aged bottle, probably looted from one of the large ranchos that had once belonged to the ruling classes.

"Olly, dear, try a sip of this medicine. It is excellent." He raised Wallby's head, then gently poured a small amount through the perennially open lips.

"Ga! Ga! Ka-aah ga! Arng! Ka! Orng! Ka ka ka. Ourng!" He swallowed the wrong way. This was terrible. Wallby was far from fully conscious. Elliot had forgotten that. "Aah-haurng! Aah-haurng! Gaarg! Guawngh!"

Elliot slapped his friend on the back several times to aid in the evacuation of fluid from his trachea. "Uahahng-graaaagh!!!"

"There, there." He slapped again and again. "It went down the wrong way. I'm very sorry." He took the glass from Wallby's hand. This had been a premature libation. Suddenly Ollie's hand took back the glass and sucked in several small sips, then a larger sip, then a full swallow. He sucked up the entire contents. His eyes were closed.

"Thank you, my people, for coming here tonight to hear the words of Che-su. Thank you, thank you."

Wallby was speaking again! It was gibberish but it showed that he was conscious! He seemed to think that he was at some sort of camp meeting, but at least he was capable of speech. "Yes, Ollie, yes. We came for Che-su. That is absolutely right. To bring Che-su to the ground-down masses."

"Che-su has come to break your chains. Che-su to free your hearts and minds! Che-su …" Wallby's hand dropped his empty glass and sought Elliot's drink. He grasped it and poured the remaining fluid down in a gulp.

"Hey! Take it easy!" For health's sake, Ollie should not overdo it at the start of his recovery. Elliot tried to take back the glass, but the reverend gentleman's hold was firm. He upended the already empty container into his mouth.

"Into this continent of suffering and oppression, after centuries of misery and poverty and total wretchedness of the destitute masses, we have brought light, hope …"

"Hope, yes, Ollie, exactly. Go on, go!" However nonsensical his speech, Wallby should be encouraged. It would help bring back his language and analytical skills.

But the holy man dried up. No more words flew from his oiled mouth. He needed more fuel. That was it. Elliot rushed back to the corner of the warehouse where the bottles were stored. He refilled both glasses.

This time he paid exact change, four cents for two brimming glasses of aged pisco. Elliot, anxious not to spill a drop, portered them back carefully to the table where the reverend gentleman lay expectantly waiting. "Drink it slowly, Ollie. That way you can drink more."

Wallby could really put the stuff away. He had a way of sucking it directly from lips to throat, entirely bypassing his mouth. "My people, we are locked solidly in a struggle against the empire of greed, against those who value only money, who are against the love and care for the masses that is taught us by Che-su." He paused to wash his words down with a good dose of the stuff. It really was excellent. "So when we pray for those who have nothing, who starve in want, our sisters and brothers, when we take up the kalashnikovs of liberation and the words of freedom, then we ..." He swallowed the remaining contents of his glass. He opened his eyes to stare at the warehouse wall.

"Go on, Ollie. Excellent, so far." Elliot was now sipping from his own glass, enjoying the sermon. It was almost like Sunday back at good old St Henry the Eighth's Church in Westwood. But Wallby seemed to have dried up. Maybe he was arranging his thoughts. "'The words of freedom ...' Do continue." Wallby was stuck at a pause. He was contemplating something beyond, looking beyond the warehouse wall, perhaps beyond history, beyond reality.

Suddenly Elliot felt a strong tug at his pants leg. He jerked back in a quick reflex. It must be rats in this old dump of a building. He drew both his legs up to the packing crate top, then peeked under it. What he saw induced fear and pity and quite a bit of loathing as well. It was poor Manolito. He looked up eagerly from a crouching position. His once gorgeous blue dress was now tattered, stained and faded beyond recognition. "You poor dear little thing! What hath berefed thee so?" He essayed a line from E.A Poe. But when he thought of how gorgeous Mano had looked in the dress before its disintegration, tears began to flow. Pisco often had that effect. It induced sentiment.

"Eh! Senor!" Manolito's voice was hoarse, as if he had been shouting for a long time. "I come to tell you de warning. Dese guy dey look for you an' de holy guy. All de Correo guy tink you wid de FARS and de CIA."

"Yes. Well we are certainly interested in FARS's ideals. Although, strictly speaking, we are only observers at this point." Mano tended to panic. Maybe because he himself was so often in trouble with the police. He was familiar with unscrupulous interrogation methods.

"Yah. I know. I git de word from de Mama an' she tell me. She the jefa of all de FARS in El Santo. She wanna see you. Bu you gotta go fine her."

"Find the Mama? Where should we look? Is she anywhere near the Carlos or the Plaza?" Elliot was confused.

"I dunno. See, we dunno wor she gonna be, because maybe de Correo guy dey fine out. So she don never tell nobodies. Then we gotta fine her. Look hard." Elliot remained entirely perplexed while he sipped from his glass of pisco. "See, if you reel tru to de FARS an wanna help de people, then you hard gonna get you to de Mama."

"I see. It is a test of valor and truth. If we are true revolutionaries, then we will find the road, the correct path."

"Yah! Yah! De tru guy gonna git it to de Mama. For de help de people."

"We shall start our quest today." Elliot took a lengthy sip of pisco. He looked at Wallby, who was still watching eternity and holding his glass tipped to the side. "Reverend Wallby was just rehearsing one of his sermons about the people helping the people to help themselves. Or something like that, it's still a bit vague."

"You go to de FARS, senor, then you gonna be good." Manolito jumped up, sucked the remaining contents of Wallby's tipping glass in one quick suck, then scattered away in the warehouse chiaroscuro. "Poody damn goo pis'," he cried out.

Elliot watched his diminutive figure disappear into the gloom. Now they were on a sacred expedition to find the head of FARS. It was a quest that would try their strength, their intelligence and their loyalty to the cause of liberation. Even the enrolled followers of FARS did not know where their Leader's head would be resting tonight. Finding the Mama was going to be an expedition that would make the moon launch look like a trip to the local store for another six-pack of beer. He was not clear on why it was really necessary.

Wallby shook his empty glass. Words formed in his mouth, but nothing came out. Maybe he was trying to communicate the fact that he needed more pisco.

Elliot stood up from the packing crate, where he was just beginning to feel comfortable, and returned to the small display of bottles. He looked at the assortment. Most of the bottles were empty. Others were rather more empty than full and had brand names like "Fuego de los Andes", "El Sueno", "Matarratas". He did not want to take too much of the good brands, the old bottles from the ranchos, least the warehouse managers, whoever they were, might think him greedy. Finally he filled their glasses half and half, half from the aged bottle, half from the remainder of the Matarratas fluid. The latter smelled in fact like pesticide.

"Here we are, Ollie. Now take a good swallow of this medicine." He put the glass in Wallby's hand and guided the hand toward his mouth. Wallby drank. The liquid gurgled down his throat to a receptacle within his large torso.

"Ack! Ack!" It had tickled the Reverend's throat, but not too much. He seemed to be arranging his internal organs and his brain for further discourse. "I …I …"

"Yes, old friend, go on. We are eager to be enlightened by your wisdom."

"I … feel the love of the people. We are rising to freedom. We must destroy the oppressors, the exploiters. Let our love free us from the shackles of …"

Elliot applied more pisco to the Reverend's filling tube. "Go on, Ollie! So far it is quite lovely. 'The shackles of …'"

"Let our love free us from the shackles of … poverty and thirst." His head slumped. Ollie needed a rest.

"Bravo! Bravo!" Elliot clapped his hands. "That was a brilliant discourse. It will make everyone think. Get to their hearts and minds first, that's the idea!" He was feeling a sort of torpor himself. Pisco could do that to you. A pint or so of the stuff and you were ready to join dreamland. It was the perfect soporific. Ollie was snoring in a heap on his table. Elliot stretched out on a neighboring table. He pulled up the packing crate to serve as a pillow. It was a very useful device.

Morning in the warehouse was much like evening. A faded light filtered through the dirty windows. Elliot was the first up. Probably because Wallby was still incapable of standing. Ah. Morning in San Santo! He felt the excitement. He remembered what Manolito had said the night before. They had to find the Mama. Only by demonstrating truth and virtue would they be able to reach the matriarchal head of FARS. And only she could put them in contact with the groaning masses that yearned for the teachings of Che-su.

Elliot slipped out of the warehouse. After a two-minute search he located a street stall where he bought two churros and two cups of coffee. Pisco was added to the coffee, as was the custom. It was cheaper than coffee. And it provided a bracing flavor. Once more, he was enraged and deeply distressed by the price the vendor demanded. Six cents for a couple of deep fried somethings and two paper cups of pissy coffee! This was incredible, it was robbery, it was murder and rape! He paid, because he knew Ollie would be hungry and barely conscious. He bore the two cups back to the warehouse. As much as he loved the people, he had to admit that a lot of them were a bunch of assholes.

The warehouse was actually the Café de la Revolucion. This was proclaimed on a sign hanging above the lockless door. Inside,

Wallby was still snoring. His mouth was only half open, unlike the unlimited gape of his oral orifice displayed at the Carlos, which had shown an expanse of unhealthy white tissues only barely crisscrossed by small red arteries. His snoring was better too. A rhythmic rumbling, not the staccato snorts and caws of before.

"Here, Ollie, drink this. And have a churro. They are extremely delicious." Ollie's mouth refused the paper cup. Probably because of the pisco smell.   He had overdone it last night. But he took in the long, fat fried churro. Once placed in his mouth, he chewed it down to the end.

The coffee was really not bad. Elliot drank his in a few gulps, then tried again to get Wallby to accept a sip. No luck. For a moment he considered pouring some up the Reverend gentleman's nose, but rejected this. It might result in swallowing the wrong way and all sorts of difficulties.

Elliot drank both cups of coffee-pisco, then, sitting on the packing crate, he considered their general situation. What is to be done? (Kto kogo?) They were almost indigent. And they were on a quest to find the Mama. They had to go somewhere today, because the managers of the Café de la Revolucion might return at any moment from other jobs or begging on the street. They would certainly press him and Wallby to spend their remaining funds on the local specialty drink. Wallby still could not walk, although occasionally he could speak. There was no way they could afford to pay blanket men (called blanqueros) to move him about, much less hire a wheelbarrow lady.

After a good deal of thought and an exact assessment of available resources, Elliot decided that the only solution to Wallby's lack of mobility was to construct a vehicle out of the materials at hand. Essentially, these were the warehouse "tables", former giant spools for communication cables. There were quite a few of them, several turned on their side. This is what gave Elliot the idea. Why couldn't a table on its side be a wheel of sorts? Other objects lending themselves to construction attempts were pieces of wood, cardboard, an assortment of trash and, of course, the dear old packing crate. After an hour of heaving and grunting and pushing and ackward binding there existed a Wallby capable carrier. It was no Cadillac. Two tables laid on their sides and strapped at the stands by bits of rope, clothing, wire and leather (Wallby's erstwhile belt) made do for the axle and wheels of the conveyance. The seat was provided by the packing crate. Although with deep regret, he pushed out one of the long sides. Then the crate was mounted on the "wheel axle". Cardboard and an old blanket stuffed into the crate would provide a more comfortable seat for the holyman. The real problem was that the seat-crate would only stay in place on top of the axle if it were held in place. There were no cords or ropes adequate to fix it. Elliot would have to do the holding *and* the pushing. Later it might be possible to hire someone to help on the manual side. Wages would have to be very moderate, however, and partial compensation might come in the form of edifying sermons emitted by the semi-comatose Wallby.

They were ready to depart the warehouse café. Elliot wheeled the "San Santo Cadillac" near to the table where Wallby lay gently snoring. With a loud huff and a tremendous effort—the clergyman still weighed more than two hundred pounds—Wallby was hoist onto the machine. "Up we go, motherfucker." Elliot was happy to use this term from home, despite its crudeness and vulgarity. In his pulpit days Olly would have said that it was not the term that was crude and vulgar, but the society that forced people to use it. "Motherfucker". It was like a breath of L.A.

The Cad would not fit through the café door. Fortunately, Elliot was able to kick away part of the decayed wall—really just mud brick—to create an exit space of adequate dimensions. Out in the street they made slow progress amidst the astonished stares of the gapers. It was a hard push. At half a block from takeoff ground zero Elliot was panting rapidly. His desperate eye caught sight of a friendly sign. "Café del Pueblo". He might just make it the last nine yards.

"Ah ah ah uh uh ah." They were almost at the café door. Unfortunately, the door was too narrow to allow passage to the Wallby Cadillac. Desperate and at the end of his strength, Elliot wheeled the vehicle to a sideways position vis-a-vis the front door and gave a heavy push with his backside. They went through. The "Cad" collapsed at the same time, spilling Wallby onto the floor. Waiters came running. The Pueblo was a class café with waiters present and working. The sight of foreign tourists and the promise of actual currency provided a strong incentive.

"Senor, senor. Lo siento. Que se sienten, senores." Two waiters carried Wallby to a chair. Elliot was able to follow under his own power. He dropped into a chair opposite His Rectorship.

"Dos piscos. Grandes." He had not lost the power of speech.

The waiters bowed, smiled, retreated.

Tears formed in Elliot's eyes as he viewed the ruin of the San Santo Limo. The two halves, formerly tables, were lying asunder near the entrance. The dear old packing crate had crashed onto the ground with untold damage to its slats. The cardboard and old clothing were scattered about the street, blown on every current of air. The waiters had not bothered to clear the wreckage. After all, no other customer was likely to enter for some time.

Wallby was awake. His hands made gestures of equity and assurance. "People, are we not one with the One? Are we not ..." A smiling waiter deposited a large glass of pisco in front of each of the guests. Although far from totally compos mentis, Wallby took in the significance with animal instinct. He was able to grasp his glass with good coordination and apply it to his lips. He murmured appreciatively.

"Gracias." Elliot nodded to the waiter. The drink, as usual, smelled a bit of matarratas, but the taste was not bad at all. They had found refuge in a high-class establishment. On the wall was a large portrait of the beloved leaders, the Correo brothers, and a smaller one of the Jimmy smiling toothily at the two Lideres maximos. Here there was no sign whatever of dart produced damage. Clearly the riffraff were kept at bay.

After a period of recuperation, Elliot concentrated on their next move. The search, the cruzada to find the Mama was the ultimate goal. In it was subsumed the idea of joining FARS and spreading the gospel of Che-su. He counted his fingers to mark the stages and possibilities of their quest. They were moving toward the Mama, but geographical progress was not more important than moral progress. The *way* they proceded weighed just as much. They had to show revolutionary virtue. Love for the people. All this had to be balanced against practical matters, such as where to sleep each night, how to fix the Cadillac to provide transport for Wallby, how to make their money last. He was deep in reflection when a particularly loud slurping sound broke his concentration. He looked up to see that Wallby, although still only semi-conscious, having quickly drained his own glass of pisco, had now taken possession of Elliot's glass and was dispatching it at an alarming rate.

Che-su! Could he put the stuff away! "Hey, slow down a bit! You're still pretty sick, you know." Walloby grunted agreement, although he continued to drink from his friend's glass. Maybe it was time for lunch. Just like in a hospital, a patient had to have regular nutrition. He signaled the waiter.

"Senor. Un poco de pan, por favor. Y un plato de pollo frito." Ollie could have the pollo. Maybe it was nutritious, even if the taste was nauseating. "Y pisco otra vez."

The glasses came first. Elliot grabbed his ration of pisco and drew it out of the Reverend's reach. Strangely, Ollie was no longer interested in aguardiente. He looked toward the ceiling of the café. Maybe he was asleep, even if his eyes were open. There was at least a possibility that he was communing with the all-one and that he might soon have new revelations on the doctrine of Che-sus.

The waiter brought a steaming plate of pollo. Elliot held his napkin in front of his nose to avoid triggering a gag reaction. "Look,

Ollie, lunch! My, it smells delicious." He moved the napkin from his nose to his mouth. For a moment he felt he was going to regurgitate.

"Ahi esta!" the waiter beamed brightly and deftly deposited the plate in the center of the table. "Que disfruten ustedes." With a swift turn worthy of a toreador, he withdrew.

A largish gray mass squatted on the plate. Someone had sprinkled the carcass with small red flakes. Probably red pepper, or bits of dried red paint meant to imitate the high priced condiment. An acrid column of toxic smelling smoke rose from the smoldering remnants of what had once been a living creature, although certainly not a chicken. Whatever it was, it must contain quantities of protein. This is what convalescents need.

"Ollie, please take just a small bite." The minister was still contemplating the heavens, eyes open, mouth half closed. "Look, I'm having some." Elliot chewed a portion of brown flatbread. At least it was tasteless.

No go. The holyman obviously preferred communing with the beyond to an earthly communion. But Elliot had an idea. Wrapping his white napkin around the lower part of his face, including nose and mouth, he cut a large portion of pollo and raised it to Ollie's mouth with a fork. In a movement that might have been an unconscious reflex, Wallby took the meat between his teeth. It paused there for several minutes, trapped between sharp incisors and powerful molars. Then, to Elliot's horror, the piece of pollo began to disappear slowly into the cavernous maw.

Aghast, terrified, nauseated, Elliot braced himself with large gulps of pisco.

Soon the protein had submerged entirely into the ministerial mouth. Maybe Wallby ought to be given another piece, to load up while he could. They might have to exist in the streets for weeks on churros and coffee. Elliot cut a second large piece and conveyed it to his friend. The teeth, astonishingly well preserved for a man of seventy something, clamped onto the offering. Elliot watched in expectation and hope. He sipped from his glass—jolly good drink—and waited. But this time the pollo was stuck within the efficient dentition.

"Now, Ollie, please give it another try. You need lots of good fresh nourishment to make you healthy and strong."

Held between jaws that would have aroused the admiration of a shark, the second portion of pollo refused to budge. It stood suspended in mid-dentition. It was tilted slightly upward, as if it were in a sense an offering to the Spirit.

The waiter reappeared. He viewed Wallby with benign interest. "The senor like mucho de pollo frito." The second piece was still stuck in the clergyman's mouth. How strange were the ways of gringo folks!

"Oh yes. He's wild about it. And it's just what he needs."

"You like more pollo?" The waiter was eager for a second order. With the commission on five cents a plate, who wouldn't be?

"Thank you, we're still working on the first plate." The waiter saluted unhappily.

"Now, Ollie, please give it another go. It's prime protein." For his own nutrition, Elliot dunked a piece of flatbread into his pisco and swallowed it.

The second piece of pollo still had not budged from the entrance. Wallby said something but his words were muffled by the pollo-plug. The poor fellow might be trying to communicate something important. It was contrary to manners, but Elliot wrenched the hunk of pollo from the vise-like jaw.

"Nang ump fa. Gorng ol fo."

It was disturbing to note that the act of removing pollo from Wallby's mouth had damaged several teeth and bruised his gums and other soft tissues of the mouth. After mushing air for several moments, Wally tried again to speak. "Mus fee th' staring mess's."

"Yes, Ollie, you are right. We certainly must feed the starving masses. It is in our doctrine. But nutrition begins at home. Try another small bite of pollo." He replaced the second piece, and waited in desperate expectation. Nada happened.

Another bright idea came into Elliot's mind. If pisco could make the local bread more palatable, why not the pollo? He removed the pollo, this time gently, from the liturgical mouth, wiped off the red stains, then poured a good dose of pisco directly down the churchy throat. Ollie had this amazing capacity to swallow pis' with hardly any activation of the normal throat muscle process. Then Elliot replaced the pollo.

At last, slowly, gradually, but undeniably, the meat began to move down the track.

"Good show, Ol'! We are absorbing our nutrition very well!"

The waiter returned. He admired the disappearance of the pollo. Wallby was just then chewing the last bit of plug. "Postre?"

At first Elliot shook his head. By his calculations the bill so far would top seventeen cents. They had to conserve their cash for an indefinite period. Then, a second thought. Why not dessert? The pisco was doing Ollie a world of good. "Dos piscos, otra vez."

The waiter smiled, bowed, withdrew.

He might well smile. So far the bill was up to twenty-one cents! But it was worth it to see Ollie happy again. The heavenly gentleman was once more deep in contemplation, but for some unknowable reason his head faced down, not up. Maybe he was communing with chthonic spirits? No, he was holding his glass in a low position, that was the secret.

Elliot sipped his drink slowly, savoring every drop. It was not the old rancho stuff, but it was a very good vintage, doubtless aged for several weeks at least. He was looking over the top of Wallby's contemplatively bowed head when he saw it. A poster on the wall. At first he believed it to be an advertisement for a bull fight, a corrida. When his eyes focused he saw that it was a notice for a theatrical performance. The Teatro Travesti de San Santo. He remembered that the Minister had explained all about it on the plane. One of the planet's greatest transvestite drama institutions. The poster proclaimed that they were giving the famous *La Paca*. It was to TV (transvestitism/

transexuality) what Hamlet was to Elizabethan drama. Why not take the Reverend to the show? It might awaken his mind, still so numbed by the altitude.

"Ollie?" He shook his friend's shoulder. "How would you like to see some transvestite theatre? There's a performance tonight."

"Excellent. Quite marvelous, very." His head was still turned earthward, in the direction of his glass. The easier to suck up pisco.

"It's not 'Jueves'." Olby had mentioned Un Jueves de Todos los Jueves as his favorite TV drama.

"I am very much in agreement even though." Head still down, the last of his glass of pisco disappeared in an extraordinary display of suction power.

"Then we will try to get tickets. I hope they're not sold out." Elliot had seen transvestite theatrics in L.A., but really only amateur camp drag. This would be art. If Stockholm had not yet taken notice it was because of their inveterate conventionality.

The next morning they woke up numbed by the nine thousand foot coolness of the night. At least Elliot woke up. The ecumenical agent was as yet snoring while his body sought warmth under old clothes and cardboard. Last night they had been unable to move on. Wallby was immobilized by the unwanted activity and the pisco. The waiters had been so good as to allow them to sleep in the inside patio for an extra three cents each after it turned out that *La Paca* had been sold out long in advance, and it was too late for them to go back to the warehouse. The doors opening to the restaurant had been locked behind them. El Santo people were not fools. The kitchen contained a valuable store of pisco.

Elliot banged on the glass paned door for a lengthy period. He was cold. He was hungry. He was thirsty. At last a figure, probably the waiter, appeared on the other side.

"Si?" The man was suspicious. Were they more beggars infiltrating the patio by night?

"Traiganos unos cafes." Bring us coffee. "We are guests here. We spent a lot of money here last night."

"Ah. Si si si. Los gringos." He he made a clucking noise with his tongue, then unlocked the door.

After a lengthy explanation he agreed to help drag Wallby into the restaurant. It was a heavy go, even with each of them pulling a leg. The theological apostle was miraculously heavy despite his recent weight loss.

"De santo hombre got de brick in de belly."

Finally they set Wallby up at a table. Exhausted, Elliot collapsed into a chair. He had fallen asleep again—it was only eleven-thirty—when the waiter came back with two coffee-piscos.

"Ahi los cafes!"

Ollie woke up and smelled the coffee. "Tomorrow we shall begin our ascent of Everest. Inform the guides. The base camp is at least three days journey from Kathmandu on donkey back."

Elliot was shocked and frightened. Ollie apparently believed that he was back in Nepal. That had been almost twenty years ago. "Yes, dear friend, the Sherpas are breaking camp. We'll soon be on our way." It was best to humor him.

When the coffee-pisco had been drunk, Elliot set about reassembling the Cad. Wallby was humming to himself fragments from Mozart's Great Mass.

Putting it all together again was no easy task. The various pieces, tables, rope, wire, packing crate, old clothes and cardboard were scattered around the patio. Finally, after a difficult struggle, it existed again. Panting from the high altitude activity, Elliot wheeled it to their dining room table.

Everything was ready to start the quest again, but Elliot hesitated. Wheeling his friend on the improvised vehicle was heavy work. His back and arms were sore from yesterday's brief transit. Anyway, there was the final bill to settle. The waiter had twigged that the two were on their way out and rushed to attend. He stood smiling in the doorway.

"Is eight cents. No, eight y medio." Eight and a half.

The bill was exact. Elliot pulled a few coins out of his pocket. He was sorry to leave the Café del Pueblo. It had been like a home to them. In a gesture of extravagance that only yesterday would have seemed criminal folly, he deposited a dime in the waiter's palm.

"Gracias, senor." He looked at the dime. He had always been intrigued by the fact that a dime—the U.S. dollar had long been the legal standard in El Santo—although smaller than a penny or a nickel, was worth much more. It must have special power. "Dejenme ayudarles, senores, adonde van?" He would help them go where they wanted.

At this point there was no reason not to be frank. "El Teatro Travesti."

"Oh oh!" The waiter winked, smiled. He had suspected as much. Maricones. Otherwise, why they no bring de mujeres, eh? It made no difference. A customer who tipped one and a half cents was an amigo anytime. "I give de help. It is teatro magnifico. Nod de far."

"Thank you, but I couldn't take you away from your work, the customers ..."

"Nada. No cliente come here in the early. Maybe two three hour we got prostitutas for big table. Y militares."

The waiter was eager to help propel the Cad to the Teatro Travesti. Elliot explained the principles of the vehicle's construction and method of empowerment. The trick was to hold the packing crate in place while pushing the wheels and the axle.

"Ah." The waiter was not encouraged.

The Cad sailed from the doors of the Café del Pueblo. Wallby, seated in the padded crate, waved a white paper napkin. Was he, at least in his own mind, greeting the masses for Che-su?

The waiter, Frediberto, held the crate while Elliot lent his shoulder to the table-wheels. It was rough going.

Frediberto was puffing with the effort. "Senor, why you no pay de blanket men?"

"Impossible. We are not millionaires."

They were pushing the contraption across the poorly pavemented street to reach the next sidewalk corner when the Cad split into its two component table halves, at the same time spilling Wallby into a large pothole filled with water from the last rainy season. It took many minutes of hard effort to reassemble the Cadillac and to extract and replace the Reverend. At least he seemed unhurt.

"I want to thank all you good people for coming here tonight. Thank you Lord, thank you Jesus."

A small crowd gathered to watch the strange vehicle and its odd passenger. They began to make bets, depositing piles of scrip and pennies on the ground. Some shouted encouragement, others jeered. At last they reached the corner. Elliot and Frediberto rested, wiped their brows, caught their breath.

"Cross the Jordan. Amen. And I shall be with you to …"

They went on. Another half block—manzana in Spanish—and they were in sight of an impressive building. Its complex baroque façade displayed a ravishing ornamentation. It was old, but not too dilapidated. It must be the Teatro. Fredi had called it magnifico.

"It is truly magnificent. Look Ollie. The Teatro. Is it not gorgeous beyond belief?"

Frediberto laughed. "No senor. Dees not de Teatro. Dees de Iglesia de San Jose el Trabajador."

"Oh." Elliot turned to his friend. "It's not the teatro, Ollie. It's just some kind of church."

"In fact?" The Reverend was not really following events.

A few more yards and Frediberto brought the Cad to a halt. He pointed with his shoulder toward a low building dabbed with faded and scaling whitewash and a muddy purple dado. "Dees de Teatro." The tall narrow windows were boarded up, probably a response to constant vandalism, but there was a bright, multi-colored sign above the open door: Teatro Travesti de San Santo.

"Dees de place wear de womens mens. Ees muy divirtido." Frediberto grinned.

"Yes." Elliot responded cooly. He abhorred condescension.

They wheeled the Cad through the door. It just squeezed through, only slightly pulverizing the plaster of the doorway. Ollie raised his hand to give a blessing, as if he were riding in the pope mobile.

"Aqui estamos." Frediberto released his load. "Que se diviertan mucho, senores." Have fun. He exited, smiling broadly.

"Fuck you," Elliot said in a low voice when Frediberto was on his way out. He looked around the teatro. They were in a sort of lobby. On the crumbling walls posters advertised the famous La Paca and Un Jueves de Todos los Jueves and other dramatic performances. There was no light except from the open street door. At one end of the long shabby room was what looked like a ticket window.

"It looks like they're not open yet." It was early afternoon. They had come to restore Ollie's spirits. He had always shown great interest in the Santano transvestite/transsexual theatre. Elliot thought that raising his friend's morale for the long, difficult quest ahead would be worth a small detour. Besides, they could camp comfortably in the lobby while waiting. "Let's just relax, Ol'."

The Reverend Wallby had already slid off the packing crate and was comfortably sprawled on the lobby floor. Probably he was sleeping.

"Respect the cultures and practices of primitive peoples ..." Wallby was giving one of his Thursday night talks at the church hall.

"No, Ol'. Remember, we're the primitives here."

"We are all primitives in Che-su."

How right Ollie was. Elliot studied the play posters. Garishly dressed women (men?) struck provocative poses. The plumes on their heads focused attention. Indented photos showed drawing room scenes with drab, mousy men looking perplexed while well shaped actresses gave challenging explanations. It was going to be quite a show. He slouched against the lobby wall and was beginning to nod off.

"Hi am ver sorry, but you cannot esleep here. We are not de hospital clinico." A female personage was calling him to order.

"We are waiting for the show." Suddenly awake, Elliot became ingenuous and disarmed. He smiled at the "senorita".

The senorita stood with arms akimbo. She looked very much like one of the figures on the posters. "Den you come back in de nighttime."

Elliot understood that he would have to give a further explanation, but which? "We are tourists, mademoiselle. We have come from Los Angeles to appreciate your world famous theatre. Only yesterday we were at the Hotel de Carlos, but had to check out because of a credit misunderstanding."

"Why you did not assay asso." Her English was quite good, but not perfect. "Dad you fren?" She indicated Wallby. She was shocked by Elliot's taste. Certainly the Reverend was not at his best. And even his best was not that good.

"He has been like a father to me."

"Ah. Ay unnerstan." She thought she understood. She gave a grimace of distaste. "Den you come wi' me an' ay gi' you de runaroun'."

She was offering a free tour. Elliot was immediately interested by such a bargain. He gave her a closer look. She was not short, probably five foot five at most, with a strong but not heavy build. Under a turban decorated with plastic fruit her face was light brown, her features even and rounded. The breast endowment, probably enhanced artificially, had a definite distinction. Beyond doubt she was—or had been—a man. Her dress was theatrical. "Now you give you fren a wake up call so we go in tour."

"Well, you see, my friend is recovering from a recent illness and he can walk only with great difficulty. We brought him here on that sort of machine." Elliot pointed to the Cadillac.

"Ah. Den you leave de sleepin' log lie. Nobody come in here before de nighttime."

They were to proceed by themselves.

"I am Maralita. I am give you de hi."

"Charmed." He took her hand. Since it seemed not to want to shake, he kissed it. Surreptitiously, he wiped his lips with the sleeve of his shirt.

"How you are call you you'self and that one?" She pointed to Wallby with the tip of her slippered foot …

"Oh." Elliot laughed at the social gaff of not introducing himself properly. "Sorry. I'm Elliot Spenseric. And my friend is the Reverend Francis Wallby. We are both from Los Angeles, in North America."

She peered closely at Ollie. "Eh? Dese guy a cura?" She thought he was a priest.

"Um. No. Not exactly. It's more complicated than that. You see, Oliver is an Episcopalian minister. Or he was." The defrocking effort in the states may already have had an effect, but they had no recent information. "They're not canonically ordained and they have little knowledge of the historic church." He had given this explanation before. As far as he knew, it was correct. "My father was Serbian Orthodox, which is similar theologically."

This was as much as Maralita wished to hear. "Okay. Now we go see el teatro." She shook her hips and bodice in a quaint and entertaining way as she moved. She grabbed his arm. "Don worry of dat one. No body gonna wanna come near." Wallby would be just fine where he was.

Inside, Elliot was astonished by the simplicity of the audience space. There were no chairs or benches. Of course, this was common in San Santo. Chairs were always the first to go.

"De guy sit on de floor, maybe give de blanket. He gotta much confor. He lie down when he like."

"Oh. I see. How clever."

"Ya. We gotta much guy dey sleep de night some time."

Even though there was little light in the large room, Elliot could see that plaster was peeling from the walls. "It is, well, I would say very picturesque."

"De otras actrices nod aroun righ now. Dey essleep laid because dey got de much boyfren." She winked and playfully jabbed Elliot in the ribs.

Maralita marched onto the stage. Elliot climbed the four wooden steps to join her. "Okay. Ri now we are show 'La Mujer Sin Caja'. Dees a play dat dey show a women which she is ver poor an no got no money. No tiene caja. She got no money. Dey make her do de prostituta. Bu she too inteligente. She git de venganza on de stupid guy."

"Fascinating."

"Ya. We rehearse all de week. I am Nachachita, de Mujer Sin Caja. When I play de guy all cry. Lloran todos. Is make everbody too sad. You witch." Mara left the center of the stage, turned around swiftly and returned, now in character.

"Tu, chingado, me has robado! Has matado a mi madre! Has matado a mi padre." She stopped to hold back a yawn. "Escuse. Las ni', I up de laid esleep." She returned to her stage character. "Yo no tengo nada mas en la vida que ..." She made a gesture of tearing away the upper part of her dress to show "what she had left in life".

"This is very dramatic. By the way, your English is excellent. Where did you study?"

"Oh. I give de bum around L.A. for fi years."

"You seem to have learned a lot. This play, Mujer Sin Caja, has aspects that recall the best of Shakespeare."

"I am so happy you say we are like de Shatesphere. Cause I know he de guy write de bes' play all de long time ago."

"Your character reminds me of Lady Macbeth."

"Oh, dees ees maravilloso! Bud I tell you one ting. De problema we got wi de play is no guy wanna play de abuela. De abuela mu importante in de play, but de actrices no wanna play de ol lady cause dey wanna be young for de boyfren. So we gotta fine a guy play de abuela cus de play start tonight."

Elliot looked concerned. He was forced by circumstances to flatter, but his sympathy for Maralita and her theatre group was genuine. "I would almost say that Reverend Wallby could take the role of the grandmother. Unfortunately, he knows very little Spanish and his health problems would make it difficult for him to memorize lines."

Maralita grinned. The problema was solved! "He no gotta know nada. De Abuela don got no lines. In de escena, she sit on de stool an she esleep. Nachachita say a lot an de utter actrices an de boyfren say, but de ol lady, she no say nuthin."

"Like tar baby in the story." Elliot now saw the advantages for himself and Wallby. The "actrices" would doubtless be paid.

"See, de abuela she sit in de corner. Dat wud so funny. All de guy do de sexy ting an she spose watch dey don do nuthin, bu she essleep all de time. We make de fun on de 'gente decente'. Comprendes?"

"Yes, I see. You are satirizing bourgeois morality." Elliot rubbed his chin, contemplating the remaining difficulties. "Do you have a dress in her—I mean his—size?"

"Ya, we gotta dress for de Pastor, claro. We got all de sizes."

"She—I mean he—would need a wig and quite a lot of makeup."

"No hay problema, amigo. Dees el Teatro Travesti. We do de maravilloso."

"Then I can accept for my friend." He was pensive for a moment. "Of course we would require a subsistence remuneration, at least until our credit difficulties are solved."

"How much?" Maralita was suspicious.

"Oh, say five cents a day?"

"Okay, amigo, but you fren bedder be good actriz."

"He will earn an Oscar. In a sense, all of his career has been one big act."

"Den you tell me where you eleeve an we make time for de re-whoresales."

"Yes." Elliot tried to think of the best way to put it. "You see, unfortunately, as a result of an absurd misunderstanding, Ollie and I no longer have a fixed address. We are waifs at hazard."

This was not good news to Maralita. "You mean you esleep in de estreet?"

"So far we have managed to arrange temporary shelter. Last night we were at the Café del Pueblo."

"Ya. I no dees place. Some time dey got de good party." This was an impressive reference, coming from Maralita. "Bu see, I no you de good guy an you no steal de stuff. Bu mis amigas, dey no like I let de guy stay in teatro. Dey got all de dresses, vestidos, muy caros. If I letta you fren stay an he take someting, dey wanna cut off my ..."

Elliot waited to hear what Maralita's friends would want to cut off in case of a burglary. Nothing followed. "I understand the difficulty. Would it be possible for us to stay in the lobby until the time of the performance? We have our own blankets and I would watch Ollie very closely."

"Maybe dat okay. De door dat go to teatro elock wen no got de representacion."

"Thank you, that is very generous of you."

"You no, now I ethink, de wig fo you amigo, we gotta one for George Washington in de play las year. You put on you fren an he look jus like de abuela."

"Excellent. I'm sure she'll—I mean he'll—put on a stellar performance." Elliot thought about his friend—still not well—and the care that he needed. "Maralita, you have been very kind to us. My friend, Reverend Ollie, is recuperating, but he's still not quite back to health. The doctor prescribed hourly glasses of a medical drink. Would you have a bottle of pisco about the place?"

"Oh, dad de problem wi you fren? He kinna look like too much de drin. Okay I gotta botella. Hondurena. De las boyfren I got he lef it. Dees de kinna asshole stuff he drin."

Maralita came back with a bottle, but no glasses. Maybe she drank habitually straight from the bottle.

"Okay. You res wi you fren, den we git ready for de show a nueve horas de la noche. We pu de makeup too goo on dis guy. You jus tell im he not in de church ri now."

When Maralita had gone—Elliot admired the deft turns and shakes of her dress, especially around the buttocks—he looked closely at the bottle. It was about three quarters full. It was clear in color, raw pisco, and small pieces of what he hoped were charcoal from the filtering process floated in the wash. He took a tiny sip. It tasted all right. He shook Wallby by the shoulder.

"Ollie, wake up, please. You've had quite a nap and I have some important things to tell you."

"Thank all of you for coming here to St. Henry's. I hope …"

"No, Ol! We're not at your holy jamboree in Hollywood. We're in San Santo. We're here to join FARS and teach them about Che-su."

"Bless …"

"Yeah. But there's something else too. You just got hired. You have a real paying job! Here, take a drink of this. It'll wake you up." He found a small plastic container on the floor. Probably it had been used to package condoms. He poured about two ounces into the cup and brought it to Ollie's lips. Ollie sniffed it, then swallowed the whole. He seemed to appreciate it.

Elliot took a drink directly from the bottle. It was more sanitary. Really, Honduran or not, it wasn't bad at all. Then he poured a couple of more shots into the condom container and handed it to the Reverend. The clerical gentleman's motor skills always improved with a sip of the stuff. It steadied his hand. "You see, you are going to be Abuela in the play. It is an important role—the show can't go on without it—and you will receive top billing."

"Then I shall … I shall … "

Elliot poured another slug into the condom pack.

"Do what I can to be theatrical."

"Right on, Ol! And you are getting five cents a day. Not bad money, eh? We can get quite a bit of pisco for five."

"But, are there lines to learn? Such as in Shakespeare?"

"Don't worry about that. That's all settled."

When it was dark, Elliot left the lobby. He walked along the poorly lighted streets until he found a corner café where he could buy churros and some meat filled pastries. They would wash it down with what was left of the pisco and they would be all set for a spectacular performance.

While Elliot was out, Wallby had gathered from the lobby floor what looked like burst water balloons. "I do not know what these are."

"Drop them, Ollie." Obviously they were used condoms.

"We could fill them with liquid for later refreshment."

"Drop them, Ollie!" When the deflated condoms lay on the floor, Elliot kicked them out of sight. The minister's sense of sanitation had been badly targeted in his general deterioration.

"Have a churro, and one of these pastries. They're much more nutritious."

Wallby swallowed several. His plastic cup had to be refilled four times.

"Yes." Elliot had been looking at his friend's face and imagining him in the role of the Abuela. The soft features, the evident great maturity, the gestures, would make a very credible Abuela. "Ollie, they will sing your praises in Hollywood."

The Reverend was pleased but obviously had no real understanding of the matter. He smiled, then looked perplexed, then smiled again. Elliot laughed at this ingenuous display.

"Perfect, Ol', keep it up, old friend."

Suddenly the old friend's face reflected terror. Elliot turned around. Maralita had returned.

"We gotta one hour before cortina." She extended an arm downward to where the ecumenical friend sat on the floor. "How you? I yam Maralita. You play de good Abuela, eh?"

"He's perfect for the part. We were just talking about it, and Ollie has been reflecting on his role. He does method acting. Just before you came he asked me, 'What's my motivation?'"

Wallby drew back. He began searching for his "water balloons". He seemed to derive a certain comfort in handling them.

"Forget it, Ol!" Elliot grabbed him by the clerical collar and shook. "Be polite to the lady. She is a very accomplished actress."

"How ...?"

"So now we gotta go. You come wi me, senor Pastor. We all get ready for de show."

"As I explained, Maralita, Ollie is still very much under the weather. He has limited self-mobility."

"Ya, you tell me. Okay, no problema. We gitta couple de guys bring im backstage." She turned to Ollie. "You gotta get de dress, den de make-up. Maquillaje." Swift turn with skirts flouncing and she was gone.

"Just do what she says, Ol'. She's a nice lady. You're on the road to stardom."

Ollie began to whimper when Maralita came back with two burly fellows apt for carrying. One had a wheelbarrow draped over his shoulder.

They were short, but strongly built. They began by grabbing Elliot by the legs.

"Whoa! It's not me. Yo no soy la actriz."

Maralita disabused them in what must have been choice local Spanish. They looked close to a general retreat. "Eet de oder guy. He gonna be de abuela." She translated so that Elliot would be aware of her management of the matter.

They moved toward the ecclesiastical person. Wallby was still highly complexed. He began to whimper again, but with more motivation.

"Ollie, really, there is absolutely nothing to be scared of. The nice men are going to take you to the backstage area. Maralita will see to your outfit and external preparations." Elliot allowed his friend to take one of the "burst water balloons" with him, even though it was highly unsanitary. It did seem to give him a certain feeling of emotional comfort.

"De maquillaje is gonna make you look beautiful, sweetie."

Once in the wheelbarrow, the Reverend relaxed. He rather seemed to enjoy the ride, like a captain on his own fast scudding boat. He made friendly comments or questions to the carriers, but they remained mute. Although they were well disposed to the passenger, their English was limited. The "Barrow" sailed out of view.

"Don' worry bout you fren. He gonna bring down de house. Ay never see no guy be a better abuela."

"Thank you. I think the experience will be therapeutic for the old gentleman. But, by the way, could you advance the first night's pay? You see, we have to have all our meals catered and it's not the cheapest way to live."

"I know he gonna act real good, but where you meet dis guy?" Wallby's sadly dilapidated condition remained a shock to Maralita.

"He was once an impressive man who officiated at our local church." Elliot lied. Wallby had never been good looking, although his discoveries in the field of spirituality had made points with scores of journalists, leading them to write of him as "the Holy Atheist". It was true, however, that just a few months ago he had been in much better shape. That was before the national scandal of Naked Mass. "He has had personal misfortunes."

"Ya, he go real fast."

Elliot nodded. But business affairs couldn't be put aside that easily. He addressed Maralita without a genuine smile. "About the five cents?"

"I pay you after de show. Ri' now ay don got change."

Late the next day new posters were put up in the Centro, the downtown area of San Santo. "La Mujer Sin Caja." Beneath photos and drawings from the play, there was a rave note. "Y con la muy famosa Olivia, Arzobispo de Hollywood, en el papel de La Abuela!"

Ollie was getting special billing. In fact, he was creating quite a sensation. The playgoers, a diverse lot including curious and slumming bourgeois, cultural advanceniks, the sexual minorities including transvest and transex, odd individuals—primarily those who thought they were at their neighborhood church—and police spies, were bowled over. During intermission Elliot heard them discuss the play and laugh while smoking their little hand rolled cigarettes and enjoying a pisco or two from the buffet. "La Mujer Sin Cajones," they jibed. "La Abuela, quien es? Que tipo raro!" They were impressed by Ollie. He had stolen the show. Even though he had no lines to speak, he managed constantly to change his facial expression and the position of his head in such a way as to monopolize the attention of the audience. He was a terrific success.

On the day of the third performance, Elliot demanded full payment from Maralita. He threatened that his friend would go on strike unless given "her" full wages to date. Maralita capitulated with bad grace. "Okay! I gi you de fuckin fiteen senz. The arte of the teatro is not jus for de dinero, hombre. Fuck, dees is our hole life! But I tell you, lotta de actrices, dey no like he make de head move and make de funny face. De people only gonna look at im."

Her very colloquial English was disagreeable, but the dime and nickel would help eek out expenses. Late that night, after the crowd had left, Elliot celebrated by giving Wallby an extra glass of pisco or two. In fact, the stage hands had begun to prime "Olivia" with glasses of the stuff between acts. They thought this would contribute to the amusement La Abuela was providing to the audience. At this point, she was feeling no pain.

"To be or not to be. That is the question." Ollie was taking to a dramatic career like a fish to water. His college drama class memories of the Bard were starting to flow back.

"Yes, the very question indeed. I just hope this interlude will advance us on our real quest, to find the Mama and to join FARS."

The fourth performance was an event of epochal triumph. It was almost the Santano equivalent of the Academy Awards. There was standing room only. Since searchlights were available only to the military, a bonfire was lit outside the teatro. From the back of the audience space, Elliot watched the beginning of the play that he now knew by heart. Maralita and her boyfriend exchange witticisms. She warns about the Abuela. He disdains caution. They embrace. She turns to the audience and exposes "todo lo que tengo". It is a faked scene.

Much of the play dragged, in the original sense of the word. When the famous drawing room scene came on, all eyes were focused. In this scene the actores/actrices gallivant and chit-chat while Wallby, adding his own interpretation to the character of La Abuela, makes a series of droll faces and amusing head rolls.

According to the stage directions, La Abuela was asleep. This allowed the amorous couples to flirt without the inhibiting influence of a chaperon. Maralita's character was hugging Alfredo between the legs.

"Hombre! Que me gustas! Me muero sin ..."

Before Maralita could say what she would die without, audience laughter reached a deafening paroxysm.

Unknown to Maralita and Alfredo, who were facing the audience, behind them La Abuela was using one hand to play with her wig while sticking her tongue out at odd angles. Maralita, good trooper that she was, played on despite obvious audience preoccupation with something going on behind her.

Wallby, although a gifted amateur, was not a seasoned player. It was at this point that he/she decided to embellish the role of La Abuela by the addition of more lines from Shakespeare. The Reverend chose a passage from Macbeth. She/he began to declaim Lady Macbeth's lines beginning with the line "I who have given suck". Many in the audience, especially the students and bourgeois, had enough knowledge of English literature and slang to send them rolling in the aisles.

For a minute, Maralita, finally convincing herself that it must after all be her stellar performance that had impressed them, smiled and bowed to the audience. Then she realized that she and Alfredo could not be that funny. She turned around and saw the Abuela and heard her reciting. Ollie had switched to Richard III. "What though he hath widowed and unchilded many a one/ Yet shall he have a great name."

It was lucky that at this point even the audience didn't have a clue. Richard III was seldom played in San Santo. The Correos wouldn't permit it, since it has to do with the assassination of heads of state.

Maralita shrieked at the canonical gentleman, "Calla, desgraciada! Tu que sabes del teatro?" She rushed toward the center of the stage and once again bared "todo lo que tengo".

There was some applause. The performance might have recovered, but Maralita's outburst drew the other actrices back onto the stage. They too were breaking character, letting go of their pent-up resentment at Wallby's success. They shouted obscene insults at him. They threw stage props. They brought empty bottles of pis' and flung them at the old Abuela character. A couple of the brawnier ones grabbed Wallby by the legs and started to drag him offstage. It was a rebellion. The pueblo/actrices were rebelling. They demanded their rights. They demanded the end of oppression. Save the world now, not *manana*. All of it, not just a little.

Much of the audience, although they had greatly appreciated Wallby's performance, could not resist an hereditary urge to join the uprising. They stood up and began a general bombardment of the stage with old cans, empty bottles, newspapers, candy wrappers, used condoms, religious pamphlets. One novia even threw part of her dress, the part left intact by her eager young novio. Oddly, half the crowd was pro-abuela and the other half pro-actrices. It was like a battle over abortion, but no one was sure of the battle lines.

Elliot watched from the back of the hall. He had no particular opinion on the subject of abortion. He was anxious for the fate of his friend. At one moment it looked like a group of enraged actrices would hurl him into the audience pit. Then a group of sympathizers stopped them. An actrice snatched Wallby's wig. Another tore his dress off. Pathetic petticoats flailed impotently. It was an exciting drama, but Elliot's sense of duty led him to advance toward the stage, to try to rescue his friend. The slogging was very heavy between the thick crowd of machito boyfriends and enraged/aroused novias. Then the lights went out. Someone, bless her/him, had chosen the simplest way to stop the revolution. Groaning and shouting filled the dark air. Lighted pitos—little cigarettes—provided the only points of light.

Elliot was pushed back by a flood of theater leavers. The flow carried everything in its wake toward the lobby. Suddenly the electricity came back on. He managed to cut loose from the floes, with the intention of picking up their few pitiful belongings from a corner of the lobby floor. He broke into tearful smiles when he looked up to see his dear friend resting comfortably in a wheelbarrow. "And this above all else: to thine own self be true." Wallby's head was covered with pieces of trash, strips of newspaper, candy wrappers, parts of used condoms, but his mood was joyous. He had found his life's path.

Beyond any doubt Wallby would have made a perfect Polonius. Could they have reached Off Broadway, the show might have gone on for decades. From their gestures and elementary English Elliot learned that, in gratitude for the pleasure he had given the audience, the stagehands had rescued Wallby from the mob and the enraged actrices. Elliot distributed a small handful of pennies, purloined from the pocket of an abandoned costume dress, to several outstretched hands. They bowed theatrically, departed.

Just in case the cast decided to rally for another attack, Elliot grabbed the handles of the wheelbarrow and rushed Wallby out the door. "Parting is such sweet sorrow".

They were half a mile from the Teatro Travesti when Elliot stopped. He was exhausted, panting, his numb arms hanging from aching shoulders. What were they to do now? If Wallby showed his face in the TV theatre again, he might be pulled to pieces by dionysiac furies. Elliot sat on the sidewalk to rest. A few faint lights illuminated the bare, crumbling houses. There wasn't even a bottle of pisco handy. Elliot fell into a desperate sleep. "Goodnight, sweet prince."

His BMW was parked in the driveway of their Beverly Hills home. Maxine was in the doorway, a glass in her hand. It was empty, but she didn't know it was empty. She said something sarcastic. He returned the compliment. She said something else. "What?" He couldn't make it out. It was particularly nasty. She was smiling. Then he woke up.

"I said, we shall have to leave soon. They are sweeping the sidewalk." Wallby pointed toward a small group of broom pushers coming near. The recall of Beverly Hills had only been a dream. Blue dawn was breaking on the frigid San Santo streets. Wallby was resting comfortably in the hollow of the barrow. He still wore petticoats. Had he slept? For Wallby, there was no clear division between sleep and waking.

"Let us take up our burden." J-P II.

Elliot grabbed the barrow handles and pushed.

"Turn left on Vernon Avenue." Wallby was hallucinating. He thought they were in L.A. In a way, they were.

At the end of the street a faint glimmer appeared in the pre-dawn. Elliot rushed for it. He thought he knew what it was. After a good eight minutes of hard shoving, they were close. It was! Thank God for miracles. It was a café. Elliot steered the barrow through the doorway. He rushed to the bar. "Dos piscos. Grandes."

He sat at a table, drawing a comfortable packing crate under him, as before. Wallby lounged in the barrow on the other side of the square table. He waggled his tootsies in the air, hummed a popular tune.

"Seriously, Ollie, we have to think of what to do now. If we could find the Mama, and contact FARS, we'd be right on course. We're somewhere in the middle of San Santo, but I'm not sure where."

The waiter reappeared. He was carrying two glasses full of pisco. "Cuatro." Four cents. Naturally he wanted to be paid in advance before delivering the pisco. Elliot dragged four big ones out of his pocket, put them on the table. The waiter put the drinks down.

"Gracias."

Elliot sucked up a bit of the juice. He felt better. Wallby's glass had a straw. He was making his drink disappear like a party magic trick. "Bueno, no?" asked Elliot.

"The Sherpas will guide us to the foothills, but the ascent will be our work."

"No, no, no. We're not in Nepal anymore, Ollie." The Reverend was still not connected. Unless he was speaking in metaphors. Elliot looked around the café. There was the usual enlarged photograph poster of the Correos. A large banner with the slogan, "La Revolucion es La Revolucion". A small sign put up by the Departamento de Salud Publico advised, "Beba Menos". Drink less.

The grey-brown walls probably had not been painted since Pizarro, but there was a huge stain in the middle of the wall opposite. This disturbed Elliot. It looked as if someone had lobbed an enormous clod of earth against the wall, then spread it around, then covered it with acrylic. It was obscene. The staff had tried to hide it with a small banner bearing the slogan, "Stalin con Nosotros", but the banner had soon come loose, again revealing the nauseating stain. Stalin was the nice one.

Elliot drank more slowly, trying to make it last. Maybe the Mama was watching them. Maybe she would reveal herself when the moment was opportune. While he was daydreaming, a group of women entered the café. They were stopping for refreshment before beginning their workday. One of them wore a badly mended blue dress. Manolito.

They rushed up to the bar and ordered coffee. Café. Of course, this was understood by the barkeep to mean pisco, which was cheaper. He poured a clear liquor into four glasses with brown stains at the bottom.

Manolito tossed his drink off in half a second, then remarked, "Que tengo sed! Anoche, trabaje hasta las tres." He motioned the barkeep for another drink. This disappeared in less time than the first. He looked dazed for a moment. It really was strong stuff, as Elliot was able to confirm. Were they cutting it with gasoline? Probably not. Gasoline was more expensive. Only Wallby could drink this pisco without any noticeable effect.

Mano finally was able to focus. He looked around the bar. Suddenly he looked at Elliot and Wallby. He rushed to their table. "Amigos, que bueno verles!" He was glad to see them.

"Hello Manolito. How are you?"

"Bien. You are de look ver good. Especially de Pastor. He look so much de better."

Elliot looked at Wallby as if noticing him for the first time. "Yes. He does look better. He has had considerable success lately, in the field of acting. As a matter of fact, he just completed a triumphant tour at the Teatro Travesti."

Manolito made a face. "I don like dat place too ver much. They kick me out too many many time. But I like you fren have de act dere. Wad he play?"

"He played the role of La Abuela in Mujer Sin Caja."

"No me digas! I see dis play two million time."

Elliot thought of the profusion of used condoms on the floor of the lobby and in the theatre. "Really?"

"Ya. It like my favorite."

"Ollie did so well that, unfortunately, he aroused jealousy in the other players. There was almost a riot and we had to flee at the end of the last performance."

"Ya. I no how dis guy is. Mujeres sin Cajones. Bud I feel real sorry for you cause dese de real bitch. Wad you guy do now?"

"To tell you the truth, we've lost our compass. We don't know where we shall go. Can I offer you a drink?" Elliot knew that they could hardly afford the loss of two pennies, but Manolito was their last friendly local contact. He signaled the bartender for a general refill.

"You see, we want to establish contact with FARS, as I told you, and to do that we must find the Mama, just like you advised us. But here we are, and we don't know which direction to take."

Mano licked the mouth of his refilled glass. It looked like he was used to intricate tongue action. A pro. "Ya. I tell you dis again. You find de Mama. She no you here, but she don do too quick. She gotta watch first, cause is like lotta dirty guy too much."

Elliot thought of what they might do until the Mama decided that they were trustworthy. The Teatro Nacional, a rival to the Teatro Travesti, was doing a performance of El Libertador, which was advertized on every lamppost. Wallby would make a fantastic Bolivar. Certainly they would be able to mount him securely on a papier mache horse. All he would have to do was to swing a sword. Or, since they now had a wheelbarrow, the two could go into the transportation business. This did not seem promising. Elliot rubbed his aching upper arms.

"Ya. Bu le me tell you de nother ting." He drained his glass, looked up to make eye contact with the bartender. "Dis guy Jonathan, he no good, no bueno. He tell de Correo guy dat you wi de CIA. Ya, dat you work for de imperialismo, an dey no like dat. See, de Jonathan wark to de droga. He not too much happy you no help im. He tink you work for de udder guy."

Elliot rubbed his chin. "This is indeed worrisome. In truth, we are not involved with the CIA in any way. We are here strictly for the revolution and we are very anti-droga."

Mano drank eagerly from his refilled glass. Small tears formed in the corners of his eyes. "You wanna de revolucion, dis de place to come."

"A horse, a horse, my kingdom for a horse!" Wallby was awake. His Shakespearian side was flourishing.

"Oh no, senor," Manolito laughed. "You no gotta pay a whole kingdom for de whores."

"Camarero! Otro pisco para el senor." Elliot ordered another drink for Wallby. He was so much more sensible when he had had a few.

Manolito grabbed the glass meant for Wallby as soon as it was placed on the table. "Le me taste dis one. It look kinna funny." He swallowed half the glass. "No. It okay."

"What you have told me is disconcerting. You see, to speak quite frankly, the Reverend and myself are on a mission to teach FARS about the doctrine of Che-su. Have you heard of that?"

"Mebbe. I dunno."

"Well, the short definition is that it is a combination of the revolutionary theory of Che Guevara with the religious doctrines of Jesus. Wallby knows more about it than I do. I think if we could make contact with FARS we could add much to their efforts."

"Le me tink a liddle."

Elliot signaled the waiter to bring Mano another pisco.

"Okay. Mebbe I see. How much money you got?"

Red alert. This was a subject fraught with danger. "Only a few dollars."

Mano thought about it. "You guy go here from de Nu Yor and you no gotta no money?"

"We're from Los Angeles. Our credit was stopped by North American Express. Reverend Wallby has identity problems."

"Oh." Mano groaned. "Dat not de too good."

In fact, Elliot wanted to bring Wallby back to the NAMEX office to try again to withdraw money. But, although Ollie was more presentable now, he was rather less reasonable. What if he started to spout Shakespeare to the clerks? They would think he was *non compos mentis* and refuse to deliver any money.

"I godda gi de work soon. Okay, I tell you wha you do. Dis gonna get you mas closs to get de Mama. You go to Café Andino.

Avenida General Jose de San Martin. He got statue on de whores. You loo fo dis guy he name …" Manolito laughed. "You tink I say Carlos. No, no senores. You loo fo dis guy Antonio. Ya. Antonio. He maybe no trus you too much. He no de gringo come for de droga, de CIA. You giv im de pisco, like de fren, an you tell im Manolito you fren. So den he sen you to de FARS, mebbe."

"Eh! Borracho! Ven. Se hace tarde." The senoritas were calling their friend.

"I go. Suerte." Mano joined the others in a flutter of dresses towards the exit. Mano's often mended blue dress now looked quite shabby. If only he could earn enough cash to buy another outfit, he might have more success in his chosen profession.

"Ollie?" Elliot poked his friend with a finger to wake him up, although he wasn't sleeping. "We have a plan. Manolito gave me the name of a contact who can help get us in touch with FARS." White morning had broken in the street. Crowds of beggars and unemployed were massing on the corners.

"Yonder breaks the moon and sweet Juliet is the sun."

"Cut it out, Ollie. Have another drink." Elliot signaled to the waiter.

Ollie drank greedily. God he loved the stuff. This certainly wasn't something that he learned in Seminary.

"How about a nice hot churro? It's time to think about breakfast."

Ollie stared at the ceiling, or through the ceiling. Was he thinking of mystical doctrines beyond Che-su itself?

"Yes. Breakfast. I'll have a double."

"Chees, Ol'. Take it easy on the stuff. We're still eleven hours till cocktail time. Besides, at two cents a glass, you'll be drinking us into …" It was hard to think what Wallby would be drinking them into. They were already in the street and the country of El Santo had no poor house. In a sense, El Santo was a poor house. "Let's remember that we came to begin the New Life. I don't think cirrhosis was part of the original plan."

They left the café in an optimistic mood. Elliot believed they were finally on the right path. They were on their way to meet a man who would help them get in touch with FARS. Ollie intoned folk songs as he was born along in the hollow of the wheelbarrow. "I'll taste your strawberries, I'll drink your sweet wine." At the café, his intake had caused raised eyebrows even among the waiters. Apparently, though, all that pisco did him no harm. Just possibly it raised his level of philosophical insight.

"So we've got to find this guy called Carlos—I mean Antonio. He can put us in touch with FARS, the Frente Armado de la Revolucion Santana."

Ollie twigged. "If we raise the Masses to a higher level of consciousness, we will have raised ourselves with them. Revolution is an air pump."

Too true. Although this apothegm was not transparent in meaning, it required assent. Even if the air pump metaphor was not reassuring. "All we have to do is to walk to the Café Andino. We'll have a refreshment." He said this to rally Wallby's morale. The Reverend would soon feel the need for another infusion, even though he insisted on having several of the "water balloons" that he had brought from the teatro filled with pis' before they left the café. The waiter had handled it with surgical gloves.

They were three blocks gone before Elliot realized that he had no idea of where they going. The Café Andino was on the Avenida General Jose de San Martin, but Manolito had neglected to tell them how to get to the Avenida. Doubtless he assumed that everyone knew. "It can't be far. Mano never leaves the barrio. Remember how he told us that in other parts of the city the policia aren't so friendly?"

Ollby was sucking a transfusion from one of the balloons. "Cherrio!"

The hard part was crossing the intersections. Elliot could push the barrow along the sidewalks, the aceras, without too much effort, but the streets were potholed and uneven. Once, Wallby almost went down as the barrow got twisted by forty-five degrees above horizontal, and he with a pisco balloon in his mouth like a suckling enfant. The passersby, whose predominantly Ameridian descent was highly noticeable, laughed good naturedly.

The barrow was set to right and pushed to the next sidewalk. It was getting to be a trudge, although not nearly as bad as the Cadillac. On the corner Elliot looked for some likely person to ask directions of. A small, elderly, black clad lady was roasting tiny chestnuts (cockroaches?) in a smoke darkened metal drum. Three indios dressed in ponchos and baggy pants leaned against the wall of a house, their hands extended in hopeless expectation of alms. Possibly they were only pretending to be "working" (in El Santo, begging was an officially recognized profession) in order to avoid being rousted by the police. A man dressed in shabby Western style offered passer-bys a chance to bet on a handmade roulette wheel. None of these seemed a likely choice. The lady was more approachable, but Elliot rejected the idea of eating street chestnut/cockroaches, or even of trying them on Wallby. He stood on his toes, trying to see beyond the immediate forest. Then he saw it. Just barely in view, blocks away, was the raised sword of an equestrian statue. "Whahoo! C'mon, Ol'."

Even with the barrow in front and rushing over rough sidewalks and lunar street crossings, they now made fast time. Elliot rested, heaving and panting at the entrance to the plaza. Right there, smack in the center, was the horse borne statue of an antique military man with extended saber. General Jose de San Martin. He was one of the many men on horseback who made all El Santo proud. "The guys that brought the freedom".

"So here's the statue. The café can't be far away."

"Thirsty." Ollie looked it. He was probably pretty dehydrated after only six piscos for breakfast.

Once again, Elliot took up his burden. "Keep a lookout for something that looks like the Café Andino." They ventured slowly along the sidewalk. The crowds were thick and poor. Once, Elliot was moved to give charity to an extreme case. He offered two pennies, the price of a drink, to a badly dressed and unkept man sitting on the sidewalk. The man held a handmade sign on his bloated stomach. "No he tomado desde cuatro horas." The poor guy hadn't had a drink for four hours!

"I'll taste your strawberries, I'll drink your sweet wine."

"Cut it, Ol'! Change the record." Elliot was feeling the need for a drink himself as he pushed along, and not a suck from one of your water balloons either. Then, another hallazgo, a lucky find. Just behind a crowd of dismounted llama jockies and rather attractive, albeit poorly clad mamacitas, hung a sign that showed a profile of the High Sierra. El Café Andino.

Through the doors of a café in the center of the former Inca capital pushed a man intent on a mission and another man majestically mounted in a wheelbarrow. Both were damn near dead from thirst.

The Andino was unlike most cafes that Wallby and Elliot had known in San Santo. There were chairs, one or two at every table. There were customers, at least a dozen, resting in happy gloom beside their drinks. There were decorations beyond the usual posters of the Correo Brothers and slogan banners. A large photograph of snow covered peaks hung above the rows of bottles behind the bar. A portrait of noble, heroic, mustachioed General San Martin was mounted to one side of the mountains. A picture of a beautiful lady dancer with fan, comb and long red dress graced the opposite wall. Was she dancing a zarzuela? Elliot resolved to look it up in his dictionary, when he got one. The bartender twigged immediately to the presence of tourists—again, a sure source of hard currency.

"Senores, por favor, sientense." Please be seated, gentlemen. He indicated a nice central table with two chairs. Although Wallby didn't really need a chair. It was convenient and more comfortable for him to stay in the barrow. "Traigo la carta de inmediato."

"Dos piscos. Grandes." No need for a menu. Elliot knew what he wanted. Wallby was starting to pant from dehydration.

The bartender bowed. His mustache provided an attractive compliment to thick, dark eyebrows above a narrow swarthy face.

"Take the Harbor Freeway. I have a meeting in Torrance."

"No, Ollie, no! We're not in Los Angeles anymore. This is San Santo, capital of El Santo, remember? We're here to start the New Life."

"Santo Santo," Wallby repeated.

Elliot had started to whimper from exasperation and dispair when the glasses arrived.

"Aqui estan."

Elliot pushed out a nickel. At this point he was damn near reckless. Then, timidly, almost without hope, he started to sip his drink. He felt a tiny center of relaxation that gradually spread through his nervous system. Thoughts formed. Life returned. "Now, Ol', look for a man called Antonio. Not Carlos, Antonio."

Wallby blinked. His glass was already empty. "Thirst," he declared.

"Mesero," Elliot called out. "Otra vez, dos." He was just starting his first, but you had to plan ahead.

Any of the dozen or so men and one or two women seated at the other tables might be Carlos—that is, Antonio. If he had to wager, Elliot would have bet on the tall, forty-something man who held a lighted cigarette in his mouth and had one eye closed—probably a defense against irritation from the tobacco smoke. He was talking to his table companions in a low, focused voice. He might have been arguing for an intensification of the process of building socialism through more rapid industrialization or for the creation of more collective farms to provide living space and subsistence for the many otherwise complete paupers . Again, he might have been arguing against these measures on the grounds of growing public disaffection and imperialist trouble fishing.

"If only this too solid flesh would melt." Wallby was bottoming out his second glass.

"For God's sake, Ollie, take it easy. We're not millionaires, you know." Wallby was intent on drinking *them* into the poor plantation.

When the waiter brought their third round of piscos, Elliot summoned the courage to ask a question in his bad Spanish, "Hay aqui alguien que se llama Antonio?"

"Antonio? No, no creo. Antonio? No. Carlos, si."

A woman from a neighboring table called out, "quiere decir El Choncho. Se llama Antonio de nombre cristiano." Now it was certain that she was a woman. Her moustache was very light.

"Choncho." The waiter laughed. "Esta alla." He pointed contemptuously with a shoulder to a large pile of dirty clothes lying on the floor next to the wall of the barroom. "He like too much the drink."

"Gracias." They had made contact. Or they were about to make it, if the pile of unwashed laundry actually was a human being. "Ollie, wake up dear, there's something very important."

"'When Burnham Wood to Dunsinane shall come'. Oh yes! Have I been called?"

"The waiter told me that Antonio was here. You know, the guy Manolito told us about. He can help us contact FARS."

"Oh." Olby was not particularly enthused. Just that, nothing else?

"I suppose we should begin by inviting Antonio to our table. Just remember, he's Antonio, not Carlos. Let's try to slide Che-su into the conversation somewhere, as a start." Elliot thought about the best way of inviting Antonio. Should he send the waiter with a message or should he go over and introduce himself directly? The problem was that he had never introduced himself to a pile of dirty laundry before. Were there special rules of etiquette?

He finally summoned up the nerve. He took a largish swallow of pis', then walked to the wall. "Senor? Antonio? Debo hablar con usted." He pushed into the worn and soiled pile of clothes with his foot. No response. Maybe it was just a pile of unwashed laundry after all. But a pair of highly worn shoes stuck out at one end and something like a dilapidated hat at the other. "Antonio! Wake up!" He pressed hard against the weekly washing. There was something in there. "Antonio! Quieres copa?"

There was a groan, a sound of infinite fatigue, disgust and futility. Elliot gave it another shove. This time the dilapidated hat moved. It had to be alive. "Antonio! Pisco!" He turned toward the bar and cried out desperately to the waiter, as a soldier in battle might call for a medic to aid a wounded comrade. "Pisco! Rapido!"

The medic came after a remarkably short interval. Elliot took the glass from his hands and tried to find a hole near the hat into which its contents might be poured. At last, by pushing aside a worn and discolored fabric (a ratty scarf? filthy underwear?) and hair or thick fiber, he uncovered a revolting orifice surrounded by thickish flesh of purple color (lips?) He applied the glass and let flow a stream of life-giving transfusion.

"Aunngh. Urrnnf. Garrggh." The laundry moved. Something like a face appeared at one end. Human features were almost recognizable, although apparently they had not been washed since the Cuban missile crisis.

"Mr. Antonio, I want to invite you to join me and my friend at our table. We are having something of a celebration." Mainly they had already had it. Antonio too. "A mutual friend gave us your name. We may have shared interests."

"Hanngh!" The pile shifted, tried to turn over, fell back, tried again.

"He is not feel much good for many months." The lady from a close table leaned over to make this declaration to Elliot. "It is too much working."

"I must talk to Mr. Antonio." He yanked fabric from the pile without much effect.

The lady rose from her chair. "We help him to the up." With what looked like practiced skill, she raised Antonio to a sitting position. It was beyond doubt a man, a large one, not particularly tall. "Choncho drink too much because he is sad in his life. We all wanna him to stop, but he have like de crazy love for de pisco. So far he stop a little, then a little more. We no wan eem stop, how you say, 'gold jerky'? Then he like too much big shock."

"Thank you, senorita. I think I understand. Perhaps I can help to let him down gently. I must talk to him." He pulled again at part of Mr. Antonio. He was heavy. It felt like he was made of something like wet cement.

"Yo le ayudo. Mi nombre es Maria." The lady from next door piped up again.

"Pleased to meet you, senorita Maria. I am called Elliot, and this is … " He didn't finish the sentence. Wallby was increasingly irrelevant. "Let us each take one side of Mr. Antonio, we may be able to raise …" Elliot was going to say "the dead" but reconsidered on the grounds that this would make an impression of insensitivity.

"Antonio, he not very good now, but once he very intelligent man. He study at Harvard University. Ciencia politica. Very smart wid doctor decree. They write on eem in de Time magazine."

Antonio had an impressive resume, despite appearances. He should be able to help their mission to save the people. "Maybe if each of us took a corner of Mr. Antonio, we could help him to his feet."

Maria grabbed Antonio from the back with both arms in something like a half nelson wrestling hold. "Get de legs!"

The legs were large, fleshy and covered with a rough, disagreeable material (old fabric? dirt?). Elliot gave it the old college try. Antonio rose like Sunday morning. It was fortunate that Maria was able to bear most of the load. Elliot suffered from chronic low back strain. He knew it was unwise to exert himself too much.

At last Antonio was seated at the table, on a real chair. His body was facing that of Reverend Wallby, who was musing silently about matters of the universe as he lay in the wheelbarrow. Antonio seemed to be unsure where he was or even what he was. His large, hirsute face had red patches within the dominant color, a sort of lead grey. Elliot took his seat. He was panting with the effort of raising Antonio. Maria had not been much affected by her physical effort. Of course, she must be used to it. She turned to go back to her own table. Elliot decided to play the gentleman.

"Mademoiselle Maria, would you care to join us? I would be grateful if you could act as an interpreter. Your time would naturally be compensated." She might be useful as more than an interpreter, Elliot thought. Her relationship with A. was probably something like nurse/psychologist.

Maria dragged her packing crate close to the table. She put her elbows on the tabletop. She was pale and dark haired, like many Santanos. Her long, sad face probably hadn't seen a smile since the Bay of Pigs.

"Antonio, the senores wish to talk toward you. They are Americans from de New York."

A. was still suffering a sort of culture shock. He looked at the others, grunted, made odd throat noises, tried to blow his nose using part of his mustache. He still did not understand.

"I think Antonio may need further restoration." Elliot signaled again to the waiter.

The medic brought an entire bottle and set it on the table with a loud, dull thunk. He was tired of playing jumping jack for these people. Most of the time his job consisted of staring at a wall. Elliot filled Antonio's glass.

"Drink, Antonio," Maria pleaded. "You are not like yourself. Tell them of your writings, the great filosofia."

Although torpid almost to a state of paralysis, A. was able to perform some motions mechanically. He grabbed the glass, drained it, tried to drain it again. It hadn't been refilled.

"Mr. Antonio," Elliot started the ball rolling. "This is the Reverend Oliver Francis Wallby, of the parish of Westwood in Los Angeles. He is interested in the interaction of religion and political liberation. We have heard of your writings." This part was untrue. They didn't even know his last name.

"Unh." It was not a grunt, not a groan. It was probably an acknowledgement.

"Antonio, please be courteous to the foreign gentlemen. They have underwent a long trip to see you."

A. nodded. He picked up his glass and reached it toward the bottle. He definitely needed another one. He was just starting to come alive. Elliot understood and poured to the brim of the glass. Antonio brought the glass back to base. He drank it half down with some muffled gurgling noises. In an odd way, like the Reverend Wallby, his mouth seemed to be connected directly to his stomach, without the intermediate throat step, at least as far as drink was concerned.

"Antonio is the editor of the important theoretical journal, 'Odio Asco y Rebelion'." Maria was doing her job to facilitate the "encounter". She saw this as part of her "historic role" at the moment. She did not say that Antonio had been fired by the journal's directing committee three years earlier when his pisco intake started to make his typewritten pages look like the random efforts of a rather untalented monkey.

"Oh really? Fascinating."

Antonio was making progress. Now he could grasp the bottle and pour his own drinks. The bottle's contents were rapidly disappearing. Elliot wondered if, as a result of some odd Andean evolutionary tangent, pisco served in Antonio's body the same function that air provided for others.

Suddenly he seemed fully awake. He looked at Elliot and at Wallby as if seeing them for the first time. "You are then reporters for Times?"

"Yes." Elliot wanted to avoid a long explanation. The important thing was to gain Antonio's confidence. Then he might risk putting them in contact with FARS. Correo agents were everywhere and trust was a rare thing.

"I have spoken with your colleagues many times." A.'s English was excellent and almost without accent. "In truth, their understanding of our country is not highly developed. I have the impression sometimes that they are Coca-Cola salesmen." Not that he drank much Coca-Cola.

"You may be right. We are from the religion department, though, not the political events department. We are more interested in your country's soul than in its consumption of beverages."

"Unh." A. poured himself another. "Your friend is a priest? Ah. I myself once studied in a seminary. Then I discovered that to save the bodies of the people is necessary before saving their souls."

"Alas, poor Yorick. I knew him well, Horatio."

Elliot laughed. "Reverend Wallby is quite an accomplished amateur actor. He was quoting from his last stage role." Elliot didn't mention the "triumphal tour" at the Teatro Travesti. That would have introduced complications.

Antonio gave the sacred man a close scrutiny. His mouth dropped open in surprise. "It is commendable that your journal has engaged a man of such great age. Here we are only beginning to combate the age discrimination." He took a large sip. "But, of course, our people are mostly under fifteen years, not ninety."

"He's very spry for his age." Slumped in the wheelbarrow, Wallby hummed to himself, looked at the ceiling, twiddled his thumbs. In fact, Ollie was not yet into his mid-seventies.

"Wait!" A. took a large drink of pisco. "I must ask you a question. I ask this same question of all whom I think are sensitive and intelligent. It is this: do you love God first or man first?"

"God is man," Maria put in.

"You," A. pointed a long bony finger at Maria, "I have talked with before on this subject for thirty-six hours. Let the foreign gentlemen give their answer."

"I'm Elliot and this is Oliver."

"Yes, then, Mr. Elliot and Oliver. Whom do you love?"

Elliot had to think about this one. He took a big hit from his glass, re-poured from the largely empty bottle. "God or man?" He was going to say that he hadn't met God yet, but realized that this would sound flippant if not blasphemous. "I think I would say Man, but only as he is in the image of God and receives the Spirit."

"No! Not in 'images' or 'spirits'. God or man? Tell the truth."

It was going to be a session. Elliot had attended a few when he was an undergraduate student at Tarzana University. Then they drank beer, not pisco. "Okay. Then I'd say God." He looked at Antonio to see if he had guessed right.

"God is your god? Okay, I see this very well. You are responding in the conventional Judaeo-Christian orthodoxy. But with your God, in what miserable disastrous bottomless pits you have left man! Man has suffered a billion crucifixions and still he must beg for pardon! Oh hopeless man, hopeless God!" He collapsed onto the table, held his head in his hands, wept, heaved with emotion.

Elliot knew that this was blasphemy, but they had to play their lead. They were on a mission. Later, the Inquisition could deal with Antonio. Hopefully it still existed. He refilled A.'s glass. There was only enough pisco for half a refill. He signaled the medic. "I can see you are a man of passion, Antonio. You have very deep emotions. Perhaps a little drink will steady your spirits."

Antonio drank.

"Our friend Manolito told us you were a great intellectual."

"Hah!" Maria spat. She took a tiny sip from her glass. She drank rum, not foul pisco. "When he is dead he will be great intellectual!"

"Ha ha ha. You both have a wonderful sense of humor. But, to return to our topic, we have come on a mission to find how the people will receive the message of Che-su."

"Che-su," A. half grunted, half snorted. "This I have read of in a thousand periodicals." He waved his hand as if chasing flies from a plate of pollo. "This is a doctrine of the eunuchs of the seminaries! Che is the gun. Of what good to add God to gun? Gun is gun and God is God."

"Ollie, could you repeat to our friend your doctrine? Just as you stated it to me on the plane."

Wallby looked pensive. He put a finger to his chin, then into his mouth. Elliot was amazed that he seemed to have followed the conversation at all. He spoke, but incoherently. Elliot distinguished the words Columbus and Marx-mas.

"My friend has not yet recovered from the change of altitude, but he says that the Christianity that arrived with Columbus was exploitative and destructive of the spirituality of the native peoples as well as of their class interests. He sympathizes with the view that Che Guevara rounds out the message by adding a clause encouraging the people to defend their material interests, just as Jesus chased the money-changers from the temple."

"Unh. Yes. I see you are speaking conventional view." Anthonio spat onto the floor. "No! What is the journals is ink and paper. What I have seen is life and blood! When patrols scout the jungle and fire machine guns at liberation forces, they have no thought for weeklies and monthlies!"

Antonio was wandering. Best get to the point. "It would help our reporting mission greatly if we could interview members of this group called FARS. The Frente Armado de la Revolucion Santana. Our readers would be highly thrilled." Elliot leaned over and whispered, "Manolito told us that you were a contact."

Antonio reared up his great unkept head. "FARS! FARS! FARS is shit! That is what this group is."

"Shh!" Spies were everywhere.

"They do of nothing! The people live in misery while the Correos and the party leaders swill champagne. FARS is a dance in the mud. FARS is lunacy within the lunacy."

The waiter brought a second bottle. He was impressed and envious that anyone could afford to drink such large amounts of rotgut at one sitting.

Without waiting for an invitation, Antonio grabbed the bottle and drank from it directly. About a quarter of the contents disappeared in one huge suck.

"Antonio is a swine," Maria shook her head with an amused smile.

"Puta de Manolito. Do not believe anything that is told to you by this, this, this … this this." He made a gesture with one hand, probably intended to be obscene. It was difficult to interpret with any precision.

"What's wrong with Manolito?"

"A man who is not a man is not a man! Once Mano was a friend. I loved my friend, a poor campesino, an indio from the villages. Mu' guapo, hombrito joven, carinoso." He swigged from the bottle. God, he could put it away. He made Wallby look like Carrie Nation. Tears swelled in Antonio's eyes. It was hard to tell how much, since they were normally inflamed and watery. "Then he is met this otra puta, this mujer sin verguenza that now are his mujer." He spat. This time on the table. As a precaution, Elliot divided the remaining pisco between the four glasses. "She is of forcing him to such dishonorable prostitions! Pobre muchacho, tan amado, tan cuidado." He heaved with silent sobs. His head sagged.

Elliot clicked his tongue in sympathy. Actually, Manolito seemed to be doing rather well. He might have been able to use a new dress. "But, to return to the subject of Che-su. Our editors are interested in discovering how far the new religious ideas have taken a deep and permanent hold within the working class and peasant masses. Have they entirely replaced the age-old grip of the Vatican hierarchy?"

"Uh?" Antonio was genuinely confused. He grabbed the empty bottle and sucked air. Then he searched the table with his eyes. His glass had to be somewhere.

With the tip of one finger, carefully avoiding the contaminated rim of the glass, Elliot pushed Antonio's glass toward its owner. "You see, if we met with some representatives of FARS, we could write our investigative report and file copy."

"Puta madre chingada!"

"Antonio is aware of your requirements," Maria said. "He is thinking how he can help you."

A. took hold of his glass and raised it toward his mouth. He gave it a curious look, as if he had never seen a glass before. Then he drained it. Elliot had the impression that he looked even thirstier afterward .

"Antonio is not well. Perhaps he will give you an answer tomorrow," Maria put in.

Now Antonio was asleep. His head drooped onto his chest. Deep snoring drew his mustache into his mouth and pushed it out again.

"I think he will not speak to you any longer this day," Maria informed them. "When he has passed out three times, there is usually no more. This is bad, but at least Antonio is now drinking less each day, so that I have hope that he will be, what you say, 'social drinker'."

"I am very glad to hear that Antonio's condition is improving, but we have important questions to ask him. For our mission. Manolito said that Antonio is a contact for FARS."

"Shhh!" Maria put a raised finger in front of her lips. She was right. Correo agents were everywhere. "You are to pay the waiter then we walk out in slow."

Elliot put two quarters on the table. Again, he grabbed the barrow handles.

"Is your friend incacacitrated?"

"No. I'm fairly sure of that." Elliot sniffed the nearby air.

"Do not speak of our conversing with no ones! If you do, my life is into the danger. I have message. Do you the follow." Maria headed for the door. Elliot took up the wheelbarrow and followed.

While they headed for the door, Reverend Wallby turned toward the drinking masses and made a sign with his hand that was folded into something like the boyscout pledge. "Ego te absolvo," he intoned.

Outside, dusk was falling in high altitude, tropical San Santo. How long had they been drinking in the Café Andino? Elliot had only a vague idea.

"I am walking. Please do this as well." Maria set out at a fast pace along the sidewalk toward the statue of General Jose de San Martin. Elliot followed as closely as possible. It is difficult to push a large clergyman in a wheelbarrow at nine thousand feet when you have imbibed a considerable amount of pisco.

Maria stopped near a street cart that displayed melons and yams of unknown varieties. She appeared to examine the vegetables without much interest. Probably she was not a great vegetable eater. Antonio certainly wasn't.

Elliot caught up. "Whew! I'm still not used to the height." He panted for several minutes.

"Listen. I must only tell you once. Antonio knows of your mission. He is aware that Manolito has given his name for you. Antonio was making only a pretense of drunk man and is actually to sober. He gives me a sign to pass to you information. If you are of wishing to contact the FARS, you are to go to the Iglesia de Santa Gregorio."

"*Santa* Gregorio?"

"It will all be explain to you. In Santa Gregorio, seek of de Padre Rigoberto Bagaje." She grabbed a small yam from the cart, threw down several dozen scrip, then turned away quickly, direction Café Andino. "Adios!"

Elliot stood on the sidewalk next to the street cart as he tried to assimilate Maria's information. Now they were to look for *Santa* Gregorio. This was puzzling. Did it have something to do with the Teatro Travesti? Anyway, they had a lead on FARS. They could very well be on their way to synapse with the revolutionary movement and to start the landslide of the peasants, workers, political activists and—face it, the alcoholic masses—toward Che-su, the theological New Deal. Would they meet the Mama at Santa G.? Mano said that the Mama had to be very discrete because of the intense repression practiced by the Correos. Maybe she would be in disguise.

"C'mon Ol', we're on our way." Elliot pushed the barrow a few more feet. "Except I don't really know where we're going to."

"Just get to Wilshire. I can direct you to anywhere in L.A. from Wilshire Avenue."

It was dark and they were looking for a church in the San Santo night. The temperature was dropping rapidly, which was not favorable to Wallby in his delicate condition. There didn't seem to be any alternative, so Elliot steered the handles toward a café. He was reluctant to do this because Wallby's intake was already reaching Olympic/cirrhosis levels. His own consumption was definitely in the regional finals. Also, their cash reserve was decreasing inversely with the rise of their pisco consumption.

One of the wonderful things about San Santo is that there are many cafes. They are the centers of communal life. By now Elliot could spot them like a condor in search of prey. Two blocks ahead was a likely sign. He couldn't read it from the distance, but it generated an unmistakeably happy energy.

Elliot forced the Wallby-mobile along an uneven sidewalk. There were unaccountable bumps in the poorly lighted night. Elliot hoped they weren't straying over the feet of outside sleepers, of whom there were many. He had heard several sharp cries as they passed, but those might have been caused by something else. Also, Ollie had developed a disturbing habit of putting his hand out at every likely occasion as if begging for alms.

"Really, Oliver, I wish you wouldn't do that. We have to maintain our dignity if we want to carry out our mission. Besides, we're not really indigent, not by local standards."

"Blessed are the poor, for I am with you always."

"You're mixing quotations." Elliot was becoming worn down by long blocks of pushing the Wallby-mobile. It was time for another break.

The sign in the distance was like a harbor light, a beacon to guide wayward barks. "Café Rebelion de las Masas". It seemed a safe, homey sort of place. A soft light showed empty tables and scarce, relaxed patrons. They made it through the door. Elliot parked the mobile at one of the unoccupied tables and headed for the bar. Man he was thirsty.

"Dos piscos, grandes, dobles." The routine of ordering drinks in a café had become second nature to Elliot. He had definitely mastered the Spanish necessary for this action.

The bartender nodded. He was short, plump, covered below the waist with a brownish apron. Probably it was supposed to be white. He turned, grabbed the bottle, brought up two glasses. Or, rather, she did. It was really a woman, Elliot finally noticed. She had short hair. Plumpness confused breast development, perhaps big rather than fat.

"Aqui tiene."

Elliot put down four cents. She counted and recounted carefully. These cafes had a narrow profit margin. "Busco una iglesia. Puede ayudarme?" Could she help him find a church?

She nodded. "Gringo? Whaddidy church you likes?" She preferred her broken English to his massacred Spanish.

"Santa Gregorio."

"La Iglesia de Santa Gregorio? Iss nod de too far. You go make Confession?"

"Sort of."

"Then good. Ladda de penitentes dey go Santa Gregorio. The Padre always busy wit de bad ting dey do. Santa Gregorio giv de penitencia for the pecados, muchos, muchos. So many dey like drink too much. Borrachos." She spat on the ground. Several drops landed on the bar top.

"I see." Elliot responded coolly. It was unacceptable for a bartender to call a customer a sinful drunk. He picked up the two glasses.

"You go tree block, then doble to the lef two more block, then you see the Iglesia. It gotta torres. Big ones."

"Big ones. Thank you. I'll look for them."

Elliot brought the drinks back to the table where Wallby was parked. There were no chairs in sight. As before he used his foot to push the single available packing crate close to the table. He sat down and took a sip. It was good. "It's really tasty," he told Wallby, who was drinking through a straw. "Like Coca-Cola." He observed the other customers for the first time. Four or five were huddled around a table. It was hard to tell if they were awake or not. One of the worldwide effects of imperialism is to spread the most degrading poverty imaginable. They were dressed in rags, unwashed, sitting on the floor. They were so downtrodden that they had not even tried to take advantage of the café's single packing crate. They sat under the table as if it were a beach umbrella.   From time to time the lips of one moved and a sort of buzzing could be detected at a distance. It might have been sleep talk.

"I think we're making progress. Ollie, don't you?" Ollie seemed to be sleeping, although he was still drinking. Talk about borrachos with muchos pecados!

"Santa Gregorio is really very close. The bartender told me. He said it was five blocks away." After the Teatro Travesti and Manolito, the pronoun gender question hardly seemed to matter.

An interrupted sucking sound may have indicated assent.

"The only problem is that it appears that we will be expected to confess our sins."

The straw dropped from Wallby's lips. His eyes and mouth opened wide. There was a look of terror. "I have a conference at La Canada Flintridge. Urgent."

Elliot tried to think of sins that he could confess—drink was so common as to be banal—just to satisfy local custom. Perhaps association with a defrocked clergyman? In fact, after Vatican II and a sequence of "reformist Popes", it was hard to be sure what would and what wouldn't be considered a sin at Santa Gregorio. Wallby, in his more intellectually active years, had mentioned certain R.C. developments also propounded by theologically evolved sectarians, including himself. "Acts harming the environment of the earth" were a mortal sin. "Failing to help the condition of the downtrodden" was another. Visiting persons of "ill repute" might not be a sin, depending on the context and intentions. But theology was like breakfast cereal. You could choose between dozens. Besides his friendship with Reverend Wallby, Elliot could confess to poor tipping habits, depriving the masses of pisco through his own intake, which although not large by comparison with some of his acquaintance, was certainly above the statistical average. Maria had mentioned that the per capita pisco consumption locally was no more than six liters per year. Antonio did that in a day.

While Elliot was examining his conscience and those of others, an odd, rag-clad figure had crawled along the floor and reached the space under the table occupied by the gringos. Something had been tugging at his trouser leg for several minutes when he first became aware of it. He assumed it was just Manolito again. "Not now. I'm thinking."

The trouser pulling continued until Elliot put his head under the table for a look. His surprise bordered on shock after discovering that it wasn't Manolito at all. It was a sort of moving coffee sack with dark, shriveled protrusions that resembled hands and a head.

"Limosna, senor, limosna." It was asking for spare change.

Elliot straightened up and took a large drink. It was embarrassing to have to choose between what doctrine said was right and an act that degraded the people's dignity. He decided to compromise and handed down four cents. Certainly not enough to degrade to any serious extent. Not at current pisco prices.

"Gracias," a voice answered from within the sack of Maxwell House. "Santa Gregorio, do no go. No. No."

"What? Why?"

The sack, already crawling toward the bar, doubtless to get a well-merited refill, gave no explanation for its sybiline statement. You got a fifty percent discount on your tenth drink of the day. That explained its eager advance.

"Ollie! Wake-up!" One of Ollie's eyes was open, but he was snoring loudly. Elliot shook the shoulder nearest the closed eye. "Something spooky just happened."

"Rest, my child, rest."

"Como muchas personas, dos caras tiene la Iglesia de Santa Gregorio." This was from a novel that Elliot had been reading between pisco breaks. Now they were standing across the square from the church. It was broad daylight.

"Jeez. Wow!"

Two towers, and big ones. The façade was baroque. Glorious decorations reached to the sky. A dense crowd of charity people surrounded the front doors and covered most of the church steps. These were the indigents who "come to get the food", according to the bartender of the Rebelion. "He" said there were far fewer now that weekly "work squads" were being sent off to the Amazonian People's Plantations (APP). The problem was how to get inside the church. Maria had told them to contact Father Rigoberto Bagaje, *cura* of Santa Gregorio. He could put them on the path to FARS. But they could hardly charge through the blocking mass of alms seekers to reach him. "Looks like we'll have to wait until things cool down. The masses are massing a bit too much around the entrances." Elliot looked around for a café.

Oliver was paying more attention than he had for many days. "The poor you have with you always." After many years of directing charitable endeavours at St. Henry's, he had come to the conclusion that most of the poor were a bunch of frauds. Now he suggested a direct charge, with himself a wheelbarrow mounted cavalier. "Andiamos!"

"You said that before. It would hardly be practical to charge up the church steps, even if the flock scatters like quail. What if we crushed some tiny old lady under the wheels?"

Wallby made a raspberry. Maybe he had misunderstood. While they were discussing strategy, a gentleman clad in a relatively new coffee sack came near. He wore a derby and carried a string of handmade tourist trinkets around his neck. He offered the trinkets for sale to the foreigners. They were mostly crude carvings of animals and humans made of wood and stone.

"No, thank you, I already have quite a few."

"Turistas? You wanna go in de church?"

"Yes, if at all possible. We have a letter of introduction to Father Rigoberto Bagaje."

"Bagaje? Si! Si!" He smiled from ear to ear. "I ged you see el Padre Rigoberto. Hombre santo. Tan amado de los pobres. He love de pour. Dey all love him like de fodder. Me, I lucky I have business. He shook his necklace of crude carvings. Tengo negocio. De udders dey got too much poor."

Elliot made a clucking sound with his tongue to express sympathy. "We are here to help the poor. That is why we wish to speak to Father Rigoberto."

"Ya." The trinket seller looked at the thick crowd pushing toward the church door. "See, all de door lock, so de poor don do de rush. Dey wan de food."

"Poor things."

"Ya. I give you de help to de get inside wen you are de pay me so little."

"Okay. How much?"

"De twenny?"

"Twenty dollars? Preposterous!"

"Twenny sen."

"Oh. That's so much more reasonable. Thank you for your offer."

"We gotta get en de church de odder way. See de place?" The seller pointed to a house next to the church. It did not adjoin the church, but it was close to it. Its upper stories were only a few feet from a sort of balcony that was attached to the side of the church near the roof. "We gone in de house, den we go up de stair to de turd flo' an' crorse on de cuerda to de church. We go dis way get to de balcon."

"You mean that we will go into that house and climb the stairs to the third floor," he pointed, "then we will cross the space to the church balcony on a cuerda or by some other means." Cuerda: rope.

"Like de Spiderman." The trinket seller grinned.

"I don't believe Reverend Wally will be capable of gymnastics of that sort." They both looked down at Wallby as he lay in the wheelbarrow. "The Reverend is the source of our ecumenical project."

"Don't worry about me, Jack. I was decathlon champ in seminary for two years running."

Wallby's recovery was amazing. He was making progress every minute. Just days before he had been a semi-comatose mummy. Now he thought he was Spiderman. "Don't take things too fast, Ollie. You might fall into a relapse."

Another raspberry.

"Despite his religious vocation, my friend is quite a daredevil," Elliot told the trinket man.

"Ya. He gotta lotta cojones."

"All right." Elliot had his doubts. "Come on, Spidie." He grabbed handles and pushed the barrow toward the house next to the church.

The door of the house was open. In fact, it was half off its hinges. Past scuffles, perhaps attempts at forced entry—or exit— probably had caused the damage. They entered and found themselves in a sort of "salon". There was no furniture, although there were pieces of wood and fabric that might at one time have formed part of furniture. No one was about.

"See, one time a lady run dis house, but she gone long time to Amazonas for de droga. Now all de girl work for she-self."

"That's interesting." Elliot believed it was a good idea always to show interest in local customs.

"This would be a fascinating *locus* for the Naked Mass," Wallby put in, admiring the surroundings.

Elliot delivered a withering stare. "Let's not start that again! Don't you remember how we got here in the first place?"

Wallby seemed about to deliver another raspberry, but thought better of it. Instead he grubbed a "water balloon" from the bottom of the barrow and squeezed out a few last drops.

The trinket seller—they learned latter that his name was Jose— had not understood much of this exchange. "Now we gotta git up the escalera. We go to turd floor."

It was a practical problem that only Elliot had foreseen. How to get Wallby, who still had only limited use of his lower extremities, up the stairs. Pretty clearly there was no elevator. Even the escaleras were in an advanced state of dilapidation. "Can you walk a little, Ol'?"

Wallby tried to raise himself from the wheelbarrow, but without effect. "Altitude," Wallby explained. He had learned this diagnosis from Influenzia and Doctor Zapatero.

Jose considered the situation. He rubbed his chin with one hand and shook his head. "Dis nada gonna be easy." He grabbed a barrow handle and shook it. "Demasiado pesado." Too heavy. "Okay, wa we gonna do is, I take de arm, you take de leg, and we git im outa de machine. Da way we go up."

It was the only likely solution. Jose would hold Wallby's arms and Elliot would support his legs. Jose would go first up the stairs. He knew the territory. Like Hiawatha in the Lewis and Clark Expedition.

The lift off was the hardest part. Wallby still weighed a ton. Both the carriers groaned. "Boy, this guy big," Jose complained.

Elliot looked back into the bottom of the barrow, now unoccupied by Wallby. There were used "water balloons", empty bottles of pisco, crushed bits of churro, a local newspaper, a sock. Then they were on the stairs and going up, step by step, slowly.

After quite an effort, they made it to the second floor. They stopped to catch their breath. Elliot advanced a few steps down a corridor and looked around. Rooms were connected to the corridor on both sides. Most of the doors were open, or non-existent. Inside the rooms, on the floor, were mattresses or sometimes just blankets. Many were occupied. The women, short and abundantly fleshed, had discarded unnecessary clothing, which was just about everything. The men, their customers, were also in "summer attire". As a precaution against robbery by some intruder during a distracted moment, many held their wallets between their teeth as they used their hired time with the women occupants.

"De guy gotta be careful," Jose explained. "Too many much robber go run in de rooms. De guy lose de pantalones an' de cartera." Cartera: wallet.

"It's quite clever of them to take that precaution."

"Ya. De guy no too stupid."

"Oremus." Wallby was having a flashback to the "Naked Mass". "Let us pray."

"Perhaps we could pray higher up." The bodies of the men, taut dark-red masses of brawn and the ballooning bellies and breasts of the other sex, were repellent to Elliot. However, their quest for social-sexual joining did have a tinge of religious morality, after all. He seized the Reverend's legs. "His Reverence forgets that we are not in the church yet."

They took the second flight at a slower pace. Jose was panting as he climbed ahead. He seemed an asthmatic Sherpa. The walls of the stairwell had shed most of their paint, a sort of dull green. Graffiti artists had been at work. Elliot could not make out the messages, except for the frequent use of the words "puta", "madre" and "chingada".

"Okay, now we take long rest." Jose put his half of Wallby on the floor of the landing. Elliot rested the reverend legs on the top steps of the just ascended stairs.

"Is it very much higher?" Elliot was puffing too. There was a window from which they could see part of the church wall. Maybe they could jump from here.

"One more piso. Den a little more."

Wallby pointed to his open mouth. He was thirsty. Evidently he had mistaken the word "piso", floor, for "pisco".

"Oliver is rather dehydrated from the altitude. Is there any way we could get a drink?"

"Drin? No, I don tink so. Unless you wan de wader."

Wallby shook his head emphatically. The very thought made him nauseous.

"Once we are in the church, we'll ask for a glass of altar wine," Elliot said. "Or something stronger," he added upon seeing Wallby's disagreeable reaction.

The third floor was far less densely populated than the second. A few of the rooms had closed doors. This was scary. Sounds of heavy breathing and moaning came from within the rooms.   "This house seems to be a quite popular place. At least some parts of the population are doing well."

"Dey got sometime de stud'nt from de army. Dey are de have goo time."

Elliot did not understand this statement, but refrained from asking for an explanation. "How are we going to cross to the church?"

"Oh. Dat no gonna have problem. You see." He took up the clerical arms. Elliot followed with the legs. Jose had to pull and Elliot's job was more in the way of pushing. Elliot was developing painful spasms in the small of his back. If Ollie had cut down on his pisco consumption a bit, he would have lost weight.

The last part of the ascent was the hardest of all. Both carriers were nearly exhausted. Even an old San Santo hand like Jose could be affected by the altitude. Then they were at the top. It was a small landing on the stairway, under the roof. They dropped Wallby like a sack of potatoes. He was not hurt. He even started to make pleasureable sounds, something like a cat purring. Maybe it was the stimulus.

"Hokay," Jose gasped. "Dere de got de church." He pointed toward a window. You could see the church roof and a small balcony at the back of which stood a little door. "We jus gid over dere."

They only had to cross the open void to the church balcony. It seemed simple, at least to Jose. This is where Wallby's vaunted Spiderman skills would come in handy.

"I suppose if we had a rope we could lasso the balcony and cross hand over hand. But Ollie can't use his hands very well and he has very little strength in his arms." It would be terrible if they had to leave the saintly Reverend in this house. Elliot thought of the moaning and groaning in little rooms below. His voice was inflected by a noticeable whining.

"Calma!" Jose was getting annoyed. He expected a tip at the end and he knew that Elliot was aware of the protocol, but this was turning out to be a bigger job than he had imagined. "Doan I tell you I got all de plan?"

"I apologize." Elliot nodded toward Mr. Jose. "But how exactly are we going to get across to the church?"

"It gonna be like wan doo dree." Jose stood up. It was a considerable effort. Then he lumbered back to the stairs. "You wade here."

Jose was gone for what seemed a long time. Elliot talked to Wallby and tried to keep up his spirits by recalling some of the comic moments they had lived in Los Angeles. "And remember when your cook went to the police and said you were running a drug brothel? Ha ha ha!" But the Reverend was asleep. It was comforting to note that he now slept with his eyes shut.

From below came shouts and dull sounds as if heavy objects (bodies?) were being thrown about. Jose appeared at the top of the stairs. He was sweating, panting, and appeared to have several new bruises on his face. In his arms was a large bundle of clothes.

"I burrow dis from de guy that come here for de lady." He threw a collection of shirts, trousers, underwear and blankets on the floor. "So de ting we gotta do is make de knot so we got de rope." They were to tie the various pieces of clothing and blankets together to form a kind of trapeze wire or something of the sort. Jose showed how to do it. Pant legs could be knotted to shirt sleeves. Some of the pieces of underwear were large enough for the purpose. Blankets gave extension to the line. Elliot did his best to follow Jose's artisanry, but he was not an expert at this type of work. Jose examined and pulled tight on each of Elliot's knots.

At last the improvised rope was ready. It was at least thirty-five feet in length, enough to span the distance from the "house" to the church. Elliot thought of having Wallby bless the device to ensure heavenly help, but scrapped the idea. It would be virtually impossible to make the minister understand the purpose and context of their efforts. From all that Elliot could make out, Ollie, despite some improvement, still thought they were back in L.A.

"We gotta poody damn goo cuerda. We go soon, cause de guy need de clothes back. Esperen. Dis de wun las ting." Jose disappeared down the stairs. Esperen: wait, command form, plural, formal.

What would it be? Elliot had a bare hope that the "one last thing" might involve a bottle of pisco. This hope was dashed when Jose reappeared carrying what looked like a large rock. He let it drop on the darkened and scuffed wood floor. It rolled over to Wallby. On the surface of the rock were carved what looked vaguely like human features.

"This de idolo come from de tribu in Amazonas. Dis de god dey sell to comerciantes."

Elliot stared in admiration. The rock was actually some sort of "idol", that is, a diety worshipped by a non-monotheistic religion. Indigenous peoples had traded it to middle men. You could actually make out a mouth, eyes, nostrils. It was wonderful. The difficult part was to understand what they were supposed to do with it. Elliot's guess was that they were going to pray until the rock opened an aerial path to the church. Ollie would like this idea and it was cute, but not likely to work.

"Todo listo." Everything was ready. Elliot watched as Jose rolled the idolo near to the window. He grabbed one end of the "rope" and tied it around the Amazon divinity. "See, we gotta tro de idolo to the balcon on de church, den we go on the cuerda." They were going to use the sacred native object to project one end of the clothes-rope to the church balcony. The other end would be made fast on the house side, probably tied to the top of the stairs. They would then cross hand over hand on the "cuerda".

"You and I may be able to cross on the cuerda, but what about the Reverend? He is largely incapacitated."

Jose smiled. Gringos could be so stupid. "Doan worry. Dis got de perfec plan. We gonna get like walk on de rope, den wen we on the balcon, den de Pastor come."

"Oh." Elliot stared in perfect confusion.

"Ya. Es ver simple. We pood dis end on de soga (rope) on de fat guy, el Sacerdote, den when we on de balcon a de church, we pull and he come over." It was difficult to visualize in detail, but apparently Jose's plan involved tying one end of the rope around Wallby's waist, then throwing the other end, knotted to the pre-colombian deity, to the church balcony. When the other two arrived safely at the church balcony, they would pull on the rope and cause the Reverend to take off from the top floor of the house and fly across to the church. To Elliot, however, the strategy seemed to defy physics.

"Jose. If you and I cross to the balcony and then pull strongly on the rope, Ollie will certainly fall into the space between the house and the church. He may be seriously damaged."

"No, senor." Jose laughed. He had good teeth, although they were yellow in color. "See, the rope fall again de balcon, he swing for a minute dis way dat way, den we pull im in balcon."

"Ah. I see." It was not such a crazy idea after all. Once the able-bodied two were on the balcony of the church, they would draw strongly on the cord and Wallby would fall at first, then the cord would be caught in its fall by the balcony rail high on the side of the church (the narthex). Wallby would swing back and forth and finally they would haul him up to safety. "It is very clever of you, Jose." Jose smiled again.

Elliot still had misgivings about sacrilegiously using a native deity for mundane purposes. Anyway, the Indians, like some others, had sold their God.

They rolled Wallby—apparently he was still sleeping—over to the window. One end of the soga was tied tightly around his waist. He groaned and exhaled largely. He could not fall out of the window, which reached to the floor of the third story, because a short metal railing guarded the lower part of the window opening. So everything was set. All they had to do was to launch the idolo toward the church balcony. Elliot tried to help Jose raise the diety from the third floor landing.

"No, boss. You lee dis to me."

Taking the non-monotheistic god in both hands, Jose gave a muscular two-arm push. The object of worship sailed into space and landed on the church balcony.

"Bravo! What a shot!" If they ever got back to L.A., Elliot swore he would contact the Dodgers recruiters and describe Jose's major league skills.

"Okay. Now we poody reddy. I go de first. Siga usted." Without further ado, Jose slowly let himself into the space between the two buildings, as if lowering his body into a swimming pool. He held firmly to the cuerda with both hands. He started to move, hand over hand. Elliot stood for a moment at the short window railing. He looked down. He felt dizzy and nauseous. If only he had been able to start with a tiny drink of pisco. But there was nothing for it, he had to follow.

"Wait up!" Elliot didn't want Jose to get too far ahead, in case of unforeseen problems at the start point. Elliot entered the "pool" and began to advance, moving hand over hand on the cuerda. Soon he was close to Jose, who had travelled more cautiously. They were both near the middle space. The cuerda then started to swing back and forth. The effect of two bodies hanging on the rope at almost the same place had set up a strong periodic motion. They could hear the idolo rolling back and forth on the church "balcon".

Jose slowed in his Tarzan style advance. The movement of the rope made it hard to grab hand over hand. His body was swinging too. Elliot, now just behind the guide, was starting to weaken. Although he had enrolled in ROTC at Tarzana University in order to dodge the Draft, he dropped out after two months when he discovered that his religious principles entirely forbade military service (drills and exercises were particularly odious). He felt his hands beginning to slip. In a panic, he grabbed Jose with both hands. Oddly, at least to the non-Physics major, placing the combined weight of the two at one point on the line caused it to stabilize. The swinging became minimal. Jose crept ahead, more slowly now, placing one calloused hand over the other.

"Doan git me on de cuello, boss." Jose was being strangled. Cuello: neck.

"Sorry." Elliot realized he had been choking the guide. He grasped Jose around the shoulders.

They were making progess, but they had a distance to cross. Elliot looked down. A crowd had gathered. He could see faces turned to the sky. They expressed fear, surprise, contempt, amusement, a desire to witness a spectacular finish. But Jose kept on. It seemed hours, but it was only minutes before they arrived at the other shore. Jose climbed over the balcony rail. He and his papoose passenger dropped onto the balcony floor.

For several minutes they lay gasping for breath. At least Jose did. Elliot's role had been more passive. He looked back at the house. He thought he could see Wallby lying next to the window railing. "I hope Ollie's all right. To watch all that swinging back and forth must have shaken him rather roughly."

Jose was reviving. He sat up. "No joke now, boss. Dis de hard part."

"Of course. Now we have to find Father Rigoberto. Can we be sure he is in the church? He might have gone out to make a pastoral visit."

"No. I mean you fren." Jose pointed with his shoulder toward the upper floor of the house opposite. "We pull on de soga so ee git eem agross." Soga: rope.

"Oh yes, yes. Let's give her a heave. At this point we are safe from harm."

With a gesture, Jose gave Elliot to understand that he was to take a position behind the guide. They would give a strong pull on the soga and bring Wallby, who was tied to the other end. "Hokay!"

They yanked. Just as planned, Wallby's body crossed over the short railing and fell into space. They watched as the oecumenical object swung toward the church wall. It was a relief. The plan was working perfectly. Then the Wallby projectile moved below the balcony in the final phase of its swing. Two seconds later sounds of smashing glass reached the balcony. At first Elliot thought that the crowd, impatient of waiting endlessly for entertainment, had begun to break the church windows.

"The mob is attacking Santa Gregorio!"

"No, jefe, you fren hit de ventana." Ventana: window.

Elliot understood now. Instead of swinging harmlessly under the balcony before being pulled up, Ollie had gone right through a large stained glass window! "Oh my God! Ollie wasn't feeling well even before. He is … probably … gone!" Tears poured along the curves of Elliot's already emotionally stressed face. Jose gave him a pat on the shoulder. Elliot nodded. "Yes, you are right, we must accept the inevitable. God's will." Elliot looked contemptuously at the clothes-tied stone diety where it lay on the balcony floor. Non-monotheistic deities were notoriously unpredictable.

The door leading from the balcony into the church was open. The guide led the way. They walked along a narrow corridor that twisted within stony walls. Elliot told Jose that Wallby had been like a father to him. He sniffled back tears as he described how Ollie had dandled him on his knee—figuratively. He was a great theologian, but he was also very knowledgeable about the secular world. At every turn there was a holy statue in a little niche in the wall or a holy picture hanging on the corridor wall. This made the task of mourning easier.

"Ee ess ver grade hombre, de Obispo."

Elliot considered this. "Well, anyway, a very human man."

They went down a flight of stairs and turned a corner. "We go ged Padre Rigoberto. When you talk im, you say you gonna pay de ventana when you git de money. Si no, he ess muy enojado." Enojado: annoyed

"Of course. The church must be reimbursed for the damages. It would be very nice, too, if a memorial plaque could be erected to the memory of dear Ollie. Perhaps Padre Rigoberto could conduct funeral services." Elliot was thinking of the money on deposit at North American Express. He might be the legal beneficiary.

At last they were on the ground floor, within the nave. You could see the large stained glass window that had been burst by the Reverend's aerial entry. Strong daylight threw its blinding rays into the dark corners of the ancient church. "Wow!"

"Dere de Padre Rigoberto!" Jose pointed to a figure dressed in a long black gown standing next to an enormous tub made of stone or cement. The baptismal font. "He make de bautizos." Although they stood forty yards from the font, they could make out that the Padre was ministering to a very large object within the stone tub. Probably an adult baptism. The historic church did not require total immersion.

They went ahead. The light from the smashed window soon gave them the details. The large child or late baptism in the font was none other than the Reverend Oliver Francis Wallby! Gawking in total surprise, Elliot approached with tiny steps. It was, well, so unexpected.

"It was at a spot in Nepal known locally as a *locus dei* that I was enlightened after long hours of meditation. At last I learned that the All-One was one of us. That we were part of it, and that we were all …" Wallby stopped talking. Padre Rigoberto, who had been listening with astonished interest, turned to follow the former Hollywood holyman's line of sight. Wallby was staring at Elliot and Jose as if their presence in the church was a complete surprise. As if they were revealed as extra-terrestrials.

"Ollie, thank God you're all right!" Elliot took in the scene in its totality. "But what are you doing in that little swimming pool?"

Padre Rigoberto was a short man, not stocky. A large supply of dark brown hair surmounted his face of regular but not particularly pleasant features. His complexion was pale. Perhaps he spent too much time within the cloister. "Mr. Reverend Wallby is propelled through the great window of our church by bandits. He has explained it of me." The Padre spoke very fluent English.

"Oh." Elliot thought it best not to contradict this version, even in the interests of truth. Anyway, the real explanation would have been extremely lengthy.

"It is fortunate that he fell into our baptismal font. I have rushed to his safety and he is explained to me the event."

"As long as Ollie is okay, that's all that matters."

"Buenos dias, Padre. Estos extranjeros quieren hablarle. Yo los he guiado aqui." Cringing to show subservience, Jose had given an account favorable to himself.

The Padre cut Jose's explanation with an abrupt gesture. Not for the likes of Jose to address the Padre directly. "I am Father Rigoberto, cura of Santa Gregorio." He was the curate, not the pastor.

"My name is Elliot Spenseric." Jose was slinking fearfully behind Elliot. The Padre had put him in his place. Elliot backhanded Jose a five-dollar bill. What Jose had accomplished was at least the equivalent of Stanley finding Livingston.

"You are welcomed to our church. The Reverend Wallby has said that you are missionaries."

"Yes. Exactly. That is, sort of." Elliot turned around. Jose was gone. A dark figure was slinking away behind the right side columns of the nave. It was just as well, since it would have been unwise to speak in the presence of third parties, even Jose. "Antonio said you could help us. We want to make contact with FARS. He said you could help us get in touch with the Mama. Has Reverend Wallby explained our idea, the doctrine of Che-su?"

"What is this interruption, Padre?" Wallby looked uncomprehendingly at his old pal. Faint signs of recognition at last appeared. "Ellie, I have asked you not to come to Saint Henry's during service hours. It is embarrassing."

Elliot ignored this. "My friend is not well. It is the altitude."

The Padre nodded. He understood. "The Pastor has been revealing to me his quaint and very spiritual experiences in Nepal." He seemed not to have understood the reference to FARS and the Mama.

"His visit to the Himalayas had a transforming effect on Ollie." Elliot thought of the Reverend's three-week run of diarrhea in a Kathmandu hotel, then his emergency air transport to a hospital in New Delhi by Medecins Sans Frontieres. Afterwards, Ollie would never eat local food without a large prophylactic dose of strong drink.

"The moment that I discovered that the All-One had innumerable faces, I dislodged spiritual doubt." Ollie.

"Quite," Elliot told the Padre. "But Ollie should not remain within this large bath. He is susceptible to colds in his weakened state."

"I understand of your concern." Padre Rigoberto turned toward the sacristy end of the church, cupped his hands around his mouth and bellowed, "Pinche!"

After several minutes during which Elliot tried to lift the spiritual leader's soggy legs out of the tub, a small figure came running. It was Pinche. He was short enough to cower beneath the Padre with room to spare. In fact, he was remarkably similar to Jose, physically and mentally. Perhaps they were at least primos. I.e. cousins.

"Si excelentisimo." Pinche bowed a dozen times. He too was afraid of the whip.

"We have a guest of great importance." Padre Rigoberto spoke to his servant in Spanish for several minutes. He did not smile. Pinche ran off toward the sacristy. The Padre turned to his visitors. "He is loyal servant and often useful, but I must exhaust all the strengths to make him understand of a simple thing."

Elliot sympathized. The problem with servants at his mother's Beverly Hills home had been a continuous trauma. "Yes. They never seem to understand the hardships that we endure."

The Padre grasped this at once. "And I have raised this Pinche Cabron since when he is even smaller, perhaps ten or five years old. His mother was a woman lost to morals and his father was the whole city."

Ingratitude was always shocking. "Ollie, try to hold on. Help is on the way."

Wallby dabbled his toes in the baptismal water. He hummed a tune that sounded like "Sunset Beach".

"What is Che-su?" Rigoberto asked. He was intrigued, but also a bit suspicious.

"Ollie knows more about it than I do. It has a lot to do with oppression and religion, about joining the peaceful teachings of Jesus with the more militant doctrines of Che Guevara."

"To totally liberate the masses," Wallby added from within the waters.

"Ah." Rigoberto rubbed his chin. "I have read of this doctrine before. It is very popular in Harvarwood."

The good padre was confusing Harvard and Hollywood. Elliot suppressed a laugh. "Yes, and in other places as well. You see, we wish to bring the idea of Che-su to FARS and to the people. Ollie says that it will increase pacifism *and* militancy, thereby triumphing over our cynical adversaries."

Wallby clapped his hands. Or maybe he was just playing in the water.

At last Mr. Cabron reappeared. He was pushing what looked like an antique wheelchair that was almost as tall as he was.

"This is chair belong to Obispo of nineteen censury," Pinche explained. "We have keep it as a holy relic. Many prays are to it for the cure." Elliot assumed he was referring to venereal disease.

The sides and back of the wheelchair were composed of carved wood that featured biblical scenes. Elliot thought he could make out Jonah swallowed by the whale. The Padre gave further orders in Spanish to the attendant. Pinche raised himself on tiptoes and managed to grab part of Reverend Wallby. Then he started to pull with all his strength. Evidently Mr. Cabron's plan was to tip the holy foreigner out of the baptismal font into the antique wheelchair, which would make transportation more practical.

Elliot watched as both Wallby and little Pinche groaned and twisted. "Our original plan was to have the Reverend cross on a rope to this church. If it had succeeded, this ackward manoevre would have been unnecessary," he explained to the priest. "We could not enter through the church doors in the normal way because of that mob of alms seekers. The rope business was Jose's idea."

"Yes. This is very thoughtful of you." With some dissatisfaction, the Padre watched Pinche work. "Do not inconvenience his worship, Pinche. He is a very great spiritual man."

Pinche was hauling on Wallby's arm as if he planned to dismantle the minister piece by piece in order to remove him from the baptismal font. Wallby groaned with increasing urgency. Padre Rigoberto gave Pinche a swift hard kick. "Basta!"

"This man receives a bed and food and even propinas, but he is irresponsible and vicious. And this in a socialist society!" Vocabulary: propina—tip.

It was shocking. Elliot considered giving the ungrateful runt a kick. "Perhaps they will learn in time."

The Padre shook his head. He was skeptical. "I have small reason to hope. You say you are here to meet FARS and to enlighten them as to Che-su theology?"

"Yes. That is our goal. Together we will work to help the people. As I said, the Reverend knows the details of Che-su thought much better than I do." They watched as Pinche struggled with one of Wallby's shoulders. "Liberation is a long task."

"You have spoke truly. But while this idiot continues to his task, I will point out the glorious features of Santa Gregorio." He gave Pinche another kick, not as strong as before, and simply to encourage him. "When the Reverend has seated in the silla de ruedas, we will go to the rectory, where I may help to satisfy your wishes."

Padre Rigoberto led the way along one of the side aisles. He pointed out several of the baroque marvels. "Santa Lucia. Make by a local artist in sixteen censury. Those carvings that you may see above the holy image of the saint," he raised his riding crop toward the arched roof of the church, "show the local people being converted after the conquest." He was pointing toward a sculpture in stone that seemed to show small figures being beheaded and burned at the stake by armored Spanish soldiers. Suddenly they were distracted by a loud noise, something like a large wet sack being being dropped onto a hard surface. They rushed back to the baptismal font. Wallby was now in the wheelchair. His head lolled to one side in an unnatural way. It was not certain that he was breathing. Pinche's chest heaved in an effort to replenish his own oxygen.

"Now we are fitted to continue toward rectory." Padre Rigoberto took Elliot's arm. They walked ahead. Pinche pushed Wallby in the silla de ruedas. While the Padre explained something about Unesco and Santa Gregorio as an internationally guaranteed "patrimony of humanity", Elliot turned his head back. Pinche was limping as he pushed the wheelchair. One of his legs was shorter than the other. Wallby slept, eyes open. "This church is a marvel of the great art of the baroque age and we must do what we can to preserve it for the Santoran people and all of those who are humans." Was this expression intended to exclude Pinche, who certainly exhibited simian traits?

They were approaching a dark wooden door in the wall near the head of the church's side aisle. It was attached by strong iron fixtures and looked very heavy. The door to the rectory. A dozen feet away, in the space under the choir loft, Elliot saw a figure lying face down on the ground. It was almost certainly Jose.

"Do not concern yourself," the Padre Rigoberto said. "The common people often come here to rest in the peace and coolness."

Jose's body was twisted 180 degrees at the waist. His pockets had been slit open. Unseen eyes had observed the dollar transfer from Elliot.

Padre Rigoberto pulled a large iron key ring from a pocket of his cassock. It required six medieval keys inserted into three openings to turn the lock. This was an understandable security measure. Beloved as they were, and smothered with charity, the people could irrupt into irrational violence at any moment. They were deeply marked by the stain of original sin.

When they were inside, Rigoberto closed the door and slid a large bolt into protective place. Elliot looked around. He was impressed, amazed by the antique furnishings, the dark wainscoting carved with noble arms, the baroque religious paintings and statuary, the many candlesticks of polished silver.

"Let us enter my study. We may talk in greater comfort."

Pinche pushed the chair-relic into a book-lined room. He positioned it at a long table.

"Vaya, idiota!" Rigoberto gave a last kick to facilitate Pinche's exit. He just missed as the servant jumped out the door.

The Padre now closed the study door. He hesitated for an instant, then locked it. "I believe that we shall be undisturbed."

Wallby's chair was moored at the table. Elliot and Rigoberto sat in two of the high-backed armchairs. Spanish furniture of the old style is very impressive.

"Now, I to begun by asking the Reverend Wallby to define this doctrine in context of our traditional theology." He looked at the Reverend.

Wallby appeared to stare into space. Probably he was still within the arms of Morpheus..

"I'm afraid Ollie received quite a shock when he accidentally crashed through your window. Pinche's efforts to extricate him from the font didn't help much. He may be in a minor state of shock. Perhaps if we supply him with something to drink he will revive."

"Of course. You will excuse my lack of hospitality. I will bring immediately a glass of water."

"Umm, not water. Pisco would be more useful. The Reverend has had bad reactions to the local water."

The padre nodded. He went to a sideboard, which was heavy and dark to match the other furniture, and retrieved a large glass carafe. He brought three glasses. Into each he poured an ounce of pisco.

"To your most extreme health!"

Elliot picked up his glass—more like a thimble—and matched the padre's salute. Wallby sat impassively for an instant. Then some internal mecanism sorted the incoming data. He ignored his glass. Without blinking, using only his mouth, he picked up the carafe and quickly guzzled freely. The padre stared in amazement.

"Oh. The Reverend sometimes requires large doses to revive, especially after a very hard ordeal."

Rigoberto's mouth dropped open. He had heard that the gringos were barbarians, but nothing had prepared him for this.

Ollie put the depleted carafe back on the table. He burped.

"Oliver? Padre Rigoberto was just asking about the Che-su doctrine and how it fits into conventional theology. You know that part much better than I do."

Wallby looked around with an air of frank incomprehension. He may have been trying to understand where he was and why. "I cannot miss my meeting in Monterey Park with Reverend Jones. Contacts with the AME are so valuable."

"We're in El Santo, Ol'." Elliot was close to crying from shame and embarrassment. He turned to Padre Rigoberto. "I'm sorry, my friend really is not well. There are even a few shards of window glass in in his head. Perhaps." He picked up the carafe, applied it to Wallby's mouth. The Reverend drank like a baby from its bottle. Much of the remaining liquor disappeared.

"Ah. Yes. That is the question," the Reverend Wallby began. "In fact, we look upon Che-su as complimenting, even as completing the historic teachings of Jesus. Jesus taught love, compassion, forgiveness and peace. But he did not give definite instructions on how to deal with exploitative imperialist aggression. Che finished the formula. In Che we see that taking up arms is like chasing the moneychangers from the Temple. It is restoring holiness."

The Padre nodded. He understood. "Non-violent violence. It is like Mr. Stokely Carmichael." This reference to the iconic black activist of the sixties stimulated the Reverend Wallby.

"Yes. I knew the man." Wallby was warming to the discussion. "A brilliant peace activist. Seminal among men as well as women."

"You will have learned much in Nepal, in due course."

"Ah. My time of study. The Tibetan monks showed me a glimpse of the all-one. But true and entire knowledge of the One is being the One. Without otherness."

Elliot scratched his head. What the hell was this about?

"The many ways are only manifestations of the one way. Transcending the illusion of appearances to reach the truth beyond the world of appearances."

Padre Rigoberto drank it in. The Pastor had acquired so much knowledge in his travels. Pad'Rig had studied for years in a Jesuit seminary, but he had never been able to travel outside of El Santo, except for a three-week junket to Lima in the company of a certain person. Even there … but that was buried in the confessional. Back to business.

"I have understanding that you are looking to meet with the forces of the organization called FARS? That I am told is your search."

Wallby was about to speak, probably something about the One, maybe the Two, but Elliot cut him off. "Exactly. We think that only FARS can help us spread the Che-su message. We were told that we must find the Mama, the local leader, that she would know from our quest if we were sincere, which we certainly are."

"Yes, I am advising of this." Rigoberto held his forehead between his hands. "This undertaking you are make is of danger, you are understand? The government of the Correo have this group in opposite. I do not critique of the Correos. The Correos have brought much of Socialism to our country. They now have almost fulfilled the phase of destruction. Of the old regime."

"Yes." The destruction had been without obstruction. Maybe it was a type of reconstruction?

"The Correos fear the FARS because of sidestepping from the goal of the Revolucion. They are suspect FARS has envolved with the CIA. But me, I am favorable to FARS. I am Frentista."

"Oh no." Elliot touched several of his teeth, the weaker ones. He thought the Padre had said "dentista". "Nothing really necessary for the moment as far as our teeth."

"I say I am follower of FARS!"

Wallby leaned forward and once again seized the carafe between his teeth. He pulled back and the remainder of the pisco poured down his throat. It wasn't much. The equivalent of three or four shots of pure alcohol.

"Ollie! We are guests of a distinguished individual. Let's watch our p's and q's!"

Wallby looked at the ceiling. He might have been unconscious. Father Rigoberto was no longer surprised by these antics. He thought they might in some way be the result of too much Eastern Philosophy. He wanted to end the session.

"I am in entire sympathy with the goals that you have to FARS. Happily, I am able to give you a counsel on this achieving. When you are leave of Santa Gregorio, you are to proceed in the path of

Avenida de las Expropriaciones. You are walk several streets in the straight. Then you will meet of El Café de los Rechazados. Enter into the inside. Ask for a man who call himself," the Padre broke into a brief and unaccustomed smile, "You think I say 'Carlos'. Ha ha. A man who call himself Eduardo. He is not Carlos, verdad? Eduardo. You say to Eduardo that Padre Rigoberto is you fren."

"Eduardo," Elliot repeated, as a memory device. "How will we recognize Eduardo?"

"Because you ask to speak to Eduardo!" The Padre was becoming pissed. These crazy foreigners had already drunk twenty-five cents worth of his pisco. And pisco didn't grow on trees.

"No. I mean, is he fat, does he have a beard, will he be wearing a poncho?"

For a second, the Padre hesitated between shouting insults and profanity and simply leaving the room. Pinche could throw them out. At last he controlled his anger. "Do as I have told. At the Rechazados you will ask of Eduardo. Adios!" In a swirl of his black cassock, Rigoberto left.

What the hell had got into him? "Ollie? We're on the march again. We've got to find the Café de los Rechazados. It's not supposed to be far from here. Let's hit the road before it gets dark." Elliot checked the cabinets of the Padre's study. Not a drop of pisco.

Elliot wheeled the Reverend Wallby out of the study. He was certain that the rectory must have a separate street door. He did not want to leave through the church. Whoever waylaid Jose might still be slinking about, ready for more prey. The study opened into a large room graced with antique furniture and baroque art. The nineteenth century silla de ruedas belonging to the saintly Obispo rolled beyond into a reception area. A large door at the other end might open to the street. What furnishings! They were worth quite a bit. Whether God had given Padre Rigoberto the money or someone else had paid, it was a cool fortune. Counting in pisco prices, Elliot estimated that the furnishings of the reception room alone would yield enough to buy five hundred gallons of pisco. Wallby sat slumped in the ornate rolling chair. It seemed like a tiny galleon, a miniature version of one of the sixteenth century treasure ships that had brought the hard-mined silver from El Santo to Spain. Again, Ollie's eyes were open even though he was probably asleep. This might have been an effect of dehydration. He hadn't had anywhere near his usual load of pisco today. The "galleon" was approaching the large door when a small but loveable figure erupted onto the scene. Mr. Pinche Cabron.

"No senor. Lo siento mucho, but you can nodda take the silla de ruedas from de rectoria. Eez belong much to the Senor Padre."

Surprise changed Elliot's face. He hadn't thought that the Padre would insist on the return of the silla. The first wheelchair, the one they had got from the Teatro Travesti, was still in the "house". "It is impossible for me to carry the Reverend for more than a few feet. He isn't exactly a lightweight. How are we to leave the rectory? Padre Rigoberto gave us instructions to go to the Café de los Rechazados."

"Eez much bad, but de Padre make de many trouble for me iz you leaf wi silla."

The solution popped into Elliot's head. The only real solution for just about anything. He pulled a quarter from his pocket and offered it to Pinche. Pinche looked behind him, grabbed the coin, bowed. He was happy, smiling from ear to ear. His expression was something like Ollie after a liter or two of pisco under his belt. Stretching on tiptoes, Pinche opened the door. Outside was the calle, the bustling street. Sr. Cabron stood for an instant beside the doorway. Dear Pinche! Tears welled in Elliot's eyes at the thought of the goodness of the little fellow.

"Senor," Cabron whispered. Tears of gratitude were in his eyes too. "Doan go to de Rechazados. No. No good, no bueno."

Elliot had no idea what Pinche's warning, similar to the one he had received from a certain sack of coffee beans, meant. Perhaps he was referring to the Reverend's exorbitant pisco habit. In the street, pushing the ackward and ancient vehicle, Elliot made a quick mental calculation of their finances. With Ollie's Pantagruelian intake and the other things, their small hoard of cash was melting like snow in the tropics. If only they could get to the Mama, their worries would be, well, at least alleviated. She might be able to help them access the account at North American Express.

It was late afternoon. The ill-clad crowds were bustling in a last attempt to obtain limosna or the sale of trinkets. In high altitude San Santo, evening came quickly, bringing cold from the upper peaks of the Andes. The instructions were that they were to follow Expropriation Street for several blocks. Elliot put his shoulder to the wheel. Man! He wondered whether the old Spanish galleons had had this much trouble sailing the Main. His elbows and shoulders were giving distress signals already.

"Padre Rigoberto is an informed theologian, but I have doubts about his understanding of the new theology." Oliver gave out this remark. Sometimes a lack of pisco could make him hallucinate.

"He gave us directions to FARS, Ollie. What more could you ask? Most of that stuff's a lot of mumbo-jumbo anyway."

"I beg to differ. The doctrines of Che are rooted deeply in Trinitarian theory and historic versions of Christology. The attributes of the Father include the imposition of punishment to wayward believers and to unbelievers. Christ partakes of the Father. He may at times assume attributes of the First Person of the Trinity. Padre Rigoberto's understanding of our doctrine is superficial."

The galleon struck a deep hole in the sidewalk. One of the wheels was badly bent away from its axle. Elliot pushed on, even though the chair wobbled at every revolution of the wheels. "Some of the pre-Colombian deities could be kinda mean at times, too." He remembered the Amazonian rock-head and its possible role in propelling Wallby throught the church window.

"Theology is not your subject, Ellie." This use of his old and private nickname softened Elliot's feelings.

"I guess not. But I didn't major in pisco, either."

The silla de ruedas was becoming increasingly unwieldy. Elliot considered renting one of the llamas ordinarily used to transport contraband in order to carry Wallby the rest of the way to the café. But it would have been expensive and, at the Rechazados, they would probably have to put out more money for pisco expenses.

"Ollie, it would help if you could lean to the left. The right wheel is about to fall off."

"Trinitary ideas have been the source of secular confusion. Who knows how many thousands died or were miserably executed to make one version or another prevail for a time?"

"Yeah. Exactly. Uh!" With a breath-removing heave, Elliot pushed the rueda off a curb onto the street crossing.

"By the way, where exactly are we off to? I'm simply curious." Reverend Oliver.

"We're going to the Café de los Rechazados. I told you. Padre Rigoberto recommended it. We're supposed to ask for Eduardo. He'll help us find FARS."

"Another café? Are you forgetting what you owe to the Diety in abstemiousness?"

Elliot halted two thirds of the way to the opposite curb. Bicycles and pack llamas whizzed past. "If that isn't the kettle calling the pot black!"

"References to color, sex and class are opprobrious, Elliot. Have I not sermonized on the subject many times at Saint Henry's?"

"You have." Elliot pushed on. "Argh!" A grand shove with his back raised the galleon to the leeshore. Now they were treading sidewalk again. "But you will permit me to observe that your preaching has seldom resembled your practice."

Oliver was silent. Elliot feared he had gone too far. They were in serious difficulties in a strange land and now they were starting to snipe at each other. "I'm sorry Ollie. I should not have said that. It was unfair. In fact, this is the third café on our search. Each one leads to the next." He thought of a good simile. "Like bottles of pisco."

"The One is present in every action." The Reverend would say no more. It was an indication of forgiveness.

Elliot looked around, trusting in his eagle eye knack for spotting bars. There was something. On the next block three or four llamas were tied up in front of a door. The Rechazados, beyond any doubt. Every llama driver from a hundred kilometers around would probably want to tie up there, from what he had heard. He pushed toward port. The chair was now wobbling so badly that Ollie's head swung from one side to the other with every revolution of the warped wheels.

`"I feel that an epiphany is close."

"Yeah?" Elliot was impressed by this statement. His sacralized friend was rarely mistaken about epiphanies. "Then it's just what was promised. I had a feeling Padre Rigoberto was a very holy guy."

Like Yosemite Sam pushing through the swinging doors of a saloon, they rolled into the Café de los Rechazados. The place was dark. At first they could see almost nothing. Loud noises were coming from the other end of the barroom. Had applause broken out? Perhaps news of their heroic mission had preceded them. Then they heard dull thuds, sounds of breaking glass, shrieks of pain and fear, noise of a hard material knocking against bodies. When their eyes became accustomed to the darkness, the scene became clearer. At the far end of the Rechazados, an entire group was rolling on the ground, pummeling each other. The aim of the contenders seemed to be to destroy a maximum amount of furniture and other objects—of very little value anyway---by breaking them over the heads of opponents. A waiter rushed up. He was all smiles.

"Are you please take seat, *messieurs*." With a sweep of his arm he offered them the choice of the café. The space was filled with broken bottles, junk, smashed wooden crates, the remains of ancient chairs and pools of blood and vomit.

"Thank you." Elliot gingerly perched his rear on part of a still intact crate. As before, Wallby needed no additional seating material.

"Whars are you will drigging?"

"Café."

"Bien, senor."

An object flew through the air and smashed against the nearest wall. It seemed to be a llama bone with a good deal of meat left on it. "I am sure we will enjoy ourselves here. It is certainly a lively place," Elliot ventured to the minister.

"I cannot vouchsafe violence to animals or wasting food." Wallby nodded toward the percussed bone.

The wrestlers at the other end of the barroom quieted suddenly. Two were embracing each other with maudlin looks. Others searched for bottles. One was still struggling, but alone.

"Apparently it was just a misunderstanding. Such things occur everywhere." Elliot.

Their drinks were served. Pisco, of course, which was always understood by "café". They had to drink from large brown shards.

"Cheerio!" Elliot raised his glass in salute.

Wallby's portion disappeared so quickly as to raise doubts that it had ever existed. Again, they would have to order a full bottle. This would save the waiter innumerable trips.

Elliot looked around the barroom. He was now savouring his third shard-full. Which one was Eduardo? Elliot's guess was that Eduardo was the one with a huge bird's nest beard and rounded body. He looked like someone who could declaim ideology for hours without a pit stop. He wore something on his head that looked like a hat with a broken crown and without a brim. His stained face bore witness to past combat, or at least to sloppy habits. "It is time to ask the waiter about Eduardo. You'll have to do the talking, Ollie. This whole trip was your idea, remember, and your Spanish is better." Elliot was shy of waiters, after their past experiences.

"I fail to comprehend the advantage of this exercise." Wallby swallowed from the bottle. A little less than half remained.

"You'll pick it up." Elliot signaled to the waiter, who came up eagerly.

"Otra botella?"

"Not yet. We are looking for a man called Eduardo. Is there such a person here?"

"Eduardo?" The waiter scratched his head. "No creo. Eduardo? No. No hay nadie de este nombre aqui."

Elliot was crestfallen. Then the whole search ended here, among debris and shards.

"Ah! Espere." He turned toward the bar and yelled. "Chicha! Te piden!" To Wallby and Elliot: "Ella se llama Chicha pero tiene Eduardo de apodo." She was called Chicha but her nickname was Eduardo. After a pause of several minutes, enough time for another shard full of pisco, a large figure emerged from the backbar. It was a woman. A large woman. Larger about the middle than at the extremities of the torso or the head. She came up to the waiter. She wore a sort of cow blanket with stylish folds and cuts. The effect was spoiled by several large stains.

"Si?" She was not enthusiastic. In fact she was restraining hostile feelings.

The waiter gave her explanations/instructions in highly colloquial Spanish. He went back to the bunker.

Eduardo looked them over with an unsmiling gaze. "Y que?" It was a challenge, as if to combat.

Elliot turned to the Reverend in a desperate appeal for aid and advice. Ollie was staring at what remained of the ceiling. "Um. Nothing, really. I mean, we were told to come here to find you."

"Mierda! Que quieres, puta de gringo?" Untranslatable.

"It's just, well, I mean, Padre Rigoberto of Santa Gregorio said you could help us." He placed a hand to cover his mouth from general view, then whispered, "he said you could help us find FARS."

"El Padre?" Eduardo brightened and relaxed immediately. "Wire you no say? Amigos, I am harpy to see of you." She squatted next to Elliot's crate seat. Man, what thighs. If ever she decided to go in for Big Time wrestling! Elliot made a mental note in case they made it back to L.A.

At close range Elliot could see that the stylish cow blanket actually had several large holes as well as stains. And Chicha was not wearing any underwear, unless those large dark patches were the remains of underwear.

"We had a long discussion with the Padre, on theology and other subjects. You see, we are here to speak of Che-su." Elliot paused to let this important fact sink in.

Eduardo shook her head. "Que? No comprendo. Hablas de un chino?"

Elliot laughed politely. "No. Not Chinese, although the message of Che-su is truly universal. With Che-su we humanize revolution and revolutionize humanity. Right, Ollie?" He gave his friend a strong poke in the side.

"Strashing. Abgolical." The Reverend was not connecting. This would have to do for his contribution.

"You have heard it from the source. You see, our love for the Santano people is very great. To ease their suffering is our goal." Elliot swallowed the remains of his shardfull of pisco.

"Ung." She was beginning to comprehend. "Noan drink from de ceramica rota. You gut you mout." She offered a squashed and stained paper cup pulled from an inside pocket.

"Oh! How thoughtful of you." He took the cup and quietly let it drop, touching it as little as possible. "We want to join with FARS and to work with them, and to find the Mama. Padre Rigoberto sent us."

Eduardo's head drooped slightly. She rubbed her head briskly with both hands. She made indistinct sounds. "Ay. Ay. Ay doan no wat I yam think. How ay no you nod espias? Somebody say all de gringo wark for CIA."

"Perfectly preposterous." Elliot gave a high and emotionally charged laugh. "Our only goal is to help the Santano people."

"Okay." Eduardo/Chicha seemed to accept this. "Butt dey all say de same. I gonna tell you ware to go. Bu you never say I say you, cause de Correo make much big trouble."

"Heap big trouble," Elliot corrected.

"Eh. No make de laugh on me, senor. I am work here and ver poor for no get money."

This was true beyond any doubt. It was possible that she worked strictly for drinks and tips. Such an arrangement would be considered advantageous by many Santanos. In earnest of his sympathy for the Santano people, Elliot deposited a quarter in her lap. She picked it up, bit it, slipped it under her bosom.

"Uhng." She was pleased. She almost smiled. "You fren nex swallow de bottle." She pointed to Wallby. In fact, the entire neck of the pisco bottle had disappeared into Wallby's mouth. Not a drop remained.

"Ollie, dear, I think this one's finished. Try to be sensible." He pulled the bottle from Wallby's mouth. There was a small amount of blood on the rim. The Reverend had never had his tonsils out. Elliot tossed the empty toward a corner of the room. It crashed amid a pile of others. He signaled the waiter.

"Otra!"

"You are ver goo an kine to you fren." Chicha.

"Ollie and I have been inseparable for many years, although at times he can be difficult to manage."

"Yah. So I give you de place. Den you go der for de FARS. Bu lissen me. Any guy ask you, you say I am Carlos."

"Carlos," Elliot repeated. That should be easy to remember.

The waiter brought a second bottle of pisco. Wallby took it from him and tried a bit, just for the taste. It was surprising, but his motor skills improved substantially with the intake of pisco.

"We're not going to have to go to another café?" Elliot was wary.

"Ha ha. No, amigo. I am not so stupid. Why I tell you go café? Dis café aqui." She looked around. She was aware of the unsavory impression that the place would create in the minds of ninety-seven percent of the earth's inhabitants. "Wha you wan do, is you go to Ministerio de la Justicia."

"Ministerio de la Justicia," Elliot repeated.

"Is big edificio of the gobierno. Bad you no fraid. I god fren work inside. Just say you wan talk wi Juan."

"Juan."

"Si. You talk wi Juan. You say you like to meet de FARS. You wark wi FARS."

This was going to be easier than he expected. Elliot turned to his friend. "Ollie? Are you ready to leave? Eduardo, I mean Carlos, has given us instructions."

"I certainly do not intend to drag myself through ministries. We know what the officials of that class can be." Oliver.

"This is different. We have friends there." Elliot turned to Chicha/Eduardo/Carlos. "Ollie is concerned because his wheelchair, a gift from Padre Rigoberto, was damaged en route to this café and can only be moved with difficulty. The wheel is out of kilter on one side."

Chicha bent forward to examine the problem. "Ah. Veo. No marcha bien. Espera." She reached into the layer of debris that covered the café floor, felt for several minutes, then retrieved a long object with a heavy end. It was a femur bone. She used it to bang heavily on the wheel axel. Wallby, still sitting in the chair, was surprised and shocked.

"The foundation is shaking. It is probably an earthquake!" Oliver swallowed a good part of the second bottle to steady his nerves.

"Ensaya." Try it now.

Elliot pushed the rolling chair. It had recovered much of its mobility. "Thank you. That is much better. See, Ollie? We have little reason to fear ministries." Ollie did not answer.

"Ya. You say to see Juan. I am Carlos."

"I don't know how to thank you, Carlos. It is so important for us to begin our mission of bringing spiritual and temporal aid to the Santano people. Right, Ollie? You're the minister, for crying out loud."

"Supposititious. But with firm referential values."

"Ollie is still suffering from the altitude. He is in fact fully aware of our position. Ol', would you like to give us a blessing before we start out again? Like you used to do for the flock at Saint Henry's."

Wallby raised the bottle of pisco again and drank freely. An astonishing flow of the stuff disappeared into the theologically trained mouth. That would have to do. "I am really very grateful to you for your help, Carlos. Unless we get into contact with Fars," Elliot lowered his voice to pronounce the name of the forbidden movement, "and find the Mama, our mission will be a total flop." He began to wheel Wallby toward the exit. Chicha accompanied them.

"You are gritt de con, de contac," Chicha assured. She walked gracefully, despite her size and asymmetric proportions. "You go today. The Ministerio always open, like de Macdonald in you country."

Elliot wondered whether they had a drive-through window. That would be too much to expect.

They were almost out the door of the Café de los Rechazados when Chicha called them back. "Hey, my fren. Don forget dis." She held up the bottle of pisco. About a third of the contents remained. Unaccountably, Wallby had let the bottle drop. "Maybe you gonna need it."

The Reverend turned around as they passed from view. He made a gesture with his right hand. "Ego te absolvo."

"How could I have been so stupid!" Elliot repeated this to himself for the fifty-seventh time. He was in a cell somewhere in the interior of the immense, squat building that was the Ministerio de la Justicia de El Santo. A small barred window looked out onto a courtyard where, during the day, he was able to see mainly uniformed figures pass in groups or in ones. Of course they had been arrested the minute they stepped into the entry hall of the Ministerio! Carlos had set them up. Oh yes! There was no doubt. The chain of events from Antonio to Padre Rigoberto to Eduardo/Chicha/Carlos was now plain. Betrayed! The fact that as soon as they entered the ministry office they had asked for Juan (this was a code word that the police understood as a signal of those in rebellion against the lawfully constituted Dictatorship of the Correos) and, following instructions, they had declared that they wanted to "work with FARS", only added icing to the cake. Membership, association with, or even the mention of the name FARS was a capital offense in El Santo. During the first interrogation, two days ago, the Security Lieutenant let drop that this declaration had amounted to a confession. The case was legally closed. The sentencing would be made by the Commander Ixtaguirre-Rubalcava. They might be let off with a firing squad. It would be better than one of the Amazonian penal colonies.

Elliot and Reverend Wallby had been separated immediately after their arrest. Elliot missed the companionship and spiritual succor of his old friend. It was twice hell having to go through this alone. During the first interrogation Lieutenant Schaden-Ortiz had urged him to reveal the names of his co-conspirators. They would inevitably be caught, anyway. By fingering them in advance he would receive lighter treatment and save his fellow traitors from the difficult process of confession. Elliot had insisted that there was no one. They were missionaries intent on spreading the Word. Reverend Wallby was his alibi. A half-crippled, mentally impaired cleric, who would take such a person on a conspiracy expedition?

"Think about it my friend. You are going to the firing squad anyway. It will be much easier when you are confess now."

That was two days ago. Elliot was still thinking about it. He had already tried insisting on the immunity conferred by his American citizenship.

"You can't touch me. I'm an American."

The Lieutenant had spat. "We do not recognize the giant imperialist empire of the North. To us you are a worm. Do not be a stupid worm."

Then Elliot had tried naming names. He mentioned Jonathan Belcher, Antonio, Padre Rigoberto and Carlos as members of the band of "assassins, terrorists, criminals and rapists" of which he, Elliot, was supposedly also a member. Then Doctor Zapatero and Influenzia. Schaden-Ortiz only shook his head.

"No. We know that this is untrue. You are involved with persons who are not these. You will be wise to spare yourself much trouble by saying truthfully."

Who else could he name? He tried making up a few. "It was Senor Gomez who was the leader. And Andrade and Garcia and Smith."

"No. Not very smart, Mr. Elliot. We are know truth from falseness. Do not tell more falsies. We are the Policia de Seguridad. Who harve send you? You have two day to tink."

He had been tinking in his cell. Jonathan, Antonio, Rigoberto and Carlos were obviously police informants. That is why Schaden had immediately rejected them as co-conspirators. He searched his mind over and over. The only crime that he and Ollie could be fairly accused of was trying to contact FARS. Unfortunately, it happened to be a capital offense.

Elliot looked around his cell. He had to admit that it was not as small as the claustrophobic cells you saw in spy films. It was at least ten by fifteen feet. A blanket in the corner served as a bed. A lightbulb hung from the ceiling by a foot of cord. This was traditional. The food was not too bad. It was rather like the burritos that he used sometimes to buy at cheap eateries on Sunset Boulevard when he had lived with his mother in Beverly Hills during his protracted days of youth. Maybe a bit more rice. Less hot sauce.

The walls were covered with graffiti that was largely incomprehensible to him. He made out a few words. "Chingada", "cojones", "cabrones", "puta madre", "mierda". Words that told their own story. "Mierda" was more elegant, possibly the comment of a student activist, maybe a FARS sympathizer like himself.

Burritos and Beverly, he dreamed back to the days of his youth. He regretted all the time he had wasted in cafes and bars. Although he had made some good pick-ups. What he regretted most was that he had not given more to those who needed more. If you donate to the oppressed today, they won't try to get you tomorrow. Anyway, that was the theory. And Maxine, his mother, a martyr to alcohol. Could he not have done more to help her?

The firing squad mentioned by Lieutenant Schaden was making him more tense and worried every hour. He still only half believed it. Surely the Lieutenant was just trying to scare him. How could it be the end now, when he and Ollie had so many things to do, a continent to conquer? And he hadn't done anything! Except to try to contact FARS. Elliot revolved these ideas in his mind constantly. Occasionally he stood up on tiptoes to look out the little barred window. Usually you could see policemen or soldiers walking through the courtyard. Then, late on the second day, he saw something that made him blink. It looked like Reverend Wallby dressed in a black cassock. He was riding on a donkey led by a uniformed figure. Wallby was giving his blessing to nearby military figures, who piously bowed their heads.

Elliot blinked and stared. What did this mean? He did not have long to think about it. The cell door opened.

"Ven!" It looked like the two days of "tinking" were over.

They walked along the corridors, with the jailer giving Elliot a shove every few moments, even though he was walking at least as fast as the turnkey. He half turned around every few yards. Actually the turnkey was not so bad looking. Usually he was not attracted to the Santanoan type. Soon he was delivered to a small room with a desk. Lieutenant Schaden was waiting for him, with his rear casually posed on the desktop.

"Sit!" He meant on the floor.

Elliot dropped to squatting position. His legs were starting to give way in any case.

The Lieutenant stood up and walked slowly to the window, which gave onto a different courtyard of the vast Ministerio building. He lit a cigarette. He had seen many spy movies.

"Bien, senor. I am sincerely hope for the good of you and you wirve and family that you have tink much."

Elliot's brain flipped between several alibis and phony confessions. There was nothing worth mentioning. He said nothing.

Schaden sneered. "Not too bright, my friend." He tossed his cigarette on the floor and crushed it out with unnecessary brutality. "What ared you say if I tell you that Mr. Wollopy has sign a statement that you are the traitor who have kidnap him to use for the advantage of the unspeakable terrorists often call the FARS?"

For a moment, Elliot's visioned blurred. What he had heard was beyond any known reality. Ollie would never finger him. Never! Not for anything! Ever!

"That's a lie! You know it's not true! Ollie would never say anything like that!" Besides, this was a well-known police tactic, divide the accused by telling each one that the other had ratted. Good cop/ bad cop would be next.

Schaden leaned across his desk, opened a drawer and pulled out a piece of paper. He handed it down to Elliot.

"I, Oliver Wallby, declare that I was forcibly kidnapped and brought to El Santo by the terrorist Elliot Spenseric to further his concocted plans of terrorist attacks against the Santanoan people and government and beloved leaders." At the bottom was a scrawl that certainly looked like Wallby's signature.

"Ollie would never accuse me falsely! Of anything! You're a liar! A liar! Shoot me if you want, but I know all of this is a lie!" He looked more closely at the handwriting of the signature. It was a very close match.

The Lieutenant sat on his desk smiling, smoking another cigarette. "Gracias, senor. You have just seal two time you own death. In El Santo it is a pena de muerte to accuse the police of lying."

"Oh. Well, perhaps I was overly emotional. But we are tourists, only tourists! We came here because Reverend Wallby needed a long rest. He is greatly interested in the culture of El Santo. We understood that FARS was a cultural association." The last part was untrue, as Elliot admitted to himself.

"Who is now de big liar?" Schaden tossed his cigarette end on the floor. "You have already confess to wish to join the FARS."

Trapped. It was true. Elliot was a poor liar. "We came to contact FARS, as I said, but we didn't know it was against the law. Our goal was cultural and religious. Oliver is interested in the religious creed called Che-su. He thought it would help the people."

"Help the bandits to murder de rightful authorities!" Schaden screamed. "FARS is a dangerous organization! They will stop at nothing to gain power. Their goal is to control drug trade. This is why the American have give them supporters. These CIA are want to use de drug for get the many million. Then they are give to dictators."

"You mean they want to take the drug money so they can help establish dictatorships?"

"Ah. You are not entirely the stupid I have thought. It is so. They are wish to overthrow our beloved Jefes, el Senor Stalin Correo y el Senor Lenin Correo. Without hour leaders, the people are helpless. They are, how you say, only 'little slobs'."

Elliot tried to look pensive and contrite. "I didn't know that."

"There are much you are not know. But you are come to make great trouble in our land." The Lieutenant took another paper from a desk drawer. He handed it to Elliot. "I give you today to read this and put you name. It will great reduce you are sentence when you have sign first confession also."

Elliot gave the paper a first glance. "I, the infamous traitor to the Santano people …"

"Juan!" The turnkey reappeared. "Devuelve a este desgraciado a su celda."

The return trip was rougher than the trip to Schaden's office. The jailer kept pushing him, sometimes punching him in the ribs. He did not dare protest. The paper that he had been given showed clearly that he was considered a vicious traitor, the Santano Benedict Arnold, if not worse. A last shove landed him on the floor of his cell. The door slammed behind him. It was good to be home.

"But I didn't do *anything*!" Elliot repeated aloud to no one. This was not strictly true. They, or rather he, because during most of the trip Wallby had believed that they were still in Los Angeles, had been aware that FARS was determined to overthrow the Correo government, which was trying to suppress the guerrilla group with all available force. The literature Ollie had provided pointed to FARS as a true revolutionary organization. The essays and monographs convicted the Correos of dangerous flirtation with more moderate elements. That was why the Reverend had planned from the beginning to join FARS, to bring true revolution back to El Santo along with Che-su. They hadn't "done anything" so far because they had not made contact. The quest to find FARS had led to a Correo jail cell.

Elliot looked at the paper the Lieutenant had given him. "I, (space left to add the name), the infamous traitor to the Santano people, do freely confess without force or compulsion of any kind that I have planned and schemed to attack and to destroy the people of El Santo and especially their beloved leaders on the path to Socialism, that I have intended to murder, burn, outrage, rob and pillage the men, women and children of El Santo without pity or regard for human rights or international law or common decency or good taste. That I especially intended to commit rape and sacrilege and to destroy sacred monuments and cash deposits of all kinds. I have looted bars and buffets of their supplies to the great detriment of the people. I have sprawled nightly in convents. I have had disgusting relations with my mother. I have masturbated in public places. I have tortured animals. I have done this freely in the service of the imperialist powers. I further admit to the particular acts described in part 7d (see below)." Then there was a place for a signature.

If Elliot confessed to these trumped up charges, he might get off with the firing squad, the Lieutenant had said. Then they would publish his confession worldwide. Imagine how they would laugh on Sunset Boulevard. Elliot Spenseric, reduced to forced relations with Santanos and to masturbation in public places in San Santo! They'd never get over it on the strip or in Beverly!

Dazed, Elliot stumbled to the small barred window. He looked out, resting his head against the metal grill. Probably he was dreaming, or hallucinating, but down below in the courtyard he saw a figure familiar from American newspapers and television. A figure hunched at the shoulders was smiling from ear to ear at some children. His head bobbed in friendly sympathy. It looked like—my god! It was Jimmy! Jimmy Carter. Those large pearly teeth that showed between lips parted in a wide smile were unmistakeable. But those were not really children he was fawning on, they were simply undersized recruits to the security forces. This was clear from their uniforms, clear to Elliot, if not to Jimmy. Some of the Andean people, after centuries of cruel oppression and malnutrition, barely topped five feet.

What was Jimmy doing here? Was it MLK Day already? Perhaps J.C. had been appointed goodwill ambassador to help the Santanos celebrate. Elliot tried to wave from the little window. After all, he had voted for the man twice, maybe three times. "Jimmy, Jimbo! Jimmo! Yoohoo!" He banged on the window. A louder bang answered from the prison corridor. The jailor had kicked his cell door.

"Calla! Puta, hijo de chingada!"

Elliot was about to reply that he hadn't done anything, but he remembered that this excuse never worked in El Santo. He went back to his blanket-mattress. He lay down. If only Ollie had been here to advise him. He didn't know what to do. It all seemed so hopeless.

He leafed through the signature ready confession Schaden had given him. There were twelve pages in all. Part 7d was actually innocuous. Here he only admitted to having barbarously sabotaged school buses and ambulances as well as blinding elderly people in order to steal their canes with which to beat pregnant women. What if he did sign? It couldn't be any worse. After all, Lieutenant Schaden-Ortiz had told him that, strictly according to the law, he had already confessed twice, maybe three times. Okay, I'll do it. At least I'll get it over with. And they would never really actually shoot anyone just for trying to bring Che-su to the Masses. Would they? Elliot took the pencil stub Schaden had provided and signed his name at the foot of the last page. Then he added an asterisk to refer to a handwritten note lower down. "I didn't know I was doing anything!"

When the jailer brought his dinner burrito, Elliot silently handed him the signed confession. The turnkey looked at the paper for a moment and seemed about to throw it on the floor, then nodded.

"Ver good senor. You are not so estupid as we are tinking. El Teniente arf be muy contento." Then he was gone. Elliot thought he could hear the firing squad practicing in the courtyard.

Tonight's burrito had less rice *and* less salsa. He remembered reading in a news article on a page of the New York Times left yesterday as a dinner place mat, that the Money Fund was considering a loan to El Santo, now suffering from an extreme lack of liquidity. That explained the reduction in the rice and salsa ration. As for liquidation, there was no lack whatsoever. There it was again. The firing squad was practicing, beyond any doubt. Was it only practice?

Taking his burrito with him, Elliot went to the barred window. Jimmy was gone, but near the far corner of the quad, tied to a stake in front of a concrete wall, hung the body an unfortunate individual who for all the world resembled none other than Jonathan Belcher. Jonathan! A friend of the Correos! He had even met Stalin, the nice one. Now his head drooped, motionless. The rifle squad, in response to a barked order, turned about and marched away. A small figure rushed to the foot of the collapsed victim. A little person wearing a tattered blue dress. Manolito! Mano seemed to weep and to hold his hands in a gesture of prayer. After several minutes Mano looked around, then reached up and checked the pockets of the victim. Nothing.

While anxiously watching this pathetic scene, Elliot gulped the last of his burrito, like a fascinated moviegoer swallowing handfuls of popcorn. He couldn't stand it anymore! He turned away and threw himself on his blanket. Jonathan! What the hell had he done? That is, that the "Correo guy" would disapprove of. He had been an ally and promoter.

Elliot cried on scraps of the New York Times. He writhed for several minutes in painful sympathy. Then he sat up in shock. If they could do that to a friend, why not to someone tarred and feathered with the brush of FARS? Tears flowed again, even more abundantly. He might never see Ollie again. Forget L.A. Then he recalled a scene from tweny years ago. He was in the den of their house in Beverly Hills. Maxine, his mother, was stowing away vodka like a cruise ship taking on bunker oil as she watched her beloved afternoon TV melodramas. She told him, "You're gonna come to a shitty end some day if you keep on doing the same old crap." The day of the prophecy had arrived.

After about an hour of weeping and convulsing, Elliot achieved a relative serenity. He remembered hearing that in El Santo no prisoner was executed without being allowed a last personal appeal for mercy from the Correos. It was a national tradition, like Thanksgiving back home. Or Christmas. He decided to phrase his appeal for clemency on the grounds of repentance rather than mistaken innocence. After all, he had already confessed to just about everything imaginable. Fortunately, the Correo prosecutors had never heard of the Reichstag fire. In his confession, Elliot would thank the Correos for saving him from a life of ignoble collaboration with the imperialist powers. Now he would endeavour in every way to help the struggle of the people for freedom under the total command of the their beloved Leaders. He understood the path they were taking to conquer peace and democracy under their Leaders for Life. He wanted to be there in the long lines following the beloved Lifers, that is, Leaders, in total adulation. The noise of a slidding bolt brought him out of a reverie of repentance and forgiveness. The door opened . Mr. Jailer. Not a bad guy, although from his physique Elliot imagined that he must swallow a burrito for each one he served to a prisoner.

"You go." He helped Elliot exit in double time.

"But I haven't had my appeal yet! Like Thanksgiving. I want to write to the Leaders."

"Wad?" the jailer's face was twisted in irritated non-comprehension.

"Every prisoner is supposed to have the final right to appeal to the Leaders. That's what everyone says."

"Eres loco." They were walking, or rather shoving, along the prison corridor. The doors to other cells were firm shut and windowless.

"Where are we going? Why did they shoot Jonathan?"

They stopped while the jailer unlocked the barred ward gate. He spat. "De Johnun no good guy. He try cheat the Teniente on a deal." He leaned over and whispered. "De droga."

Now they were walking on a familiar path. Elliot supposed they were going to the Teniente's office for a final interrogation or confession. He planned to make a histrionic case to be followed by a last tearful appeal. He would do his best to save Ollie and himself. Poor Ollie was too far gone mentally even to think about "the Thankgiving appeal". Then, at a cross corridor, they turned the wrong way.

"Please. I have to speak to Teniente Schaden-Ortiz. It is my right. You will be personally responsible for violating Santano law!"

"Lis', gringo. We are tire of givin' food to de guy dat never work." Elliot saw that argument was futile. Still, he thought of one last plea that he could make in front of the peloton de la muerte. An officer would be in charge, a man who might understand the legal issues.

They walk-pushed along unfamiliar corridors, down stairways, through small courtyards, under gateways. A final door opened. Elliot received a last shove. He closed his eyes, expecting to fall into a pit.

When he opened his eyes again Elliot was astonished and overjoyed to find himself on the street outside the Ministerio de la Justicia. He had been released, although rather informally. His surprise doubled when he saw Reverend Oliver Wallby sitting on the crumbling sidewalk only a few feet away.

"Ollie! Thank God they didn't shoot you." He rushed up to his old friend. "What happened? They let you out too."

Wallby sat impassively, still dressed in the same black cassock.

"I saw you from my cell window when you were crossing the courtyard on a donkey and you were blessing the soldiers and everything."

"I must make my next preaching from a café. I am rather thirsty."

A folded piece of paper was hanging out of the Reverend's cassock waist pocket. Elliot grabbed it. It was a receipt for the withdrawal of tweny-five thousand dollars from the North American Express office in San Santo. "Ollie! You got the money! Bless you. At last we can live like human beings again!" He smiled at Ollie and bent over to hug the senior clergyman. "Well, to hell with push contraptions and cafes. We'll call a cab and go back to the Hotel Carlos."

Elliot smiled, patted his friend on the back. He waited. He smiled and patted again. Then, since afternoon was waning and the cold San Santo evening was coming on again, "By the way, Ol, where is the cash you got from North American Express? I'll have to pay the cabbie and they took every last cent I had in the joint." He used his shoulder to indicate the Ministerio.

"I signed a document for Teniente Schaden-Lopez in that express office. You must ask him about it."

Elliot was still smiling when the cruel truth sank in. He looked in a last appeal to the dark blue Santo sky. Of course! Schaden had stolen the whole wad. That's why he let them go. So there would be no more questions about the matter. He could have had them shot, but that always makes a good deal of noise. The news about the NO AMEX account waylaid Elliot to such an extent that he forget to stop smiling. "Then ..."

"The Teniente advised me to leave the country as soon as possible. He suggested we go to nearby Granadia. They currently have no diplomatic relations with El Santo."

Now the full truth settled in Elliot's mind. The entire balance of Wallby's NO AMEX account had been stolen by the Lieutenant, with Ollie's blythe cooperation. "Charming. I suppose I'm required to pack you papoose-style on my back over the Andes? Meanwhile selling my charms to villagers to keep you in jungle juice? When clergymen fly!"

Ollie stared impassively and mutely forward. Was he looking at the street, the buildings opposite the Ministry, or at the Beyond, the all-one, the all-none? The cassock suited him, his large white head emerging from the formal dignity of black cloth. He looked like some ancient figure from the Reformation, Calvin or Luther or Melancthon or W.C. Fields. But he continued mute. Probably Ol was simply going through withdrawals because of the long deprivation of pisco. Elliot realized he had to be practical. He had to put aside his rightful resentment. The Teniente had the cash and there was nothing they could do about it. He and the holy man had zero cash, zero assets. Or, reaching into the bottom of his left trouser pocket, he pulled up two pennies the police guys had missed. Miracles do happen. With his usual optical accuracy, Elliot spied a café in the next block, on the side opposite the Ministerio. "Wait here, Pocahontas."

Elliot tracked out to the café. After twenty minutes he was back with a plastic cup half filled with pisco. He drank his share first, the only way to make sure of wetting his throat. "Okay, Poca, here's your dream cream." He put the cup to Wallby's lips. Wall grabbed it with trembling hands and swallowed the rest in half a gulp. It was clear that he was relieved by the arrival in his blood system of the life-giving liquid, but hardly sated. He chewed a bit on the rim of the cup.

Go to Granadia, the Teniente had advised Wallby. Maybe they should walk on their knees to Guadalupe? Schaden was a vicious, greedy lout. Even if he had graduated from the Escuela Secundaria Carlos Marx, as he had bragged more than once. What to do? The Reverend could not think rationally; his various health problems were being aggravated by the altitude. Elliot, last scion of the House of Spenseric, had a duty and obligation to bring them to their goal. The goal remained as before, to contact FARS, to meet the Mama, and to spread the doctrine of Che-su. The Lieutenant could go to hell. Besides, it was highly unlikely they would be re-arrested. Schaden would not want any questions from his superiors about the NO AMEX account. They would want their share, the usual hundred percent.

The cool shadows grew as Elliot meditated on their possibilities. Providing Wallby, still unable to walk, with some sort of workable transportation, chair, barrow or blanket, seemed in itself nearly impossible. Then, to continue the quest for FARS and the Mama, they would need sustenance for at least several days, and he had blown their last two cents on lunch. Right now the only possibility was to drag the Reverend to a sheltered doorway and wait out the Santo night. Meanwhile they could beg for food or scrip. Since Ollie was round shaped and large, he might make a good barrier against the weather.

"I have definitely decided." Reverend Wallby, now harbored in a dilapidated doorway, was speaking. "It will be necessary and advantageous to establish a chapel in La Canada Flintridge. Of course the chapel will be in administrative unity with Saint Henry's."

"Go for it."

Wallby began to hum a sort of hymn. It might have been "Rock of Ages" or "Shall We Gather by the River", or an imaginative combination of the two.

"Ol? Why La Canada?"

"Because it is currently a center for youth culture. We must sow the seeds of faith while the field is fresh."

"Oh." Ask a silly question. Elliot was beginning to doze when he saw what must be a hallucination. He imagined that he saw the head of Manolito pop up from behind a rusting, highly dented automobile parked outside the Ministerio. It was a Moskovitch, a Soviet make probably on lend-lease from Cuba. Elliot knew it was all an illusion. He was suffering from pisco deprivation, just like the Reverend.

"Psst!" The head reappeared. It now appeared joined to a blue-clad torso. "Senor Elliot! Venga aqui!"

"Huh? You're an illusion and I have to think. Go away."

"Senor! Rapido! Ustedes tienen que evitar el peloton de la muerte!" They had to avoid the firing squad!

"Wha?" Elliot half crawled, half walked on his knees, Guadalupe style, until he reached the back of the Moskovich. It was Manolito, in flesh and blood. At least he had not vanished into fantasy. The blue dress was so tattered and stained it was an embarrassment to look at.

"Really, Mano, you should dress in a manner more appropriate to your station in life."

"Ay no godtime. You come quick wi de senor Pastor. De Teniente wan shoot you. He change de mine. Den he say you escape and he god de money."

"I was watching from the window in my cell when they shot Jonathan. I saw you, too."

"Yah. De Johnun, he go wi' de santos en de cielo. El Teniente god im shoot for de droga. No good, no bueno. Okay, maybe de Johnun he take kinna greedy, bu de oder guy do de same, right?" Mano smiled.

"A regrettable event. A sad loss. You were kneeling at the foot of the stake," Elliot mused tearfully.

"De guy from de seguridad le' me in cuz dey no me like lotta time." Mano grinned disagreeably and smoothed his tattered dress. "Bud I like de Johnun mucho, cuz he gi me lon time like de fren. Why I let de policia steal de centavos? So I take 'im."

"Tsk tsk." All of this was not too creditable for Manolito.

"You go now wi me, cuz de puta de policias wan do you 'por la Gloria de la Patria'. Dey change de mine, dey tink you go to de embajada an' make problemas"

"Ugh. And the Teniente seemed such a nice person. Then let's start immediately. Ollie's over there." In the dark twilight he pointed to a large mass resting on a stoop five meters distant.

"Yah. I help de Pastor." Mano made the sign of the cross over the old heretic. "Que Dios me perdone!"

They had been dragging for a long time. Wallby groaned from time to time but he had not been seriously damaged by contact with the paving stones. He was heavily padded in the under zone.

"Mano, how about stopping for a refreshment." Elliot was thirsty and in need of a morale recharge.

Mano looked away. "Me, I no gotta money." He knew that Elliot and Wallby, as released prisoners, would not have a centavo.

"We're very short on funds too. But I have a few articles to barter." Elliot reached down and removed something from the Reverend Wallby's neck. "Don't you think we could trade this for a drink or two?" He showed in the palm of his hand a silver crucifix worked with intricate skill. "Ollie brought this back from Nepal." The superstitious jailers had not dared to steal it.

"Que bonito!" Mano took the crucifix into his hand and looked closely at it. "Doan giv it for no lousy pisco. I give for you." The little tyke took a crumpled ten dollar bill out of his pocket and pressed it on Elliot.

"Thank you, Mano. It is very generous on your part. Although the crucifix is worth every penny of it and more."

"When I put de cruz aroun de neck, den I gi' proteccion, li wen de Obispo make de sign."

"Mmm." Poor Mano was incurably superstitious. It might be a good idea to have Ollie talk to him about religious matters. For now, there were more urgent matters. Elliot pushed through the door of a café. Mano dragged the Reverend behind him. "Pisco, y mucho!" Elliot cried out to the tender, whose happily surprised look turned to fear when he saw a cassock clad body being dragged into his respectable establishment. Elliot ignored this. He went to the nearest table, once again dragging a rather elegant wooden box to the table for his own accommodation. Soon Wallby and Mano had joined him.

"What exactly happened between Schaden and Jonathan?" It was a distressing business and Elliot hoped to lessen his distress by discovering the details. He felt he needed a drink. Then he realized he had been drinking pisco for several minutes already.

"De guy got no problema hasta que viene el Jimmy."

"El Jimmy?"

"Si! When de Jimmy come, he say he wanna haf de freedom for all de prisioneros, like in de democracia. So el Teniente make de Johnun talk wi Jimmy, cuz Johnun es from de People Watch dat like de free-dumb, bu he say too many ting, maybe, den when Jimmy go in de avion, de peloton talk to Johnun." Mano laughed until he fell over.

"Indeed! I'm sure we'll all remember Jonathan in our prayers. But wasn't there something about a drug deal that you mentioned before?"

"Yah. Dey always do de deal. No es gran cosa."

"No es gran cosa," Elliot repeated sarcastically. "You sent us to see Antonio at that café, and he sent us to see Padre Rigoberto, who sent us to see Eduardo. Eduardo sent us to the Teniente, who almost had us shot. No es gran cosa."

Manolito sobered abruptly. Then he started to whimper. "Yo no sabia! Yo no sabia!" He didn't know. "Antonio de guy I know in de FARS. You go to Eduardo, pero Eduardo no conozco."

"Also known as Chicha," Elliot put it more precisely.

"Yah." Mano nodded, contrite and sad. "Chicha. Mujer imprevisible."

Elliot threw back his head and swallowed a good slug of pisco. "We trusted you, Mano. We trusted you implicitly. I personally was tortured by Schaden! I was forced to sign a confession, and to accuse others."

"Wad he do?" Mano's prurient interest was aroused. He leaned forward. "Who you say?"

"The Teniente would not accept my accusations," Elliot swept the question aside. His "confession" was not highly creditable, especially since he hadn't been paid for his divulgations, unlike Mano.

"Yah, Ay no! Ay no!" Mano went into paroxysms of high pitched whinning in contrition.

This would have to suffice as far as repentance. Mano was their last local contact. He did have cash. Ollie lent support. He raised his lips from the glass for the first time in a half an hour. "Who among us is not without sin?"

"Thank you, Ol. Your remark is highly pertinent. But go a bit easy on the stuff, for chrisakes. Pisco doesn't grow on trees, you know." Ollie had drained most of a liter bottle in the short time since they barged into "The Llama".

"Man does not live by bread alone."

"Anyway." Elliot turned back to Manolito. "Whatever the past, Mano, and we are all guilty of failure in the cause, our quest remains. The Reverend Wallby," Wallby saluted with his glass, "and I are determined to find FARS and to find the Mama. We have brought the message of Che-su. All of our purpose is to spread it."

Mano scratched his head, "De guy I know is Antonio. He too smart guy sabe toda la filosofia, el Marx, el Trossie, el Lenin, todo, bu he drink too many much."

"Mano," Elliot insinuated in a teasing tone, "didn't you once tell us that you were an activist for the FARS? That you had militated in FARS and once landed in prison?"

"No. Mi, no." Manolito took a sniffling drink from his glass of pisco. "Weah, ay kinna once do de ting, lon tine ago. Bu de FARS no wan me now, dey say I deshonra todo el movimiento." Mano showed the tatters of his blue dress, raising it over naked shoulders that were far from unattractive. "Bu wha de odder ting Ay do? Ay gotta de familia, cinco ninos." He meant that financial necessity had forced him into transvestite prostitution, like thousands of unfortunate others.

"You were kicked out of FARS." Elliot said this in a tone that was sympathetic rather than accusing.

"Yah, de gick. So I don no too much many now."

"You knew the Mama."

Manolito started to whine again. Chees, what an infernal tear duct! It wasn't really the culture, either. Mano just loved a good cry. Maybe he watched too many telenovelas on TV. "De Mama gi me de gick. She call me marica!" Now he was really turning on Niagara. Elliot patted him on the back. Mano too was going heavy on the pisco, matching Wallby glass for glass.

"Mano," Elliot paused for rhetorical effect. "In this case the Mama was following a mistaken line. She was influenced by the remnants of bourgeois ideology. We can work within the movement to repair this ideological error."

"Huhg." Mano sniffled. He had no sleaves with which to wipe his eyes and nostrils. "Maybe yah. De idiotical ere er."

"Yes. That is exactly why we have been struggling to contact the movement. The doctrine of Che-su that we bring will remove those injustices within FARS that are really holdovers from the former society."

"Ahng. Ay si. Okay, den I take you to see de Mama. De razon ay no do before, she say she cut off my ballachos when she see me again becuz all de sheet." He wiped his face with his hands. They weren't exceptionally clean. "De Mama move about, to safe from de policia, bu I no where she now."

"I'm sure she was speaking metaphorically." At the same time, Elliot visualized how painful such an injury might be. In his nineteen seventies college psychology class they had mentioned the "archetype" of the castrating mother. For some reason Jung and Freud never analyzed at length the "castrating father". Maybe they were too deeply stuck in the old patriarchal culture. For them, it was usually the father who got the knife, cf. Uranus.

"No. She do one time on dis one guy. Bud I don giv de blame, cuz he work wi de policia an' de FARS."

"Someone worked with FARS *and* the policia? I thought they were enemies."

"Es muy complicado."

"Oh. In any case, you must take us to see the Mama. Reverend Wallby will explain the Che-su doctrine to her. He knows it better than anyone. Although I'm sure she's heard it a million times before."

"Yah. We go *manana*. Tonight we no wanna go, cuz on de night de policia watch an de FARS guy tink we de espias."

"Where can we pass the night?" It rarely froze in San Santo, but the nights could approach zero centigrade. "Reverend Wallby is still suffering from the altitude."

"Don worry. I got de place. Many confortable, safe, safe."

"Ol? We will have to leave soon. Mano has offered us shelter for the night."

Wallby's head was resting on the table. His glass was tipped to allow occasional resupply to his mouth without unnecessary motion.

"Ol!" Ol started to snore. "Ol!"

"I think he's had his last inning," Elliot commented. Wallby sucked up the last bit of pisco in his glass with a deft and curious tongue and lip action.

"We bring de old padre. He get good de rest."

Elliot settled the bill with the bartender by handing over a dollar bill he had inveigled from Mano. Twenty-six cents for the drinks. He asked for churros to go. They must have some solid refreshment. Ol could use one as a straw …

"Up we go, motherfucker." Elliot and Mano dragged the ecumenical gentleman by the collar. Unconscious, he held onto a quarter full bottle of pisco.

The street was dark. A faint glimmer came from distant lamp-posts and, half a kilometer away, the lights of what was probably another café, like a near galaxy shining on a clear night. "De place no muy lejos." It was close, according to Mano. Vocabulary corner: lejos, far.

After an hour of walk-dragging Manolito signaled the party to stop. In front of them was what looked like an old abandoned van. It had no wheels, the smashed windshield was covered inside with cardboard; the van had long ago rusted and faded to blue-white with large reddish brown patches. "You wade. Ay go see de safe." Manolito slowly and carefully opened one of the double-doors in the rear of the truck. He peered in, listened attentively.

"Is okay. We go have nice night." He helped Elliot drag the minister to safety inside.

Mano closed the doors when they were comfortably seated in the back of the van. Ollie naturally reclined as soon as he was not supported. Elliot leaned back against the metal side of the vehicle. Manolito was already asleep, the skirts of his dress pulled up over his ears. Unfortunately, he wore no underwear.

"Ah." The place was humble, but doubtless one could relax here. Elliot turned on his side, closed his eyes. Soon he was aware that the van was occupied by other persons. You could tell because of the moaning and hard breathing noises. There were at least two others.

By the faintest light emanating from a tear in the windshield cardboard, Elliot saw that Wallby had decided to make the most of it. He was using a churro as a straw to suck up more pisco from a bottle found on the bottom of the van. Was it pisco or gasoline? "Don't overdo it, Ol'. Remember what Doctor Zapatero said."

"Egregious quack." Ollie crunched a churro and washed it down with the stuff.

Later in the night Elliot looked over and saw that the Reverend was sleeping next to Mano. Actually on top of him. Clever way to beat the cold.

The next morning, as "Apollo's cart drew rosy rays close upon the face of drowsy earth"—but that is old culture, banned and mainly forgotten—Elliot awoke to see that the three were now alone in the van. The other guests had checked out early. Mano's skirts were still drawn over his head. So were the skirts of Wallby's cassock. Neither was wearing any underwear.

"We go." Still groggy, Manolito ate part of a churro that Wallby had dropped on the van floor. He swallowed some pisco. "Ged de early, then less trouble."

"Ready Ol'?" Elliot took a hold on the ecclesiastical collar.

"I do not understand why we do not remain in this place. It is comfortable and we are well supplied."

"Because, Ollie, we have to contact FARS and meet the Mama." In the early morning Elliot was not in a good mood. "Anyway, this was your fucking great idea! If it hadn't been for you we'd be safe and warm in L.A.! And now you've forgotten all about Che-su and the movement! You make me feel like an idiot!"

The Reverend's face showed a touch of contrition. "Che-su can infuse the flesh as well as the spirit. However, you are doubtless correct. Let us resume our search."

Manolito and Elliot each took one of Wallby's arms. He was able to help in his own transport because he had now regained partial use of his legs. Probably the pisco had done him much good, also the massage administered to his legs by Mano last night between "warming up" sessions.

In the early morning beggars and street vendors were just starting to assemble. The sidewalks (aceras) were relatively unblocked. Although the buildings, mainly of two stories, were dilapidated and faded, it was not a particularly depressed section of San Santo. Many small stores were open, their activities announced by signs. Zapateria. Libreria. Ropa. Abarrotes. Sexo.

"Why we not go inside," Mano suggested. "De get de refresh."

"Sexo?" Elliot exclaimed in a tone of revulsion and contempt.

"No. No. Abarrotes." Groceries.

"We can't afford it right now." Elliot dragged up some churro crumbs from the bag and swallowed them. "We'll just have to make do for now, like Che would have done."

"Ung."

They resumed their journey.

"Many of these Sexo shops are quite interesting. Culturally, I mean," the Reverend put in. He looked with fascination at the displays.

Elliot ignored this. At the next street corner he cut loose with a few cents to a street vendor to provide them each with a banana and a mango. Then onward.

"I'm rather dying of thirst," Ollie announced. Of course. He traveled on high-octane fuel. Elliot let Mano hold the load while he went to the take-out window of a café. Two cents bought a large plastic cup of pisco. With trembling hands, Ollie took the cup. He swallowed a good third of it in a desperate gulp. Amazingly, not a drop was lost. The Reverend never mistook his basic values.

After half an hour more of walk-dragging, Elliot was afraid he was going to have to ask Manolito to carry both of them. "Le le le's re re rest a moom." He collapsed onto the sidewalk.

"Pobre senor. Toma." Mano brought the pisco cup to Elliot's lips. Elliot took several quick swallows from what remained. He saw that a sort of dregs of churro crumbs and dirt lay at the bottom of the plastic cup. He took another swallow, but from the top. Such a thing would never bother Ollie.

"Thank you. It's the altitude."

"Yah. You feel bedder. Wad I gotta say is, soon we go de FARS guy. When we get, you gotta say you de Whoryard Universidad. You de professor from de Whoryard. Then dey no tink you wi de imperialismo. Dey know Whoryard hate de imperialismo. He giv em money." "Whoryard" was funding FARS.

"All right. I'm a professor from Harvard and I suppose Ollie is too. He could be a Professor Emeritus of Theology or something like that. And I'm a professor of Sociology."

"Yah. Den, dey no make big trouble. Like giv de beat up."

"A definite advantage. Good idea, Mano. I am no longer apprehensive."

"De FARS guy in de mecanica mebbe two three block. We show we fren. Bu you res. Yo llevo al Pastor." Manolito hoisted the Reverend onto his back. He went ahead bent almost at the waist, like an ancient Andean porter with a holy man on his back. Cassock over dress. The black and the blue.

"I am really rather thirsty."

"Shut up, Ollie. You're a professor of theology at Harvard, not a longshoreman. Remember that."

"I have known theology professors at Harvard who could drink a team of longshoremen under the table."

"No doubt. But it's important to make a good impression on the central FARS section of San Santo. Just as Manolito said, we must convince them that we come as friends."

"Dehydrated friends."

"All right!" They stopped for a rest. Mano was panting from his efforts with the Wallby papoose. "You have investigated chtonic and solar deities, and salvation deities, but this is the first I have heard of worshipping liquid deities."

"Spirits," Wallby capped.

Fortunately, cafes were everywhere. Elliot got their plastic cup refilled at a pisco station close by. You got a slight discount for bringing your own cup. Santano environmentalists had crafted the legislation.

Wallby's head lolled to one side when Elliot got back. "Aaagh." Doubtless he was faking distress to obtain more substantial relief. Such an approach had received theoretical elaboration in Wallby's article, "Suffering as Declaration" (Journal of the New Social Spirituality, Berkeley, August 1989).

"Whoa! Don't swallow the cup, pardner. We get a discount." Ollie had imbibed half the contents of the two hundred centiliter cup of 90 proof pisco at one go.

Manolito and Elliot each took a few miserable sips from what remained. Then they were off again. Soon Mano became excited.

"Alli esta, alli esta!" He pointed to a low front space in a building half a block away. A sign stretched over the half-shuttered front. "Museo de la Revolucion".

"I thought you said it was a mecanica?" A mechanic's shop.

"De mecanico ren it from proprietario guy, bu den, wen no got clientes because Correos grab all de cars, e gotta make money, so e make de Museo. Dos centavo la entrada. De Correo guy from de seccion ged la mitad, so dey done make trouble." New words: mitad, half.

They went ahead slowly, expecting to be surrounded by gun-totting terrorists at any moment.

"Homoousian, homoiousian." Wallby was practicing theological terms, the better to prove his Harvard status. Or was it Yale? The sacred gentleman was now experiencing short term memory weakness.

Elliot peeked inside the Museo de la Revolucion. It was nearly dark inside and no one was in sight. A low watted electric bulb gave off enough light to make out posters on the walls. Lenin, Trotsky, Stalin, Che, Ho Chi Minh. He stepped inside. Several glass topped display cases held relics, such as early printed revolutionary pamphlets, weapons used in actual combat, photographs of the first armed group formed in El Chinasco provincia. Mano sneaked up to provide some advice.

"Cuidado, senor. De guy hide wen he see extranjeros. I no go de entrada. De FARS guy like de hate my gudz."

"We have to make contact, Mano. That's why we're here." Mano slipped out. Slip: long female undergarment.

The place was not actually uninhabited. In a corner near the half-shuttered entrance, a very old woman slept. She was snoring. From the size and color of her mustache Elliot estimated that she must be at least fifty years old. (NDLR: the average age of the population of El Santo is twelve years, the same as the legal age for marriage. A person of fifty years is considered antediluvian.)

Elliot approached. "Senora? Senora? Excuse me, could you please direct me to the group called FARS? I, that is, we--we're professors from Harvard, Whoryard. We have come a long way to find FARS."

The senora stirred. She scratched her neck, then her back, then her lower back. She opened her eyes. "Eh? Gringos. Wha you wan?" Even the socio-economical dregs of the population of El Santo was somewhat fluent in English. It was taught in the schools from grade one. For street vendors, it was an absolute necessity.

"Buscamos el grupo FARS. Somos profesores de Whoryard." Elliot tried some of his execrable Spanish.

"Eh? No comprendo. Wha' language you speak? No se nada. Vayanse. Me debe dos centavos por la entrada."

"No. That is, we are friendly supporters of the Revolucion. That is our goal and we have brought a new doctrine. Che and Jesus. Do you see?"

The senora waved her hand in front of her face as if chasing flies away. Then Elliot felt something touch his back. It was hard and pointed. At first he thought Manolito was being playful.

"No too smart, senor."

Elliot turned his head and saw that a young man dressed in khaki was standing behind him. He was carrying a rifle or an automatic weapon of some kind. It was pointed at Elliot's back. "You will come accompany me." He motioned brusquely with his shoulder toward a door at the far end of the Museo. A prisoner again. Freedom lovers had to expect it.

"We are peace-seekers, theologians," Elliot pleaded. They were now in a bare, windowless room behind the Museo. On the wall was a poster of Comrade Abulaim, leader of the Peruvian ultra-Maoists. Hardly promising.

The man with the machine gun motioned Elliot to sit. On the floor. "We have been well advise of you coming. You movement have been track for weeks and we know that you are agentes of the CIA, that you have come to betray our people and to make the masses suffer even worse that the living death they are already suffer."

"Who told you that?"

"Silence! I will ask the questions. Padre Rigoberto, among others."

"Ah. I kinda thought he was hostile. But he was mistaken. We only want to help FARS. Reverend Wallby here," he indicated the old floppy guy, "is a famous theologian from Harvard. He and I have come to preach the doctrine of Che-su. A sort of armed love."

The trooper was busy examining his machine gun. He noisily slipped and unslipped locks and ammunition holders. "One bullet or two?" He smiled with childish happiness. "Like you gringos wi' you tea. He he."

Maybe one would be sweeter. "We're not spies! Reverend Wallby has spent all of his life trying to help the people emerge from the degrading, demeaning, humiliating, disgusting poverty in which they have been eternally submerged. Our mission is to help FARS by bringing the Che-su doctrine. Jesus and Che."

'Ha ha ha ha! Do not believe we are such fools. This is the first ruse of CIA operatives." He pulled a pamphlet from his back pocket and tossed it on the floor in front of Elliot. The pamphlet had the CIA seal on its cover. It was entitled, "Using Religious Idealism to Undermine Guerrilla Movements".

"Oh." Elliot leafed through the pamphlet. The word "Che-su" occurred several times. "Well, we didn't know about this at all. We're not involved with the CIA or the FBI or even the LAPD. I guess it's just a coincidence."

The soldier went into hysterical laughter. "Senor, you are earning the cake. Maybe one bullet." He pointed his weapon at Elliot and looked smiling through the sight. Then he looked up. His face registered an unhappy surprise. The old lady had come into the room.

With a single withered hand she motioned the armed man to leave. She took his weapon away and let him slink, head down, through an inner door. Elliot watched with amazement. From his psychology course at Tarzana University he knew that this was symbolic castration.

"Farinaceo is a goo boy, bu sometime he ack too quick. Bu we see you are wi de traidor Manolito. That tell us you are no good for us."

Elliot did not understand this. Mano said that FARS had rejected him because of his economically forced involvement with transvestite prostitution. He hadn't mentioned an ideological problem.

"I think there has been a serious misunderstanding. We have come to help with the revolucion. We met Mano at the Hotel de Carlos. He was a friend of Jonathan Belcher, recently executed by the Correo government. Manolito said he could help us contact FARS, because we wish to work with you. We are against the Correos, even more against the imperialist empire. We have been knocking around San Santo for weeks, but Mano finally agreed to bring us here. Before, he was afraid because in the past he was stigmatized for his sexual orientation."

"El marica? Si. Lo criticamos. We non wanna guy in a blue dress get wi our militantes. We are el Ejercito del Pueblo." The Army of the People.

"Yes. That is why we have come to you. I and the Reverend Wallby are seeking to find the true revolution and to help by adding the principle of Che-su. To armed revolt, we will the join the principle of non-violent humanity."

"Eh. Dis de guy wi' de Misa Desnuda en Los Angeles?"

Oh-oh. She knew. How?

"I read in El Chino." El Chino, the Peruvian tabloid, informed its readers of sensational events everywhere.

"Nothing really happened. The press and the police blew it all out of proportion. That's why we thought it best to come to El Santo." Elliot was aware that his explanation wasn't going too well. It wasn't exactly what he intended to say. From the expression on the old woman's face, he saw that he was digging himself in deeper and deeper. "I mean, Reverend Wallby had planned to come to spread the Che-su idea long ago. This just seemed the right time."

"De guy drink much much. He gonna drain de whole army."

"You have been watching us. But you see, Ollie imbibes a bit to excess because he has had a hard life. His idealism is genuine. It's also the altitude. Before he got to the high Andes, the Reverend was a very different man." Then Elliot had a flash of understanding. Things fell into place. His face brightened. "Then you are the Mama!"

The female senior citizen smiled. "Si. Yo soy la Mama. Dis mi grupo, FARS, seccion central, San Santo."

Later Elliot would discover that the very senior looking lady was in fact ten years younger than he was. She had had three husbands, all dead from the revolucion and other natural causes, had eleven children, forty-four grandchildren and twenty-two great grandchildren. Thirty-nine of the grandchildren and spouses worked without documents in the U.S. They worked at government jobs that no one else wanted.

"Okay, where you fren ri now?"

"I left Ollie just outside the Museo. He cannot walk without assistance."

"Okay, den we gotta fine you fren." They headed to the outside. "Farinaceo get happy wen I giv im de gun back. Jus he not make de trigger till I say im."

Elliot walked behind La Mama.

On the street, there was no Reverend to be seen. Peasants and proletarians passed in an unbroken stream. A few llamas, freighted with sacks, walked by with their delicate, sure-footed pace. You could see suspicion in La Mama's face.

"Where de guy?"

The same question presented itself to Elliot's mind. "This is very strange. I left him here just minutes ago. He couldn't have got far on foot."

Without a word, La Mama led the way back into the Museo. They went again through the inner door, then through another door on the far side of the windowless room. They were in a courtyard. A square piece of the dark blue sky of San Santo could be seen above. To the amazement of both, the Reverend Oliver Francis Wallby was sitting on a pile of boxes, preaching to the multitude.

"I say to you, what good is it if you win the revolucion and lose your immortal souls? Without Che-su, the revolucion will have no spirit, no eternal consciousness of the All One to guide it. It is well to take up machine guns and to oppose the forces of reaction and imperialism and the bourgeoisie, but alone it is not sufficient. There is man the spiritual being who also must rebel, who must find his new life in efforts for the spiritual well-being of the masses."

The soldiers of FARS, San Santo, seccion central, were standing or kneeling as they listened in awed respect to the words of the holy man. Most had little or no English, but Wallby had a gift for the pulpit, a presence of holiness that moved even uncomprehending crowds to awed respect.

"Dis guy mucho mucho santo. Wad he say?"

"He is saying that the revolucion must add the spiritual dimension of Che-su to the armed enterprise of Marx, Lenin, Trotsky. Something like that. I'm not sure myself."

"Los militantes lo aman mucho. He arse like un profeta."

"He had exactly the same effect on a group of sun worshippers in Malibu."

"Los Nudistas?"

"No, they weren't nudists, not all of them, at least at first."

"Ya, den we wait to he end de predicar."

Wallby went on for some time. He made allusion to the gospels, to modern theology, to the New York Times. The crowd was hypnotized. Then the Reverend fell asleep in mid-quotation. It was the altitude.

"Ollie is still not well. He is having a hard time acclimatizing." In fact, Elliot believed that the Reverend was undergoing a sort of pisco withdrawal. "Perhaps a bit of medicinal spirits will bring him around," he suggested.

"De pis'? We done let no pis' in de seccion. Reglamentos. All de militantes on de rye."

"Dry," Elliot corrected. Or maybe it was rye. This was bad. Without a modicum of pisco, Wallby would be unable fully to perform his pastoral role.

The Mama took a pistol out of the pocket of her long, folded, folklorico skirt. She pointed it at a target attached to a courtyard wall. The discharge reverberated in the closed space and caught the attention of the liberation troopers. "Okay. I tell you dis," she was facing Elliot. "I dunno w'eh you guy from. Maybe you wi de CIA. I dunno. We gonna le you a try. We watch how you do an' you tell us all de kazoo."

"Che-su."

"Che-su. But we watch an we decide. Dey come de espias, muchos, muchos."

"Comprendo." Elliot tried to salute like a soldier. The Mama turned and left. Probably she was going back to the box office. The revolutionary squad went back to their habitual activities, essentially polishing and disassembling and reassembling their weapons and gossiping to each other about the revolucion. The Mama was not sure that Elliot and Walby were on the up and up. She was granting them a trial period, like when you got a job back in the states. Elliot crept up to his old ecclesiastical friend.

"Ol? Ol?" He shook the ecumenical personage. "Ollie? Are you okay? You just gave a splendid sermon. It got rave reviews."

Ollie's head wobbled for a minute or two, then stuck up. "I should like something to quell my thirst. I have become dehydrated in this thin atmosphere."

"No luck, old friend. The Mama told me alcohol was taboo here at the seccion."

Red anger showed in the Reverend's eyes. "This is preposterous. How is one to keep off the cold?"

"I think they use blankets. But don't worry, I'll ask around. They might not be as puritanical as they say."

Elliot crept close to a camouflage-clad combatant. The man was sitting cross-legged as he polished his weapon to a shining silver color. His posture emphasized the crotch area of his trousers. Rather large.

"Hello. You are a liberation soldier, verdad?"

"Wad you wan?"

"I really like your gun." Elliot stared in admiration.

"I make kill de reaccionarios." He raised the machine gun and pretended to aim at a worthy target.

"As indeed you should." Elliot paused and searched in his pockets for the change from Mano's five-dollar bill. "We are experiencing a difficulty. You see, my friend the Reverend Wallby ..."

"El Santo," the trooper repeated in awed respect.

"Yes, El Santo. You see, El Santo is suffering from the altitude here. He is from la costa and is not used to the mountains. It would be big medicine for him if he could have a little drink of pisco. A couple of litros," he added quickly. "We will pay."

The soldier looked over his shoulder. "How many you wan? Tree, sis?"

"I think six would be a good round figure." Elliot needed no prompting. Ollie was like a power pump when it came to pisco, and there ought to be some left for his own therapy as well.

"Twunny," the trooper coughed out.

Elliot squeezed a quarter, which he had found on the holy man's person, out of his pocket, looked around and let it drop into the soldier's lap. It caught in the large space between crotch and stomach. Bravo. Elliot crawled back to his ecclesiastical companion.

"Good luck, Ollie. I found a splendid young fellow who is willing to help us with our problem."

Ollie was sleeping again. Rhythmic snoring shook his nostril hair and lips. Elliot decided to let him sleep, he looked so calm and peaceful. When he awoke he might find a very happy surprise. Elliot took a tourist guidebook from Wallby's pocket. He opened to a page at random. "It is important not to let the natives know that you are afraid," it read. He would have to remember this. He hoped it wasn't too late.

An hour later the remarkable soldier came into the courtyard bearing a large sack. Looking around cautiously, he approached the pile of empty boxes where Elliot and the Reverend were camped. Ollie was still sleeping. Elliot was trying to count sheep, or rather snores. The soldier let his sack drop into an empty box. "Deh you drink." He about-faced and left.

Surrepticiously, because of the FARS prohibition of alcohol, Elliot took a bottle from the sack. It was labeled "La gasolina". He uncorked the bottle and smelled the contents. It did smell a bit like gasoline. He tried a tiny sip. It tasted just slightly of gasoline. Perhaps gasoline had been added as a substitute for the aging process that was used to take the harsh edge off fresh pisco. After all, some of the commoner brands of pis' could easily burn the skin off your tongue. Or maybe the bottles had been re-used without adequate rinsing.

"Ollie, dear, wake up, please. You can now get re-hydrated to your heart's content."

Ollie stirred somewhat. He didn't seem to want to wake up. Possibly he was still exhausted from his extraordinarily successful sermon earlier that day. Elliot took the open bottle and passed it under the Reverend's nose. Wallby moved frenetically for an instant. Then he grabbed the bottle with both hands and applied it to his mouth. He drank steadily. His eyes were firmly shut. He continued to drink while Elliot clocked the time on his cheap wristwatch, a Chinese make bought from a street vendor.

Elliot looked at his friend with fascination as the bottle's contents quickly shrank. Wallby's large, pink, almost hairless head made him look like an infant drinking its formula from a nippled bottle. "Whoa, Ollie, take it easy." Elliot tried to pry the bottle from grasping hands. It wasn't easy. At last the gasolina bottle came away. Wallby burped loudly, then fell back into a snoring sleep. The newly opened bottle was at half-mast.

This was worrying. Was the holy gentleman relapsing into his altitude sickness, or whatever it was? Would he recover after proper "re-hydration"? Elliot drew another bottle from the sack. He took a small drink. He almost vomited. Then he sipped slowly and let the fluid flow over his tongue. No, it wasn't really so bad. It was almost tasty. After a few swallows he was starting to think it was the best drink since champagne.

As trial associates of the seccion, Elliot and Oliver were assigned daily duties. They were given light fatigue because of the Reverend's age and infirmities. Elliot had to be there to care for him and to give him his medicine—he was now on his second to last bottle of gasolina, but there was more where that came from. Their job was to clean and wash the Museo de la Revolucion. Each morning after breakfast—they were served a sort of corn mush with peppers and small pieces of animal flesh—Elliot would drag the Reverend to the exhibition room and deposit him on a bench. Then Elliot would sweep, dust, mop and tidy. The Reverend slept most of the time, although occasionally he wakened long enough to give the soldiers a little exhortatory talk on the subject of Che-su.

"We defend the people with arms, but must we not also defend the people with love? We are in battle against the bourgeoisie and the imperialists, but are we not also in battle against cruelty and inhumanity, and, yes, even against ourselves?"

The soldiers loved it. Usually several made the sign of the cross—hicieron la senal de la cruz. They murmured in sadness, even wept. Few understood his words.

The Museo did not have many visitors. It was mainly a front for the guerrilla training base. La Mama sat near the door, selling tickets to the few who came. Some of the exhibits were interesting. There were photographs, now yellowed and curled with age, of Trotsky and Lenin and others. The storming of the Winter Palace. Lenin speaks at the Finland Station. Lenin after his first stroke. Kamenev and Zinoviev smile in a group shot with Trotsky.

Oddly, the Mama never seemed to notice when Elliot stopped his labors to apply a bottle of medicine to the reverend lips. She dozed a lot. There wasn't too much to do. You could hear the weapons being disassembled and reassembled in the courtyard. Trucks passed in the street. Llamas brayed. Peatones shouted, laughed and quarreled. Occasionally one of the lookouts would shout "patrulla!" Correo's soldiers patrolled the area regularly. They knew about the Museo-base, but they received regular payoffs and were inclined to ignore it anyway. Who wanted to get into a machine gun fight over—well, over what? Any revolucion would be followed by another revolucion just as good.

Wallby was not able to shave himself. Because razor blades were in short supply in El Santo (due to the imperialist blockade as well as a state monopoly) at the moment, Elliot used their rusty existing blade to cut back the beard on the Reverend's face. This left only a mustache and a bearded chin.   Because of his light beard—light in color and texture and profusion—Elliot shaved himself only every week or two. After the Museo cleaning was completed for the day—it only took an hour or so—Elliot tried to engage the Mama in conversation. This might create a bond that would help in their mission. She too had light duties and generally lounged, half- sprawled, on an armchair near the Museo entrance. She was fond of talking, but her tendency was toward the monologue, not the interchange. "Egfritho, mi marido, he love mucho, mucho de Alpinas." (NDLR: Alpina is the name of a Santense brand of yogurt.) "He ees many, in the manana, before the siesta. Bud wen he esleep too mucho, den de tropas, dey god enojados. See, we leev in Andes, we make patrullas to de aldeas so de people love de FARS when dey see we kill Correo soldier. An Egfritho, he give de ninos the plastico from de Alpinas. Dey play wi plasticos, se divierten mucho." He let the kids play with his empty yogurt containers.

"You must have loved Egfritho very much." It was hard to understand why. Elliot assumed the husband was dead, a reasonable supposition in view of the marido's violent proclivities.

La Mama appeared to consider this. She turned her stubbly chin toward the ceiling and squinted. "Eh?" Probably she didn't understand the statement.

"When did he leave us?"

"Cuando murio?" She thought about this for some time. She scratched her chin. She spat. "No se." No doubt she was telling the truth. In an eternal land like the Andes, time was timeless.

"I suppose he was killed in combat with a Correo patrol."

"No. No creo." She thought about this for several minutes before she could think of the answer. "Ah. Now I 'memberme. He git bite by one llama. He love de llamas. He make like kiss, bu de llama bid im. Den he nose get big, big, mucho fiebre, den he die. Den we have big fiesta, wi de Padre, los musicos." She smiled at the memory.

"Sometimes I worry a great deal about Reverend Wallby. The climate doesn't suit him. For a while he seemed to be improving, but now he sleeps most of the time."

"Esleep. Wan dey no ting to do, den mucho, we esleep in de day." She dozed off as if to demonstrate the phenomenon.

At least she didn't think Wallby's condition was anything to worry about. Maybe it was just the altitude. Elliot fell into a short nap, but shook himself awake. He went to the door of the Museo, to take the fresh air. A short distance away, at the corner, he saw, or thought he saw, a short figure in a blue dress running from pursuers. He went back inside. He sat down next to the Mama. She was snoring. Elliot must have dozed off again, because when he came to, the Mama was counting the day's receipts for Museo tickets. He remembered the blue dress. Probably just a dream.

La Mama counted aloud. This was possibly a method to minimize mistakes. Or maybe a result of her limited numeracy. "Cinco, siete, nueve, once, trece, quince." She stopped to scratch her chin rigorously. Elliot thought he might offer the use of the razor.

"Is good day," she concluded. "Twunny-seven sens."

"It was that last group. The man with glasses who looked like a school teacher with the seven children."

"Yah. Senor Iniguez. He naw teacher. He like to show im to de ninos."

Elliot did not know what this meant. He did not want to ask. Suddenly he shook himself. He certainly did not want to doze off again. It was time for Wallby's medicine. "Excuse me."

He sauntered to the other end of the Museo. The problem was how to give Wallby his dose of pisco without letting the Mama observe this blatant violation of seccion reglamentos. He knelt by the side of the bench where Wallby lay deep in philosophical slumber. He took the current bottle from the bag. The Mama was recounting her pennies. He applied the bottle to the theological lips. They sucked furiously and coughed a few times.

Suddenly the Mama looked toward the ecumenical bench. "Hey! Don git im choke on de medicina."

"No, Mama."

The next day, jueves, Thursday, the militantes were leaving on patrol for San Ignacio de Jicaca. This was a small aldea located thirty kilometros to the norte. They would carry their carbines and packs. Since the Museo-campamiento was located on the outskirts, las afueras, of San Santo, they could disappear into small paths and tracks and not risk meeting their Correo opponents/colleagues on the main highway. Elliot and the Reverend were being left at base camp. Sargento Bronchez, detachment leader, gave Elliot his orders.

"Den you gi Estalino de comida. Dwon gup ery day." One cup of food per day. Estalino was the camp pet dog. He was a small, loveable mongrel who supposedly barked when the Correo patrols came near. In fact, he never stopped barking night or day. He was named after the head of the Correo government, Stalin Correo. Normally he was not taken out on walks. This was impractical for security reasons. The courtyard had to be cleaned daily with a small rake.

Then there were the deliveries. Elliot was to expect three large sacks of corn meal and one sack of chiles. The carriers would knock and give a password. "Estalino chinga en el rincon". Remember it. "Dey come fliday." Viernes.

Elliot was proud and happy that he was being left in charge when the patrol left for San Ignacio. They trusted him. Apparently these duties were not performed by La Mama because this was macho work. In many ways, revolucionary El Santo society was still unevolved.

Jueves, the detachment assembled in the central courtyard. They massed by file and rank. El Pastor was been asked to give his blessing and a small exhortatory talk. It was six o'clock in the evening. Since Ollie still could not stand unaided, Elliot helped him take a sitting position on a large box behind the improvised podium. Probably it had served at one time to transport corn meal. Elliot squatted behind the box in order to steady the Reverend without detracting from the parade detail appearance. It was amazing that Wallby, although usually semi-comatose lately, was able to give profoundly moving sermons. He had to be primed with a good deal of pisco, of course, and refreshed periodically during the talk.

Wallby looked out at the armed masses of workers and peasants—there were about eighteen of them. Suddenly his head drooped. His chest began to heave in wild emotion. Then he raised his head. His face was bathed in tears.

"Dear comrades. Dear comrades." He looked from right to left, from front to back. "Do we know ourselves what we do?

Do we even know why we act?" Dramatic pause. "It is because no one else will help the masses! No one. No one. The masses are alone, abandoned, helpless. Except with our help. The masses starve, they wallow in poverty, they stagnate in ignorance, they regress to superstition. They cannot move forward. Except with our help. Except with the armed and compassionate help of FARS." Wallby stretched an arm behind himself. Elliot pushed a pisco filled military canteen into the open palm. The Reverend drank, as if curing his throat from momentary dryness.

"Quiero decirles algo." Another dramatic pause. "Les amo. Les amo. Les amo! Siempre!"

He loved them forever. There wasn't a dry eye in the courtyard. Many cheeks flowed with tears. Soldiers moaned in emotional distress. "Adelante!"

From a corner of the yard the Mama raised her arm to bid the patrol adieu. They turned and left in formation, by file and rank. Then the courtyard was empty except for the three, Wallby, Elliot, the Mama. From a distance they heard the words of the International sung to the tune of "Don't Cry for Me Argentina".

Wallby was refreshing himself from the canteen. La Mama joined them. "Brillante, la bendicion. De guy feel like now dey gonna go to heaven. Bien, mi hijo."

The cool San Santo night was coming on. Elliot dragged the Reverend back from the courtyard to the Museo. He stretched him out on the bench. Wallby clung to the canteen. Probably it was empty. The Mama closed and locked the street door. Then they heard the sound of intense gunfire coming from the ravine that lay behind the Museo-camp. La Mama shrugged. "Maybe dey shoot de rabbit." Rabbit: conejo.

Wallby had commenced his usual baritone snore. Elliot dusted a glass display case. La Mama shuffled out of the room. "I go make comida."

The next morning, Elliot and Wallby were eating their rations of boiled corn meal. "Not bad," Elliot commented. "Perhaps a little more salt."

The Reverend was licking his bowl. "We are to share the misery of the masses."

"The patrol must be in Jicaca by now," Elliot mused. Anyway, those that made it.

The corn meal delivery was not expected until the afternoon. Elliot swept and dusted the Museo again, although there was really very little need for it. Customers were few. The Disney films playing in the cinemas in San Santo's centro were drawing away the small public that the Museo de la Revolucion had enjoyed.

La Mama walked by. She had a curious way of walking, very heavy at the feet and the shoulders, but loose at the abdomen. She stopped to look at the Reverend, stretched out on his bench, snoring at peace with the universe. "Chingada! He look jus like de Vladimir Ilyich! Maybe jus a li'l bit de old."

Elliot bent over the sprawled body of his friend. She was right. He hadn't noticed before, but Wallby was the spitting image of Lenin. The baldness and shaved upper face, the pale complexion, the mustache and small pointed beard, as well as the facial features—small squinting eyes, pug nose—recalled the famous Russian revolutionary. "Well I'll be damned!"

La Mama had a brainstorm. Since Wallby slept most of the time anyway and seldom moved around, why not put him in one of the bigger display cases, dress him in early Soviet style, and advertise him as "the Living Lenin", "el Lenin en Vivo"? "Brin de guy back from de cinema, mucho dinero."

It was too good to resist. They cleared a lot of old papers and photographs out of a large glass display case and eased Wallby in. A nice grey blanket spread at the bottom gave him a soft bed. The problem was that the Reverend had to have a steady supply of his "medicina" to keep him comfortable. There too, the Mama had a great brainstorm. They found a narrow plastic hose, stuck one end into a bottle of pisco and the other between the theological lips. Since the embalmed body of Lenin, now in Red Square, Moscow, was kept in a glass case maintained in a vacuum by suction tubes, they would tell the visitors that the plastic hose was an authentic detail. La Mama wrote out a sign on a long piece of cardboard. She was an excellent calligraphist, remarkable for someone only semi-literate. "Aqui! El Muy Famoso Lenin, En Vivo desde Moscu!" They hung the sign above the street entrance to the Museo. Tickets were to sell at three cents, with a discount for senior citizens, of whom there were very few in El Santo, an unfortunate result of the high mortality rate.

The curious started to come in. At first a few older people, probably FARS sympathizers for half a century, paid their entradas and trooped to the display case in which Wallby was maintained on a pisco lifeline. They were enthralled.

"Si! Si! Es El! Es el Lenin! Esta todavia en vida!"

"Que maravilla!"

"Yo me muero!"

It was a hit. La Mama had an instinctive sense of the commercial.

At noon they closed the Museo in order to give Wallby—the Living Lenin—his lunch. He spooned up the corn mush with real enthusiasm. When he wasn't so thirsty—as after three hours on a pisco IV tube—he could put even the solid stuff away. The Reverend was not unaware of the show. He half sat up and looked at them. "We shall be reborn in the spirit, and the dead shall come again to live."

"Es verdad." Tears formed in La Mama's eyes.

The high point of the afternoon was the entry of four school children at once. They paid twelve cents at a clip. The commercial success of the Living Lenin was beyond doubt.

La Mama put four cents into Elliot's hand. It was time to celebrate. "You go ged de cerveza." She indicated an itinerant vendor standing in the street opposite to the door of the Museo.

Elliot came back with two opened bottles of El Inca, ice cold.

"Mu ben." La Mama took a long pull on her beer.

"Si, Mama."